MW00781823

FIRST DO
NO HARM

BOOKS BY JOE KENDA

NONFICTION

I Will Find You:
Solving Killer Cases from My Life Fighting Crime

Killer Triggers

FICTION

All Is Not Forgiven

First Do No Harm

FIRST
DO NO
HARM

JOE KENDA

**BLACK
STONE**
PUBLISHING

Printed in the United States of America

First edition: 2024
ISBN 979-8-200-92436-3
Fiction / Mystery & Detective / Hard-Boiled

Version 1

Blackstone Publishing
31 Mistletoe Rd.
Ashland, OR 97520

www.BlackstonePublishing.com

I dedicate this book to my wife, Kathy,
and all the other medical professionals who spend their
careers relieving pain and suffering, and saving lives.

CONTENTS

PROLOGUE

Dear Reader,

Just a note to make it clear that this book is entirely a work of fiction, even though I serve as its narrator and a main character. Like my first fiction book, *All Is Not Forgiven* (2023), this new book marks a departure from my two previous nonfiction books, *I Will Find You* (2017) and *Killer Triggers* (2021). Like my reality television shows *Homicide Hunter* and *American Detective* (on the Investigation Discovery and discovery+ networks, respectively), those first two books featured nonfiction accounts of true stories drawn from my case files as a patrol officer, detective, and homicide detective lieutenant with the Colorado Springs Police Department from 1973 to 1996.

This book, *First Do No Harm*, offers a realistic but not real story about the early use and abuse of fentanyl, an effective painkiller in the hands of ethical medical professionals that is extremely dangerous when it is distributed by criminals and used as a street drug.

As in *All Is Not Forgiven*, I appear in this book as a primary character, but it is my fictional self as a young detective in the late 1970s. All the other characters in this book, other than my wife, Kathy—who also is presented in a fictionalized younger version—are made up, though more than a few were inspired by people I have worked with, investigated, come across, or learned about over the years.

While this tale is entirely made up, I assure you that it is rooted in the very real story of a drug that was created to ease pain and suffering but has resulted in no end of it because of corrupt criminal enterprises. Please keep all of this in mind as you read. I hope you enjoy it and maybe learn a thing or two.

Detective Lt. Joe Kenda (retired), 2024

CHAPTER ONE:

THE PAINKILLER

JUNE 1977, COLORADO SPRINGS
SPRINGS GENERAL HOSPITAL

Rosemary Calhoun did not recognize the tall young man in a striped golf shirt and black pants as he walked into her husband's intensive care room without knocking or introducing himself.

"Excuse me, who are you?" she asked politely as he approached her sleeping husband's bed.

The stranger turned and glared at her in a way that made Mrs. Calhoun cringe in fear. *What is this white man's problem?*

"I am Dr. Blair Moreland, head of the anesthesiology department, and if you want your very sick husband to survive a difficult surgery tomorrow, you should speak to me with more respect because I will be administering his painkillers and anesthesia. Normally, I wouldn't come to a patient's room, but his surgeon wanted me to check his chart and look him over now because your husband is such a high-risk patient. So, you're welcome!"

The doctor then snatched her husband's chart, scrawled something on it, and glared fiercely at her again as he rushed out the door, nearly knocking down Nurse Emily Brown as she tried to enter the room.

"What is with that doctor? Is he a racist or something?" Mrs. Calhoun asked the nurse.

"No, sister, believe me, that man treats everyone that same hateful way, regardless of race, creed, or religion," Nurse Brown said. "All the other anesthesiologists and doctors here are truly caring souls devoted to patient care, but that man, I don't know, he just seems to be a different type of person. I guess I shouldn't say more than that.

"But don't you worry, dear," she added. "He is a very good anesthesiologist. There is no doubt about that. And if you don't believe me, just ask him because he will gladly tell you himself just how wonderful he is."

The two women chuckled over this, but when the kind nurse left the room, Mrs. Calhoun wondered, *Do I really want that angry white devil watching over my husband?*

Raymond Calhoun, sixty-three, an overweight and diabetic construction supervisor with six children, was scheduled for an orthopedic procedure to repair a fractured patella and an ACL tear that he'd sustained in a fall on a job site. The fact that he loved cheeseburgers, drank a six-pack of beer each night, often with whiskey chasers, and smoked cigars at work, made his surgery even more challenging.

Dr. Moreland consulted with the surgical team prior to the operation, and all agreed that Mr. Calhoun's vitals would have to be closely monitored.

But even with extra care, the patient's condition deteriorated rapidly.

"His blood pressure just shot up to one ninety over one

hundred and his pulse is racing. Nineties and climbing," the operating room nurse said. "Pupils are dilated."

"Damn," said Dr. Ricardo Castillo, the orthopedic surgeon. "Dr. Moreland, are you adjusting accordingly?"

"I'm on it," Moreland said.

Within seconds, alarms sounded on every piece of monitoring equipment in the operating room.

"He's in cardiac arrest! Get the cart!"

Twenty minutes later, Mrs. Calhoun was informed that her husband had died of "complications during surgery."

As they washed up afterward, Dr. Castillo locked eyes with Dr. Moreland, who shrugged and said, "We knew he was a high-risk candidate for this surgery. What can I say?"

Dr. Ross Nicholas, head of the surgery department, huddled with top hospital administrators in an emergency meeting to discuss the fatality, which was a black mark on the hospital's record.

"All I can tell you is that his vitals went south during the procedure. He went into cardiac arrest and there was nothing we could do."

"Dr. Nicholas, do you suspect that the patient was not adequately anesthetized?" asked Springs General's chief physician, Dr. Randall Pence.

"Oh no, I'm not going there," Dr. Nicholas replied. "I don't want to be on Moreland's shit list. That prick is difficult to work with as it is. If he heard that I'd questioned his competence, I'd have to hire bodyguards for my entire family."

PHYSICIAN AND SOCIOPATH

My wife, Kathy, a veteran RN, worked at the same hospital as the odious Dr. Moreland. She told me that the running joke among the nurses on the surgical floor at Springs General was that he had to give up his dream of becoming a heart surgeon when it was discovered that he had no heart himself. Behind his back, the nurses called him "our ass-thesiologist in chief," among other things.

"I'd say he suffered from a god complex, but it would have to be the cruelest and most uncaring god you could imagine," fellow nurse Nancy Hickman once told Kathy.

Moreland did not shy away from his reputation as a cold and heartless bastard. In fact, he proudly posted plaques on his desk that said, "The only good patients are unconscious patients," "No pain. My gain," and "There is no joy without pain."

Even so, the medical staff and hospital administrators agreed that Dr. Moreland was extremely competent. He was promoted to lead the hospital's anesthesiology department at a younger age than other department directors. Yet nurses, aides, and other physicians steered clear of him because of his prickly personality. This suited him just fine because being left alone made it easier for Moreland to collect the opiates that fed his growing addictions.

He had begun using amphetamines to stay focused and awake while studying during medical school, and, later, he'd upped his dosages to get through exhausting double shifts as an intern. Once he was established on Springs General's staff, Moreland had discovered and embraced a new drug introduced in 1974: Sublimaze, also known as fentanyl.

"This new synthetic opioid painkiller is fifty times more powerful than heroin and one hundred times more powerful than morphine," the drug rep said in her initial pitch to Springs General's team of surgeons and anesthesiologists. "This will become the drug of choice for easing pain and suffering around the world! I promise you that!"

If it is as good as they say it is, I can't wait to try this new drug. For my patients, sure, but mostly for myself, thought Moreland during that meeting.

There were hospital rules and procedures to monitor and control the use of such powerful opioids, of course, but Dr. Moreland figured out how to circumvent them easily enough. As the head of anesthesiology, he did not have to ask anyone to write him a prescription. He had an all-access pass to the drug locker and its shelves packed with ecstasy-inducing treats.

To prepare for surgeries, he normally would draw a carefully measured amount of fentanyl from a vial into a syringe that would then be drained into an IV bag for the patient. If there was any amount left in the syringe or the IV bag after a surgery, hospital procedure called for the anesthesiologist or another surgical staffer to drain the remainder into a sink or medical waste trash can.

Regulations called for someone to supervise this process, but that rarely happened, so Moreland overprescribed fentanyl for surgical patients and collected the leftover amount in a plastic bottle for his own use.

Later, as his addiction left him craving more and more of the drug, he grew bolder, switching out drops of saline for drops of fentanyl in the storage room two or three days a week. He also covertly collected any dosages that had been prepared for surgeries that were canceled at the last minute, using the same method.

I'm not stealing it, because the hospital would just throw it out anyway. I'm just recycling it, he told himself. *And, really, if some of my patients experience a little pain, it will make them appreciate being pain-free even more! It's a win-win.*

Many of the staff members who worked with him picked up on Moreland's twisted mentality.

"I think he gets off on watching people suffer and then stepping in to play the hero who eases their pain—in fact, I've seen him linger for five or ten minutes over patients who are moaning and crying out in torment before he administers a painkiller," a surgical nurse once told my wife.

Moreland's arrogance extended to his belief that he could manage his addiction just as he managed the doses he administered to his surgical patients every day. He hid his private stash in plastic bottles in the glove box of his Porsche 911, his Jeep Wagoneer, and around his office at Springs General. He also kept an ample supply at his home in the foothills.

There was little risk of discovery there since Dr. Moreland was not married, even though he was television-doctor handsome, fit, and successful. New female nurses and other staffers were routinely cautioned by their supervisors to stay away from him, but the predatory physician managed to seduce those who did not heed the warnings.

One-night stands were his forte. He had been engaged twice in his thirty-four years, but each time, his fiancées eventually figured out that the money and social standing of being married to this doctor were not worth the hell of living with his cruel and narcissistic personality.

"I don't know how someone can be so vain and so insecure at the same time, but he manages," said Claire Behr, a pediatric nurse who had been one of Dr. Moreland's near-missuses. "I once made a joke about how skinny he is, and he went ballistic, screaming at me and telling me to get the hell out of his house. That was bad enough, but he is also a sociopathic, racist, right-wing nutcase who buys into every paranoid conspiracy theory out there."

The anesthesiologist's temper tantrums during surgery were usually directed at nurses. They occurred so often that the nursing staff had created a "Code Pink" alert that brought all available nurses into the surgical viewing room so they could support the nurses Moreland had targeted that day.

The hospital administration had difficulty keeping track of all of Moreland's transgressions. When a surgical nurse told him that a patient on the operating table was breathing erratically and groaning from pain, Moreland told her to "give him some Valium and take a couple yourself to calm down, you pompous ass."

In another outburst that resulted in a complaint filed by the entire nursing staff, Moreland screamed at a surgical nurse: "I could teach a monkey to do what you do, only better!" When Dr. Andrew Smithson, chief of surgery, called Moreland on the carpet for that incident, his defense was, "That nurse has the hots for me, and she's just reporting this to get my attention."

"That's outrageous, and I'm warning you, the hospital administration is very close to terminating your contract," Dr. Smithson told Moreland.

"And I'm warning you and those puckered assholes in the C-suites that if they come after me for simply correcting a nurse, I will gladly go public with my story about the day I witnessed your beloved Dr. Warmoski throw a bloody scalpel at Nurse Wilken because she could not find the instrument he wanted quickly enough."

The consensus among both amateur and actual psychiatrists at Springs General was that Dr. Moreland was bipolar, if not tripolar.

"I mean, he is the most aloof and antisocial guy in the world, but then he volunteers to counsel and assess patients at the recovery center for addicts. I can't figure that out. He even works a shift in a soup kitchen every week, and I've heard he hands out cash to homeless people on the streets, so you'd think he has some trace of empathy and humanity, but I swear he hates everyone," Nurse Behr told my wife on a girls' night out shortly after her breakup with Moreland.

"And yeah, he does look great in a tux, but he is an empty suit, one evil, sociopathic, soulless bastard. May he and the choke chain he tried to put on me rot in hell for all eternity."

DR. FEELBAD

Upon the death of Raymond Calhoun, Dr. Moreland's only remorse was for the fentanyl he'd wasted during his surgery.

Fuck, I didn't really mean to kill that guy, even though his wife was such a bitch to me. I just wanted to let him feel a little extra pain because she dissed me when I was checking his chart. That old dude wasn't going to live more than a few years even if the surgery had been successful, so fuck it. I saw Dr. Nicholas meeting with the brass. He may have suspicions about the doses I administered, but none of them have the balls to confront me. They will bury it to protect their asses and the hospital's reputation. That's the way it works. Screw the Hippocratic oath and all that 'Do no harm' bullshit. The new motto is "We worry more about billing than killing."

The Springs General nurses were not far from the truth

when they joked that Dr. Moreland had been drummed out of the cardiology program because he lacked a heart. Moreland didn't know the full story himself, but his own father had covertly made certain that he was not allowed to enter the surgical residency program.

Dr. Blair Moreland's father was Dr. Sidney Moreland, dean of the medical residency programs at the University of Colorado School of Medicine. Sidney Moreland had practiced cardiac surgery for twenty years before becoming a medical school professor and administrator at his alma mater. He and his wife, Dr. Caroline Moreland, an obstetrician, had guided their brilliant son's education from preschool through medical school. Their plan was for him to follow in his father's footsteps.

They saw early on that the child had a substantial intellect. With their help, he learned to read, write, and solve mathematical equations before he entered the first grade. They knew he would excel in learning. They had no concerns about his mental capacity. Tests performed at the university put his IQ at 165—exceptionally gifted—when he was ten years old.

The boy's brain power was never a question. His interpersonal skills were another matter.

"He is so smart; it is easy to understand why he can't identify with kids his own age," said his first-grade teacher in their initial parent-teacher conference. "But I have observed that he has a low regard for most adults, too. I never thought I'd worry about a child who spent so much time reading, but I am concerned that he does not seem to need to interact with his classmates, at all."

"I can assure you that our son has many friends in our neighborhood," said Moreland's mother. "I think he just feels that, while he is at school, he should be learning and expanding his mind rather than playing dodgeball with kids who will be mowing his lawn and changing the oil in his Mercedes one day."

"Well, I see where little Blair gets his arrogance," the teacher later told her principal.

In truth, Blair's parents had privately expressed their own concerns about their son's tendency to isolate himself by reading alone in his room. Those concerns grew as he entered pre-adolescence. When the Morelands invited other children over to play with their son, or took him to neighborhood or school events, Blair was openly hostile to them.

"He knocked my daughter down and kicked her when she asked him if he wanted to play kickball."

"My boy came home with a bloody lip and said Blair punched him on the playground."

And, even worse, "I caught your son throwing rocks at our cat. Please tell him that is not the way to treat pets—otherwise I will have to ban him from coming over."

A week later, the same cat was found beaten to death in the neighbor's backyard.

The Morelands consulted Dr. Judith Long, a child psychiatrist and professor, who conducted an interview with their son and offered a disturbing assessment.

"You have a brilliant son, obviously. His IQ is off the charts, but he does show troubling signs of antisocial behavior that I believe should be addressed with counseling and therapy," she said. "I'm sure you've read that cruelty to animals is one of three symptoms that predict the development of a psychopathic personality. There are therapies, but I must tell you that, with such an intelligent child, it will be challenging."

The therapist explained that the Morelands' son's cruelty

to the cat was likely not the last time he would act out in such a way.

"This is an indication that he has an underdeveloped capacity for empathy, and so he doesn't understand, or care, about the pain he is inflicting," Dr. Long said. "I would suggest psychotherapy as a first step and perhaps medication as he gets older, depending on how he responds to the therapy."

The kid did not respond well to four years of therapy, so he was eventually put on a drug program to quell his more violent urges. Little Blair, the brainy loner, grew up thinking drugs were his only friends. He routinely used amphetamines to stay awake and focused on studies during college and medical school, while smoking marijuana and using cocaine and heroin on weekends.

After his wise father slammed the door to a cardiac surgery residency, fearing that his sociopath son might be too tempted to wreak havoc on humans with surgical knives, scissors, and saws, drug-dependent Blair saw anesthesiology as an attractive alternate path.

As an anesthesiologist, I'll have access to all my favorite opiates, and, even better, I will be able to play with pain as never before, either relieving it or inflicting it at will, he thought.

His plan had worked to a point. Moreland's only miscalculation was a common one among addicts, even those who were brilliant and successful otherwise. The new drug, fentanyl, had proven to be a more powerful and faster-acting opiate than he'd expected, which made it all the more addictive.

Even though he'd become head of the anesthesiology department at Springs General and had, as he'd dreamed, easy access to powerful drugs, Moreland knew he was risking his career and his medical license by stealing from the hospital's supply. And that is why, in the fall of 1977, he found himself 120 miles south of Colorado Springs, standing between the Cucharas River and the San Isabel National Forest.

CUCHARA, COLORADO, AUGUST 1977

Moreland watched as two horses meandered down Highway 12 without apparent supervision or purpose. They stopped to graze in his yard and those of his neighbors, too.

"Did they escape from somewhere?" he asked. "Should we call someone?"

"You will have to get used to life down here, Doc," said his real estate agent, Jimbo Wentz. "Wandering animals are part of the daily scenery, especially come October when the cattle travel from high pastures down to the lower pastures for the winter. You shouldn't be surprised to see large herds passing by your place this fall."

"You mean an old-fashioned cattle drive, like 'git along little doggies,' *Rawhide*, and Rowdy Yates?"

"Naw, this is more like a cattle ramble. The livestock down here knows where it is going; no need to guide them or hurry them along," Wentz said.

"Can I shoot a steer for supper if it comes on my property?"

"That would be a no. Slaughtering your neighbors' livestock is a good way to get a visit from shotgun-toting members of the local Unwelcome Wagon."

Dr. Moreland, who didn't want anything to do with his neighbors anyway, got the message. Wandering creatures, both domesticated and wild, were part of the rural charm of this place. Not that he cared about any of that.

The front porch of his newly purchased A-frame cabin at the

base of the West Peak of the Spanish Peaks offered panoramic views of the Sangre de Cristo Mountains and the narrow but fast-flowing Cucharas River.

"You will have all sorts of critters visiting year-round, thanks to the elk, mule deer, wild turkeys, black bears, and mountain lions in the forests around you."

"Mountain lions?"

"Yeah, I was in town the other day, and the game warden was checking out a big dead cat in the back of a pickup truck. A guy said he'd shot the beast when it came after him and his dogs up on Blue Lake. The bears mostly leave you alone unless they have cubs to protect, but the mountain lions are more inclined to see you as prey. You may be getting away from all that crime in Colorado Springs, but there are things that will eat you in these woods."

Dr. Moreland and his real estate agent had just returned from the San Pedro National Bank in Walsenburg where they had finally completed the closing on the cabin and its surrounding ten acres. The property checked all of the boxes for Moreland and his ambitious plans. It was in one of the least-visited, least-populated areas of the state, and just a two-hour drive from Colorado Springs. The cabin's interior needed a good scrubbing and new furniture and appliances, but he was more focused on renovating and refitting the large, well-vented outbuilding that was all but hidden in the woods behind the cabin.

His plans for that outbuilding were the main reason Moreland had persisted in trying to buy the property for more than six months, even though the elderly owner, Joshua Collingsworth, had repeatedly canceled previous closings, saying he'd changed his mind about selling.

Collingsworth was eighty-seven years old and known to be cantankerous with outsiders.

"Old Joshua was once a renowned taxidermist in this area. The local hunters and fishermen kept him busy, so he put up that metal building in the woods for his taxidermy work," Wentz explained to Dr. Moreland when first showing him the property.

Moreland had agreed to pay the original asking price, but Collingsworth walked out during the first closing, swearing at them and their lawyer and "big city assholes" in general.

"The locals say he was an easygoing guy in his younger years, but they suspect he inhaled too many taxidermy chemicals and it eventually affected his brain, making him volatile," Wentz said.

Dr. Moreland had persisted in trying to buy the property in the months that followed. He often visited Collingsworth, bringing him gifts and offering him thousands more than the asking price.

Just three months earlier, they'd scheduled another closing, but the old guy did not show up.

"He wouldn't let me in the front door after he skipped out on us in April, but I have to give you credit, Doc, you didn't give up. You kept driving all the way down here every couple weeks, working your charms," said the real estate agent.

"Yeah, you know, I'd pretty much given up on the cranky geezer after my last visit a few weeks ago. He was adamant that he did not want to sell the place. He said they'd have to carry him out in a casket before he'd leave," Moreland said.

"I guess the old coot got his wish," Wentz said. "Sure, worked out for you, too, since they found him dead of a heart attack in his kitchen just a couple days after he told you that," Wentz said.

"Well, I would never have wished for Mr. Collingsworth to die, of course, but it did work out in my favor." And since Collingsworth hadn't paid his property taxes, Moreland just had to pay the taxes in order to get the property he had coveted for its privacy.

The remote cabin was at the base of one of the two mountains known as the Spanish Peaks, which rose to more than 13,000 feet above sea level.

"The Ute Indians named them *Huajatolla*, which some local yahoos claim means 'Breasts of the Earth,' but that's bullshit, as appealing as it may sound," said Wentz.

"I like that! Finally, my own private set of Grand Tetons!" Moreland said.

The anesthesiologist did not share his next thought with his real estate agent, but he also found it amusing that his cabin's location was between two villages with names that were very fitting, given the real reason he'd purchased the property.

What better place for my little project than a cabin between La Veta and Cuchara? The names were Spanish for *the vein* and *the spoon.*

CHAPTER TWO

CHEYENNE MOUNTAIN

AUGUST 19, 1978, COLORADO SPRINGS
CHEYENNE MALL

Lula Lopez sat in her 1968 Chevy Impala at 9 p.m. on a Saturday, waiting for Airman First Class Alfonso Peres to show up in the parking lot of Cheyenne Mall Plaza on the lower west side of Colorado Springs.

This was Lula's favorite location for selling to her regular customers. Many of the mall stores stayed open late on the weekends because it had a two-screen movie theater that brought in big crowds. Two current hits, *Animal House* and *Grease*, were on the marquees, so there were plenty of locals coming, going, and milling about to provide cover for her illegal transaction.

Peres pulled up in his 1970 Dodge Charger, blue with a white roof, and parked beside her car. He nodded. She nodded. He shut off the engine and joined her in her car.

Lula gave him a welcome hug.

"Hey, 'Fonso!"

"Hey, Lula, how's it shaking?"

"It shakes a lot more than it used to, my friend," she said with a smile.

"Ha! Looks to me like civilian life agrees with you," he said, patting her shoulder.

"I just wish my civilian job at the recovery center paid better, especially since living in the real world means I have to cover rent and groceries," she said.

"I guess that's true, but at least you get to breathe clean mountain air instead of the air *inside* the mountain, which isn't so clean, no matter what they tell us."

They had first met and bonded while stationed at the North American Aerospace Defense (NORAD) Command Center inside Cheyenne Mountain, a massive military base built in a cave cut out of a Colorado Springs landmark.

From the outside, the three-peak mountain with a top elevation of 9,200 feet seemed benign and majestic, overlooking parklands, a zoo, the famed five-star Mountain Vista Resort, and exclusive neighborhoods of high-end homes.

On the inside, however, the mountain was home to a foreboding complex created during the Cold War to protect the US air defense system and keep it operating in case of a nuclear attack.

Forces of nature built Cheyenne Mountain over millions of years. Then, in the 1960s, the forces of the US military ripped out its granite guts to create the Pentagon's biggest safe house. Fifteen steel-encased buildings constructed inside the mountain were mounted on 1,300 massive steel springs to help prevent seismic-shock damage from a nuclear blast, which is why those who worked there referred to it as "the World's Biggest Bounce House" and "Home of the Real Colorado Springs."

Peres, who spent his work hours monitoring US air traffic

on NORAD's computer screens, was among those who struggled with claustrophobia and anxiety inside the enormous cave's windowless buildings.

Lula was stationed at the base as an air force mental health nurse. She had helped Peres deal with job-related headaches, dizziness, and claustrophobia. His favorite nurse had first written him prescriptions for Valium and then introduced him to more potent sedatives—for a fee.

Their arrangement worked out for both of them until her supervisors caught Lola writing fake prescriptions for Valium that she took herself. They'd also heard rumors, never proven, that she was taking cash payments for prescribing amphetamines and other drugs to other base personnel.

They threatened to hand her a dishonorable discharge but cut a deal instead. The Pentagon didn't want the media getting wind that Cheyenne Mountain personnel were using drugs to deal with anxiety from working while locked behind steel doors inside of a mountain.

"Keep your mouth shut about why you lost your NORAD job, go through the recovery center program and get clean, and attend weekly Narcotics Anonymous meetings for a year, and we'll give you an honorable discharge and your military pension," her commanding officer said.

She took the deal.

DURANGO CONNECTION

Lula had sincerely wanted to get clean when she entered the Rocky Mountain Recovery Center outpatient program. She figured her life would be a lot less complicated without drugs, and less expensive, too.

I mean, if the US Air Force will pay for me to get straight, why not do it?

She got clean with the help of the program, and eventually took a job at the recovery center. Lula might have stayed on a drug-free, legitimate path for more than a couple months if she hadn't reunited with Lorenzo Martinez at her great-aunt's eightieth birthday party earlier that summer.

Lorenzo was a distant cousin—third or fourth or fifth on her mother's side, she wasn't sure anymore—who had moved from Mexico to Denver with his parents when he was fifteen. She and Lorenzo had bonded at family gatherings in their teenage years, often sharing a joint while their parents got drunk on tequila and beer.

After high school, they lost touch. Lorenzo stayed in Denver. He landed a job thanks to an uncle, who was one of the city's wealthiest and most respected Hispanic businessmen, Jorge Santos. His uncle was the owner and operator of Santos Heating & Cooling, a thriving installation, service, and repair operation with branches throughout the Denver metropolitan area. He also owned Santos Trucking, a freight transportation company, with a vast fleet of short- and long-haul delivery trucks that operated nationwide from a base in Littleton.

Jorge Santos's business enterprises went beyond heating, cooling, and transportation of goods. He secretly served as a *regio* in charge of the southwestern United States for the Hinojosa crime syndicate based in Durango, Mexico. This criminal enterprise was not then known as a member of the Mexican drug cartels, but one day it would be among the largest. This family's illegal operations dated back to the 1950s. They were known for running a "farm-to-arm" heroin operation.

The Hinojosa family grew and cultivated poppies for opium production. They distributed mass quantities of their final product on the "Heroin Highway," which had a series of smaller distribution hubs between Durango and Chicago, including Denver—the family's primary base of operations in the United States—where Hispanic street gangs provided security and handled street sales.

Federal and local law enforcement had difficulty investigating and penetrating this crime syndicate because disciplined members of the Hinojosa family controlled the heroin division from top to bottom. The US Drug Enforcement Agency office in Chicago estimated that their operation was responsible for nearly 90 percent of that city's heroin traffic. By 1978, the Hinojosa family's criminal enterprise generated $60 million a year from heroin sales in the US.

Led by patriarch Marcos Hinojosa, it imported an estimated 746 pounds of pure heroin into the country annually. Their product was then cut with other substances for street distribution, which increased their volume to more than eight tons of heroin of only 5 percent purity.

Much of that diluted Mexican brown heroin was transported by vehicles fitted with the syndicate's own invention, the "Durango driveshaft," a sleevelike device that held several kilos. Their drivers were also known to store contraband in hidden compartments built into gas tanks and door panels.

Jorge Santos, who had become a master of logistics as a chief warrant officer for the US Army, ran the Denver-area hub. Santos kept his legitimate businesses separate from his drug-trafficking sideline. Just for the Hinojosa family's operations, he maintained a separate fleet of eighteen-wheel rigs, as well as smaller delivery trucks and vans based in a remote warehouse between Colorado Springs and Denver.

By the mid-1970s, Lula's cousin, Lorenzo Martinez, had risen to the rank of *Los Capos* for the Santos network, serving as his uncle's second-in-command. His primary job was to monitor the heroin delivery system and the activities of both the intermediaries and the street dealers who moved the drugs and collected the cash.

When Martinez reunited with Lula at their aunt's birthday, he was intrigued that she had a military background and worked as a mental health nurse at a drug treatment center.

"You must know a lot of drug users in the Springs," he'd said.

"Oh yes, I do, but I'm trying to stay clean myself these days," she replied.

"Do you plan on staying poor, too?" he asked.

"No, being poor has never suited me, but being a mental health counselor is not the path to riches."

"I can help you find a more rewarding path," Lorenzo said. "We have to take care of family, just like the gringos do, right?"

He could see that Lula was listening and continued.

"I need someone I can trust in the Springs. I will hook you up with one of our dealers down there so you can score some brown for friends, but keep the circle tight. I would rather not position you as one of our primary dealers there because that might put you on the radar of the feds or the local narcotics cops. I'm thinking that, with your job at the recovery center and your old military connections, you could help me keep an eye on things down there."

Lorenzo also warned Lula to keep their connection quiet.

"I don't want our other dealers, or the law, to identify you as a person of interest. That would defeat my purpose for making you my Springs watchdog who will alert me to any possible threats or issues with our operations down there."

Martinez had counted on his cousin staying clean, which did not happen. Once Lula began getting heroin from his supplier, she couldn't resist "sampling" it as well as selling it.

She tried to keep her shooting up on the down-low. Lorenzo had made it clear that he and his boss didn't like it when dealers became users and addicts. They became unreliable and vulnerable to pressures from local and federal narcs eager to flip low-echelon dealers who might lead them up the food chain to their suppliers.

THE CUT THAT KILLS

Lula had managed to avoid any problems, so far.

"I have your Mexican brown; do you have the cash?"

"Right here, Nurse Goodbody," Peres said.

When he was her patient, the airman had often teased Lula by comparing her to his favorite character on the television comedy *Hee Haw*. As one of the few females working inside the Cheyenne Mountain military base, Lula was used to flirtatious males. She let it slide. *Boys will be boys.*

"Before I put this shit in my body, I'd like to know what it is cut with," he said as she handed him a sealed vial within a capped plastic bottle.

"The usual suspects, I guess. Saline, maybe. Tequila? The Mexican mob doesn't provide me with a list of ingredients, my friend."

"Yeah, yeah, I know. But a lot of dealers cut it again with their own stuff. Just so it isn't rat poison or broken glass, I guess."

Lula did not want to tell her friend that he was right. She

had cut this batch of heroin with a new drug that was inexpensive and, supposedly, potent enough that her customers wouldn't realize they were getting less Mexican brown and more filler.

Peres was the second customer to buy this new mix—she'd sold a vial earlier in the day to Buck Medina, her coworker at the Rocky Mountain Recovery Center.

"Don't go crazy with this, okay, buddy? I want you to be my customer, and my friend, for a long time."

Before he could ask any more questions about the drugs, she steered Peres on to another topic.

"How are things inside the mountain these days?" she asked.

"As claustrophobic as ever," he said. "Do you miss it? I sure as hell miss you."

"Aw, thanks, but I don't miss working in that hellhole. It's what drove me to drugs in the first place," she said. "You take care now. See you next time."

I hope, she thought, watching the airman drive away.

Lula had joined the air force after earning her mental health nursing degree. She had bought into the recruiting brochures offering the opportunity to "see the world." Instead, they'd stuck her inside a giant rock where the only views were jagged granite walls.

No wonder I lost my freaking mind and started writing fake prescriptions for myself, she thought.

"I worked inside a mountain, in a building that sits on giant springs, and we were constantly reminded that nuclear war was a very real threat, and they couldn't understand how I became a drug abuser and paranoid nutcase," she had told Dr. Blair Moreland, who volunteered as a counselor at Rocky Mountain Recovery Center.

"It is understandable that your brain would be scrambled in that crazy base, Lieutenant Lopez," said the doctor. "Everyone in there is trained to expect a Russian attack at any moment."

"Yeah, Doc. Every time they see a strange blip on the radar screen, they shit themselves," she said. "The stress is unbelievable."

Dr. B was nothing like Marcus Welby, the calm and kindly television doctor she'd watched growing up. Dr. B was out there. A little paranoid. A little hostile. She thought he was hot.

Lula liked that he had a nasty edge and a rebellious streak. When he hit on her after their third session, she thought, *What the hell, why not?* He wasn't much for pillow talk, but she was okay with sex just for sex's sake. She didn't even mind the leather handcuffs, or his slam, bam, thank-you-ma'am approach. In and out, and then out the door.

That's okay, I'm not looking for love, she thought.

They hooked up at least once a week, often in his office at the treatment and recovery center. Her treatment program didn't quite go the way the air force had planned. Lula learned even more about using and selling drugs from her fellow patients, not to mention from Dr. Moreland, who turned out to be an enthusiastic drug user himself.

Once she became his patient with benefits, Moreland offered to help her out. It was on his recommendation that Rocky Mountain Recovery Center hired her as a mental health counselor once she had completed the program.

"It takes one to help one," he told the treatment center's CEO. "You've already seen how effective former addicts with military backgrounds are in working with veterans trying to get clean. They share similar experiences and speak the same language, so they relate to each other. I'm telling you, Lula Lopez has cleaned up her act now that she is out of that intense environment at Cheyenne Mountain, and she will be every bit as effective as the other veterans who've gone through treatment here."

Moreland thought Lula would prove useful to his plans, especially after she told him about her connections to the Santos trafficking operation in Denver.

"So, you are dealing Mexican brown for your cousin, and using it, too?" Moreland asked as he retrieved his pants from the floor next to the office couch.

"Only to make sure the product I'm selling is up to my standards," she said.

"Ha! Yeah, I believe that—not!" the doctor said. "Just remember, I can supply you with some great stuff—a new painkiller that packs a punch. You could use it to cut your Mexican brown. It would boost the buzz and your profits, too. You'd double your money and double the fun for your customers. They'd never know the difference. In fact, they'd probably think it was better than anything they've ever had. They'd keep coming back for more."

"You have mentioned that shit before," Lula replied. "Maybe it is time to give your stuff a try. I could use the extra money. It's either dilute my Mexican brown or start charging you for the great sex I'm giving you for free."

"Real men don't pay for sex! But I'll give you a deal on this new painkiller. I will teach you how to measure it carefully, though, because a little of this goes a long way, and even just a pinch too much could result in a high that never ends."

"Sounds dangerous, but also . . . interesting. What is it?"

"It's just a painkiller that I use in liquid form for my patients."

"Like morphine?"

"It's a new synthetic that just hit the market a few years ago, a hundred times more powerful than morphine, so you have to be really careful with it. The drug reps claim it isn't as addictive as heroin, but I think the jury is still out on that," Dr. Moreland said.

"Where do you get it? From the hospital?"

"You don't need to know that. Just know that I can get as much as I want, anytime I want it. And, like the Hinojosa family, I control the manufacturing process from start to finish."

CHAPTER THREE

A GOOD MAN DOWN

COLORADO SPRINGS
AUGUST 20, 1978

Officers John Stuart and Mason Kane were on the graveyard shift, cruising slowly in their CSPD patrol car through Monument Valley Park, a neglected city greenway on 150 acres overtaken by weeds and despair. The park is a big attraction today after a major restoration, but back then it was no place for family picnics. Most of its visitors in those days were on the skids; homeless people, bottom-feeding predators, and drug addicts.

Officer Stuart slowed the squad car to a crawl after spotting a tall male with long black hair drop the handset of a pay phone and then stumble across the road toward the park's creek. Stuart watched as the man stopped abruptly, held one hand to his forehead, collapsed to his knees, stumbled back to his feet, then lurched into the shadows.

"Looks like the big guy is going down," Stuart told his partner.

They pulled their squad car to the curb and got out, searching with their flashlights. The officers found him sprawled on the edge of the creek, vomiting. His arms and legs were jerking from seizures. Foam bubbled at his mouth. He was gasping for breath.

"Call in an OD victim. We need to get him to the ER ASAP," Kane said as he pinned down one flailing arm to check for track marks.

The ambulance arrived minutes before Rick Becker drove into the park, searching for Buck Medina, the friend who had called him after realizing he'd overdosed.

Those cops must have found him. I hope they got to him in time, Becker thought as he watched two patrol officers help a city ambulance team struggling to carry his hefty friend on a stretcher. They loaded him into the ambulance and drove off with sirens screaming behind a patrol car that led the way through the forlorn park.

Becker struggled to keep up in his battered old Mercedes. *Damn, Buck. I thought you'd kicked that shit a long time ago. What made you start using again?*

SPRINGS GENERAL OD

Upon arrival at Springs General Hospital, the ambulance driver shouted to the ER team rushing out to attend to their passenger.

"Male. Thirties. Seizing. Vitals flagging. Possible OD."

My wife, Kathy, a veteran nurse, happened to be helping in the ER that night. She joined the swarming team but paused briefly as she caught a glimpse of the patient's face.

Oh damn, she thought as she hooked up his IV.

She recognized him as Michael "Buck" Medina, a local Native American and Vietnam veteran activist, whom she'd known both as a previous patient and as the younger brother to her friend Dr. Maggie Medina, the El Paso County medical examiner.

Kathy had treated Buck in the past, but it was usually because he'd been punched or stabbed while trying to break up a fight at the halfway house where he worked as an advocate and a counselor. At six feet six and 280 pounds, he was a legendary street fighter, but rarely the aggressor. Buck was known for stepping in to defend others being taunted or preyed upon.

Kathy appreciated his toughness and his dry sense of humor. He'd even made her laugh on the night I brought him into the ER in handcuffs after he'd punched me in the face when I tried to break up a street brawl.

"Nurse Kathy, I am sorry I slugged your Officer Joe," he'd told her as another nurse checked my face for broken bones. "I was so wound up by those gang banger assholes I didn't recognize him as a cop until it was too late, but Joe got me back good. He's a fast fucker with that nightstick, so be careful around him, little lady."

Buck had become a local hero after turning his life around. He had returned home with a heroin addiction after six years in the army, including two tours in Southeast Asia. Combat nightmares and multiple injuries haunted him along with the addiction, but with Dr. Medina's guidance, her younger brother successfully completed rehab.

After a year of clearing out his demons through therapy and community service, Buck convinced his friends and family that he was drug-free and thriving.

Buck, what the hell? Maggie said you were doing so well, Kathy thought as the ER team swarmed around him, desperately trying to bring him back. The doctors were losing their battle against whatever drugs had shut his body down. Buck was unconscious and barely breathing. His pulse was faint. The pupils of his eyes were pinpoints. His skin felt cold and clammy. His lips were blue.

"I don't get it. We saw him go down as we were driving through the park," Patrol Officer Stuart told Kathy when she stepped out into the hall. "The ambulance got there within minutes. His vitals were tanking, but this is a young, strong guy, I thought for sure he'd make it."

A half hour after arriving in the ER, Buck was pronounced dead.

Kathy allowed herself a few minutes to grieve and regroup before making the phone call she always dreaded.

"Maggie, it's Kathy. I'm working the late shift at Springs General ER, and I am sorry to call at this hour, but I wanted to tell you this before you go in to work. Maggie, it's your brother, Michael. I'm so sorry, honey. We did our best to save him, but he died from an overdose. I was shocked because I know he's been through rehab and seemed to be doing well. He just went so damned fast. There was nothing we could do to help him."

There was no reply. Kathy heard a muffled cry, then the voice of Maggie's husband, Lee Wilson, my partner in homicide investigations, saying, "What's wrong? Who was that, Maggie?" and then the line went dead.

SUSPICIOUS CIRCUMSTANCES

After learning that Buck had died, patrol officers Stuart and Kane were leaving the ER when Rick Becker approached them.

"What brings the hotshot reporter out at this hour?" Officer Kane said.

"Was it you two who found Buck Medina in the park?" Becker asked.

"Yeah, why? You know him?"

"I did a story on him and his work after he got clean. We became friends. He called me on a pay phone from the park tonight, saying he was in trouble and needed help. I got there just as you were loading him into the ambulance."

"You weren't his dealer, were you?" Stuart asked.

"Fuck you, I've never messed with that shit—and I thought he was done with it after rehab. I can't figure this out."

The patrol officers knew the local reporter well enough to give Becker a pass on the profanity, especially given what they were about to tell him.

"Well, I'm sorry to say your friend didn't make it," said Kane. "I don't know what he shot up, but it took him down fast. Most of the junkies here are on Mexican brown and I've never seen anyone have a reaction to it like that. I mean, he was a big, young guy and in pretty good shape—and if he called you for help before he collapsed in the park, it sure doesn't sound like he overdosed on purpose."

"I hadn't even thought about him doing that," Becker said. "Buck was really into his community work. He'd found a purpose, and he had some strong family support. I just don't get why he'd even start using again after all he'd gone through to clean up. It doesn't make sense."

THE WAKE

The next night, Becker and other friends of Buck Medina gathered at MacCallister's Pub to mourn the loss of a community hero. Conveniently located across the street from the El Paso

County Courthouse in downtown Colorado Springs, MacCallister's was the watering hole of choice for lawyers, judges, cops, and other sources sought by local reporters. The reporters also gathered there just to drink.

And to play darts. The pub's other big draw was its backroom dart boards and the twenty-team dart league, whose raucous members practiced and competed every day of the week. There were teams for lawyers, judges, circuit clerk staff, and court reporters in the Legal Beagles division. The Shoot First division included county and city cops from patrol, vice, sex crime, crime scene, and detective units. Local newspaper, radio, and television reporters made up the Bad News Bearers division.

Becker belonged to the Aim High team, the edgy staff for the local alternative newspaper, *the Rocky Mountain High Times*. He was their star investigative reporter, front-page columnist, and ace archer in the dart room.

Members of the local establishment, including most law enforcement officials, disparaged the *High Times* as a "hippy dippy fish wrap tabloid." Yet its reporting team, led by Becker, was known for digging deep and breaking big stories missed by the mainstream newspaper, *The Gazette*, and even the much larger newspapers in Denver.

Becker had been around. He'd worked for *the Denver Post* and gained fame there before moving to Colorado Springs. His pissed-off, smart-ass, on-the-mark columns for the *Post* were often hilarious and the talk of the town. He had a lot of fans, as well as some powerful enemies, especially among the city's entitled elite, ethically challenged power brokers and backroom wheeler-dealers who were the targets of many of Becker's columns.

He championed underdogs and minorities and called bull-shit on the rich and powerful when they deserved it, following the traditional newspaper role "to comfort the afflicted and afflict the comfortable."

His first *High Times* column after he hit Colorado Springs was unusual because it was a largely flattering profile focused on Buck Medina. Becker wrote it after the city council recognized Buck for leading a campaign to provide more homeless shelters and transition housing for the city's large population of homeless veterans and recovering addicts.

Initially, Becker thought Buck's hometown hero story sounded too good to be true, but as he interviewed him and got to know him, the cynical reporter became a believer. Buck came to trust him too, baring his soul in describing his struggles with drugs.

"I first used heroin in an army field hospital after I was shot and hit with fragments from a booby trap while chasing the VC through a swamp. The heroin was supposed to ease my pain, but it became my pain, my nemesis, and my curse," Buck told the columnist.

The column stirred controversy and drew national attention because Buck also told Becker that he and his fellow soldiers believed the US military tolerated and even encouraged drug use among soldiers in Southeast Asia. He said top officials secretly condoned it as a method for boosting the energy and alertness of combat troops, and the drugs also kept them from rebelling against "that senseless war."

Becker's column about Buck's recovery and rebirth won a national writing award from the Associated Press. While the Pentagon was not pleased with his claims about amphetamines being issued by the military, they did not issue a formal denial, or even an informal one. Buck became a hero to many Vietnam vets for daring to tell the truth about his experiences. He was invited to speak to veterans' groups across the country.

"That's another thing I don't get about him using again," Becker told friends gathered at MacCallister's for Buck's wake. "He knew other guys looked up to him, and he enjoyed being an advocate for the underdogs. He'd been approached by a couple different organizations and individuals who wanted him to run for Congress. The last time I talked to him, he was still considering it."

Becker choked up. Another *High Times* reporter handed him a shot glass of Old Fitzgerald: "To clear your throat."

"Thanks. You know, I really respected Buck," he continued. "He had integrity, and he cared about other people. He had demons. We all do. I just don't understand why he went back to heroin or how a guy who knew a lot about using drugs could overdose and kill himself."

"Come on, Becker, give him a break. Even heroes like Buck have weak moments, and given all the demons chasing him, I can understand how he might start using again and mess up his dose," said Lula Lopez.

Becker knew Lula through Buck, who had met her at the local veterans' chapter of Narcotics Anonymous. They'd become closer when they moved on to jobs as counselors at the Rocky Mountain Recovery Center, where they had both completed the program for veterans.

"Well, maybe you knew him better than I did, Lula. I just don't get it," said Becker.

Buck had introduced Becker to Lula at MacCallister's a few months earlier. Becker had often wondered if they had a thing, but he'd never asked either of them. From what he'd observed, Lula had a lot of close male friends, but she and Buck seemed to have a special bond.

He hadn't asked her about it because Lula made Becker uneasy. He didn't trust her. There were also rumors that she had been caught stealing drugs while working inside the NORAD base and that, maybe after her discharge, she had become a dealer, selling to select customers. Becker had heard those rumors while reporting a series of stories about local drug traffickers and their Mexico connections. Lula's name had come up as one of their players in the field.

"You don't want to mess with Lula," one of Becker's sources told him. "She has bad mojo, and people who've fucked with her end up dead."

Becker had not investigated further into the street talk about Lula, but not because he feared her or the Mexican mob. He'd given her a pass out of respect for her friendship with Buck. He'd seen no compelling reason to check out Lula.

But then Buck died.

FAMILY CONNECTIONS

Dr. Maggie Medina did not attend her brother's wake at Mac-Callister's. She preferred to grieve Buck privately. She tried to keep a low profile since she was a public official. She agreed to have coffee with Becker ten days after Buck's passing, but only if it was off the record.

They met at the Coffee Hut, a few blocks from Maggie's office at the county morgue. Before the waitress arrived to take their order, Becker told Maggie, "Dr. Medina, I know Buck's death has hit you hard. Me, too. After I wrote the profile of him, we became friends and, as you may know, if you saw the police report, he called me from a pay phone in the park that night. He could barely talk. He was gasping for air. Buck could only tell me where he was and that he'd shot up some Mexican brown, but he said, 'It's not like any other time, I'm in trouble. I need help. Please come.' And by the time I got there, the patrol officers had found him and called for an ambulance. Everyone seems shocked that Buck didn't make it."

The waitress came to the table. They both ordered coffee. After she'd gone, Maggie replied.

"I wish that he had called me that night, but maybe he was ashamed to let me know he was using again. My family and I are all still struggling with his death on a personal level," Maggie said. "And, on a professional level, all I can tell you is that I assigned my brother's autopsy to one of my deputies, and his case will be treated like any other suspected overdose case. There will be a lab report, but that can take weeks," she told him.

"I understand," Becker said. "I'm not pressuring you for information on the circumstances of his death. I want to write a column about his life and what he meant to people in the community and how they are mourning him. Since I've already done a column that described his experiences in Southeast Asia, his battle with drugs and how he turned his life around, I wanted to focus this story on his childhood here by talking to close family, like you, Dr. Medina."

"I thought we were off the record today, Mr. Becker," Maggie said.

She'd been a public official long enough to know that reporters often would agree to off-the-record conversations initially but then try to turn them into on-the-record interviews.

"I was thinking we were off the record on the circumstances of Buck's death, but hoping we could go on the record about your family background as army brats with a Native American mother and Mexican father. I was looking for your memories of growing up with him," said Becker.

Maggie took a sip of coffee and checked her watch.

"Look, maybe we can talk about that another time, but Buck's death has thrown me for a loop, and, on top of that, my office is very busy right now; in fact, right before I came the police said they have another possible OD victim for us . . ."

"That seems strange, I mean, how many OD cases do you get a year? I thought they were rare in Colorado Springs. Buck's death is the first OD report I've heard since I moved here a year and a half ago, though I haven't really tracked them."

"Well, they are fairly rare, but it seems to go in cycles," Maggie said. "Honestly, I don't have the annual figures off the top of my head, but I can check and get back to you later today or tomorrow."

Maggie could tell that Becker was thinking the two OD cases in a short span could be connected, somehow, and she didn't want to go there. At that point, she had no idea whether there was a connection or not, but it would be unusual to have two cases within ten days of each other.

"Is there anything else, Mr. Becker?" she asked, rising from the table after putting cash down for her coffee.

"Yes, off the record, if you want, but do you have any idea why Buck might have started using again? Had something happened in his personal life? He was private about that stuff. He'd once told me that he had a fiancée before he went to Vietnam, but the relationship had not survived his two tours. Was there someone else in his life?"

Maggie was not going there, not now anyway. Buck had protected his private life for a reason.

"As I said, I'm as shocked by this as you are, Mr. Becker. I have questions too, but you will have to give me time to grieve and to sort things out. Agreed?"

"Yeah, sure, Dr. Medina. Let me know when you are ready for an interview. I'll wait to hear from you. Thanks."

On her walk back to her office, Maggie thought of Buck's tortured breakup with his fiancée, Rachel Jacobson, while he was first deployed in Vietnam. They had dated since high school. Buck had asked her to marry him before leaving for basic training in 1970. He'd volunteered, hoping that he'd be able to eventually go to college on the GI Bill.

Maggie liked Rachel, who'd managed a downtown pizza place called the Back Porch when Buck was deployed. She knew Rachel loved Buck, but Maggie understood why Rachel broke it off.

After Buck returned from his first tour in late 1971, he was a different person. The entire time he was home on leave, he was strung out, drinking, fighting, and complaining that he couldn't sleep because of the things he'd done and seen overseas. When Rachel told Buck that she no longer wanted to marry "this person you've become," Buck had threatened to go AWOL rather than be redeployed.

Maggie had talked him into returning, promising that she would talk to Rachel and try and convince her that Buck would return and do whatever it took to win her back. But as soon as Buck shipped out for that second tour, Rachel moved to Florida and cut off all contact with her ex-fiancé and his family, Maggie included.

Buck was so distraught that he reenlisted for another three-year hitch, serving most of that time in Southeast Asia and later at bases in Europe. After returning to live in Colorado Springs in late 1976, Buck had traveled to Florida, hoping to track down Rachel, but he could not find her.

Just two weeks before Buck died of an overdose, he learned from a high school friend that Rachel had died in a car accident in Central Florida. The friend sent Buck her obituary, and in reading it, Buck learned that Rachel had a daughter.

"Who was the father of this daughter?" he asked the friend, who had stayed in touch with Rachel over the years.

"All I know is that Rachel told me she was pregnant after she left Colorado but hadn't told you or anyone else," the friend said. "She made me promise not to tell anyone. And Rachel told the daughter that her father was killed while serving in Vietnam."

CHAPTER FOUR

CRASH AND BURN

Curtis Whitford was heading to Aspen for a job interview at the Snowmass Ski Resort, planning to stay at his mother's lodge. He'd invited a bunch of friends to come and party with him, so he needed to stock up on Mexican brown. He figured he'd buy enough for the party and for a warm-up hit to relax him before driving up into the mountains.

He called his usual dealer and fellow ski instructor, Art "Edges" Hedges, but his cupboards were dry.

"Sorry, bro, my supplier seems to have retired or maybe got himself lynched for cheating the Mexican mob," Hedges told Curtis. "I can give you the number for another dealer if you promise to call me next time and not switch to her just because I'm out of brown right now."

"Sure, Edges, what's her number? And her name?"

His friend gave a local number and then said: "I only know her as Lola, or maybe it's Layla? I can't remember for sure. I met her at a party a while back. She wanted to shoot up and hook up, and she was hot, but she was too old for me. I think she's former air force, a nurse or something. I've heard she was forced out at Cheyenne Mountain for doing drugs."

"It always freaks me out to think that, while we are teaching teeny boppers and their families how to ski the bunny run on that mountain, there is this huge freakin' Cold War military base hidden inside it, right under our skis," Curtis said.

"Yeah, man, that's like some *Dr. Strangelove* meets *Downhill Racer* shit right here in the Springs," Hedges replied. "They have a huge lake in there to supply water and another one full of diesel fuel! I mean, seriously, man, you couldn't dream up something like that."

"Okay, I'll call this what's-her-name, Lola or Layla, and see if she has any Mexican brown, but you'll still be my main man."

"Thanks, Curtis. Have fun in Aspen and watch out for those hippy cops there. They'll pull your ass over and steal all your dope for themselves!"

"Right on, bro! Thanks for the connection. Talk to you later, man."

After Edges was off the line, Curtis started to dial the number for the other dealer when he heard his mother return from the grocery store. *Not cool to be caught setting up a drug deal by your moms*, he thought. *I probably ought to help her unload the groceries, especially since she isn't charging me for room and board—even though the old man says she should.*

His parents were divorced. His mother's family were billionaire real estate developers from Denver. She played real-life Monopoly too, but mostly dabbled in high-end condos and mountain McMansions in Aspen and other Colorado resort towns.

His father was vice president for the US operations of an

international pharmaceutical company and oversaw an army of drug reps. He didn't think it was funny when Curtis called them "state-sanctioned drug dealers." Curtis didn't care. His dad had been perpetually pissed off because he'd paid for his son's college tuition at the University of Colorado in Boulder, but Curtis dropped out in his junior year to become a ski bum.

"Are you ever going to stop playing in the snow and get a real job?" his father asked every time they got together.

"Dad, I have the rest of my life to work like a wage slave. I just want to enjoy life until I'm like, thirty, and then I'll put on a suit and sell overpriced drugs for you."

"Well, at least you could stop leeching off your mother, which means you are also leeching off me since she took me to the cleaners in the divorce, even though she is a rich bitch by birth," his father said.

"I've been working at the Mountain Vista's ski area, and I'm moving up, at least in elevation. I've applied for a ski instructor job in Aspen, so I won't be living with her anymore—if I get the job, that is. But I might need to live in her family's vacation place there for a little while. Just until I find my own crib somewhere."

"Yeah, sure. Once you move into that palace, you will never leave. I have no doubts about that," said his father. "And to think that I once figured that would be my retirement home."

"It probably would have been, if you hadn't been boffing every female drug rep between the Springs and Fort Collins."

FEELING THE HEAT

Lula Lopez called Edges after hanging up on some dude who called, asked for "Lola," and said Edges had given him her number.

"Who is this Lance Reese dude, and what are you doing givin' my number to people I don't know, you dumbass?"

Edges laughed at the name Lance Reese. Instead of giving her his own name, Curtis had used the name of their goofy supervisor at the Mountain Vista ski area, whom all the guys called "Lance Romance" because he was always bragging about his après-ski conquests.

"Hey, Lance needed a hookup, and I thought you could use the business. Like, you're welcome, okay? I thought you could use another customer while I waited for my shipment, all right? Geez. Thought I was doing you a favor."

"I am very careful about who I do business with—and you should be too if you want to stay out of prison and alive," Lula replied.

"Look, I didn't give him your real first name or even your last name, and besides, Curt . . . I mean Lance, is cool. He's a ski instructor at Mountain Vista, and everyone loves the guy. Plus, he comes from a rich family, so you know he has the cash. So relax. Call him back and charge him double if you want. That way I know he'll come back to me for his next buy. Ha!"

Lula hung up and asked herself why she'd ever tried to hook up with Edges.

Ski bums! Why do they all sound like they've bashed their heads against too many trees and rocks? What was I thinking?

Lula hadn't told Edges, but she was especially wary of new customers because, over the weekend, she'd developed a serious problem—two of them, in fact.

She'd sold heroin cut with Doc's painkiller drug to only two customers, who also happened to be her friends—Buck Medina and Airman Peres. They had died within hours of each other. Both from overdoses.

Buck had gone down in a city park the day after she'd sold him a hit. Two cops had been watching him, and they got him to the ER quickly, but he'd died anyway.

Peres was found dead in his apartment later that same Saturday after failing to show up at his NORAD post. His death had not been covered in the media, but Lula was sure the military would put its investigators on his case because the air force supposedly drug tested the Cheyenne Mountain base personnel regularly. They'd want to know how Peres's heroin habit had gone undetected.

Buck was an even bigger problem. His death had been widely reported in the local media. On top of that, the county medical examiner was his sister. She had the power to order an autopsy. If it showed traces of the new drug along with the Mexican brown, it could trigger an investigation.

I gotta lie low until things settle down. Maybe I should even leave town. But I can't be certain their deaths had anything to do with that new drug. The doc told me to be careful in measuring it out, but what the fuck do I know about chemistry? I went into mental health nursing so I wouldn't have to go near a lab or learn how to measure shit.

The more she thought about it, the more Lula worried that maybe she'd used too much of the new drug in cutting the heroin. And the more she worried about that, the more Lula fretted about the cops coming after her.

I mean, sure, I knew Buck from Narcotics Anonymous and the recovery center. Everyone knew Buck. He was like the St. Francis of Assisi for all the miserable wretches in town. Except he beat the crap out of anyone who preyed on them, so maybe he was more like a guardian angel or something.

Lula had never had a customer die of an OD before Buck and Peres went down, and she'd sold Mexican heroin to a few other acquaintances since the air force had kicked her out. She'd also never known the cops to care much about OD cases. They figured most junkies were dead men walking anyway.

Still, Lula considered blowing off Edge's friend and not calling him back to set up a deal and a meeting place. Then it hit her that she didn't have enough in the bank to pay her bills and get out of town if necessary. She needed to unload the rest of her Mexican brown.

It would be safer to sell it to someone like Edge's friend who couldn't be connected to me if this shit is bad. So maybe I go ahead with this deal but have someone else make the sale.

She called Aurora, a junkie she'd counseled at the halfway house. She'd always talked about needing money. Aurora was a former stripper who'd put on too much weight. None of the clubs would hire her to perform, so she'd been waitressing and hooking on the side.

"Aurora, I want you to meet a guy and do a deal for me tomorrow night. I can't make it because I have other commitments. But if you handle this one, I'll cut you in on the deal, and there might be more opportunities like this in the future."

A VISIT FROM THE DOCTOR

The next morning, Lula met with Aurora in a church parking lot near the Rocky Mountain Recovery Center. After giving her a packet with the cut brown heroin and instructions on where Aurora should meet with "Lance," Lula went to work at the center. She was in her small office preparing for her first client meeting of the day when Dr. Moreland opened the door and entered without knocking.

After locking her office door, coming around her desk, and looming over Lula in her chair, he said angrily, "Have you moved all of the product I gave you?"

His sudden appearance and menacing tone startled Lula. She hated it when Moreland was so volatile. It was usually an indication that he needed a fix.

Moreland moved closer, pushing between her legs, forcing her skirt up, pinning her against the wall in her chair.

"Are you following my instructions about mixing it carefully? You can't fuck around with this shit, Lula! It could kill someone if you added too much."

For a second, Lula feared that Moreland had heard about the overdose deaths of Buck and Airman Perez. She had been counting on the fact that the arrogant doctor often bragged that he didn't have time for "all the bullshit and liberal media hype" in newspapers or on television. Even the resident clients of the recovery center picked up on Moreland's cluelessness about the world outside his workplaces. One resident client had told her that when he asked Moreland for a weekend pass to attend the Willie Nelson concert in Denver, he'd said, "Who the hell is Willie Nelson?"

But Lula's fears of being blamed for the two OD deaths proved groundless. Moreland had already moved on from his concerns about her heroin mix. He was pawing at her crotch now, clumsily trying to remove her panties. She instinctively pushed him back and knocked his hands away.

Immediately, she regretted resisting him.

He slapped her with the back of his hand.

"You lowlife bitch! I could kill you right now and not a soul would care," he said. "I own you."

Moreland's eyes were twitching. His breathing was erratic. He pushed her back against the wall again, forcing open her legs, and then buried his face between them.

She gave up fighting him.

Better to just let it happen and appease him . . . for now.

CHAPTER FIVE

ANOTHER DAY, ANOTHER OD VICTIM

On the morning of August 25, 1978, my cantankerous partner Det. Lee Wilson and I were dispatched to investigate a body found in a vehicle parked at the Garden of the Gods Overlook Motel.

"I've been to this no-tell motel on calls before, and I think the city should at least sue the dump for false advertising," Wilson said as we drove south from the Colorado Springs Police Department headquarters.

"Yeah, but I don't think they'd attract many tourists if it had a more appropriate name like 'The Dead Doper Dump,'" I replied.

I'd only had time for one cup of coffee before we got the call from dispatch, so my rapier wit wasn't as sharp as usual.

Then again, by this time I'd been a homicide detective for the city of Colorado Springs for more than three years, and I'd been a city patrol officer before that, so I was less than excited about another report of a body found outside a seedy no-tell motel in my city.

Det. Lee Wilson, who was ten years my senior, had guided me through my rookie year in Homicide and brought me up to speed. I'd proven myself as a detective and won his approval as well as his friendship. We had become a full-fledged team, solving dozens of difficult cases together. So he no longer hazed me, maligned me, used me, or abused me— at least not any more than he beat up on other members of the CSPD.

We even socialized frequently given that Kathy and his wife, Maggie, had bonded over the challenges of being medical professionals married to homicide detectives who were married to their jobs.

"How's Maggie doing, by the way?" I asked on our way to the day's first corpse. "I know she and Buck were pretty close."

"She's taken his death harder than I would have expected, to tell you the truth, pardner," Wilson said. "She'd always held out hope that Buck would get his shit together and go to college. She'd even encouraged him to apply to nursing school, but Vietnam kicked his ass. There were too many ghosts chasing him."

Wilson paused for a second. I knew what he was thinking. We'd spent a lot of nights sharing our own haunted thoughts drawn from the murders we'd investigated. We dealt with those demons daily, and we understood that Buck's years in Southeast Asia included endless periods of intense combat in thick jungles rife with horrors.

"I mean, he really was an advocate for the most down-and-out people in the city," he continued. "Buck did a lot of good, so he wasn't wasting his life. He was making a difference and that gave us hope he was on a good track. I'm telling you that neither one of us had any idea he was doing heroin until it killed him . . . I guess I shouldn't say that until Maggie and her assistant Amy finish the autopsy and get the lab reports, but that's sure what it looks like."

"Yeah, if it turns out there is some bad batch out there, we are in for some long days and nights," I said. "It's crazy how much cheap Mexican brown heroin is available around town. They must be bringing it in convoys across the border from Durango. The shit is everywhere including, in all likelihood, the veins of today's leadoff hitter."

We were driving past the entrance to the Garden of the Gods nature center, which was a terrific park, a national landmark on more than 1,300 acres within the city limits. In the days before the pioneers came in covered wagons, it was the hunting grounds and home to Native American tribes including the Utes, Apaches, Cheyenne, and Comanche.

"The scenery is priceless," I said. "Kathy and I took our kids there to climb Steamboat Rock a few months ago. The views of the red sandstone rock formations and Pikes Peak were spectacular."

I loved the history of Colorado, and I went on a run, telling Wilson that those incredible geological features dated back to the Ice Age when the parkland was covered by an ancient sea . . . until he waved me off.

"Sorry, Joe, but whenever I think of that park I think of all the bodies we've found dumped there, not to mention the suicidal maniacs who've jumped off those beautiful cliffs. Or got thrown off."

He was right. We'd found so many bodies on the park

grounds that patrol cops referred to it as the "Garden of the Stiffs." The park's real name supposedly came from the fact that only the gods deserved to live in such a beautiful place, but that didn't stop the angels of death and the dirty hand of man from visiting.

The city's criminal element had figured out that the park was a great place to dump their victims. This tended to disturb the tourists who stumbled upon their bloody bodies.

"Not much we can do to stop that. Providing twenty-four-hour patrols for more than thirteen hundred acres of park isn't in the police department budget," I said.

The areas bordering the park were home to some of the city's most expensive neighborhoods where many of the rich and famous lived in multimillion-dollar mansions, but if you drove just a few miles south, as we were doing, you hit the crappiest and most dangerous parts of town.

The Garden of the Gods Overlook Motel was one in a series of beds-by-the-hour joints on the far outskirts of the park. About two miles south of the park's entrance, the run-down motel consisted of a dozen one-bedroom, one-bath stucco cabins with clay tile roofs.

From a distance, the place looked decent enough, but it didn't pass the smell test when you got close enough to detect the mildew, piss, and rot emanating from every crack and crevice. The pile of used hypodermic needles in the dumpster was another clue that this was not the Ritz Carlton.

Patrol Sgt. Marvin Manley had been the first officer on the scene, and he was waiting for us near the Jeep with the body found in the hotel parking lot. He and his partner, Officer Jason Rodriguez, had sealed off the area with yellow crime scene tape while waiting for the techs and someone from Maggie's office to show up.

Marvin had grown up in the toughest neighborhood of Colorado Springs. He'd managed to fight off both the Black gang recruiters and the hillbilly racists before joining the marines where he became a drill sergeant. No one messed with Marvin.

"Good morning, Detectives," he said. "I arrived on the scene shortly after the sun came up after the hotel custodian notified our dispatch that he'd seen someone unconscious or possibly deceased slumped over the wheel of a Jeep Cherokee parked in the lot here. I checked it out upon arrival and found a young man unresponsive. The vehicle door was unlocked, so I investigated further and found that he was deceased.

"His name, according to the driver's license found in his wallet on the seat next to him, is, or was, Curtis Whitford, twenty-eight, and his driver's license indicates he is a resident of our fair city's exclusive Mountain Vista neighborhood."

"Unless he still lives with his parents, my guess is that's an old address dating back to when he first got his license," I said.

Patrol Officer Manley had more.

"I did notice that he has an employee parking pass for the Mountain Vista Resort in the window of his Cherokee, and it has a bumper sticker that says, 'Ski Cheyenne Mountain at the Mountain Vista,'" he said.

"That's where our whole family learned to ski," I said. "It was close to home, not crowded, and their bunny hill was a good place for our kids to ease into the sport."

"I wonder what a young guy working at that fancy place

and living in that neighborhood was doing in this shithole?" Wilson asked.

It was a rhetorical question. My partner understood the only reason someone with a fancy address would be at the Garden of the Gods Overlook Inn was to buy drugs from one of the many street dealers who used it as their base of operations.

Officer Manley confirmed this.

"While waiting for you detectives and the medical examiner, I did a quick inspection of Mr. Whitford's fully tricked-out Jeep Cherokee Chief and found drug paraphernalia, including a silver spoon with char marks, a spent hypodermic needle, and a disposable lighter. There was also a plastic bag with a quantity of a white powdery substance. It would appear that the deceased could not resist sampling his purchase by heating up and liquefying a bit of it and then injecting it into his bloodstream with the hypodermic needle, but I'm sure you veteran detectives already figured that out," Manley said.

"My quick inspection of his body detected needle tracks on the inside of his elbow. There were no signs of bullet wounds, stab wounds, or beating, so it appears to be, wild guess, a drug overdose."

"Really?" I said. "Most of the bodies found at this dump are the result of drug deals gone wrong and the carnage that ensues when a dealer and a customer cross swords. Overdoses are rare here."

"Yeah," Wilson said. "Dead junkies are bad for business—and the Mexican drug lords at the top of the food chain have a low tolerance for anything that hurts their bottom line."

"If that's the case, the big dogs across the border in Durango may be howling," I said. "With Buck and the NORAD guy dead from overdoses, and now this kid, their Mexican brown business may be taking a serious hit. No pun intended."

A KILLER CUT

Our chief told us to make the three OD cases a priority even though we had no proof so far that anyone was intentionally targeted. It is tough, though not impossible, to make a murder case out of an overdose.

We might have balked a little at diving deep without more to go on under normal circumstances, but this investigation was also personal given that one of the victims was the brother of Dr. Medina, our medical examiner and Wilson's wife.

Yet, as usual, we were working other murder cases too, including one in which a low-level drug dealer was shot and killed. We didn't have any reason to think that murder was connected in any way to the OD cases. However, we did know that most of the drug trafficking in our fair city was linked to the Hinojosa crime family based in Durango, Mexico, which was just a twenty-hour drive straight south.

Our victim in the shooting was one Carlos Gardner, who got himself killed for failure to pay his cocaine supplier in a timely manner.

"I hate that we have to spend our time trying to figure out who killed this lowlife instead of working Buck's case," said Wilson as we discussed the case in our office at police headquarters.

"I hear you, but as you once told me in my rookie year, we don't get to choose the quality or quantity of our victims. We are required to investigate all murdered humans, whether or not their lifestyles meet with our approval."

"Did I really say that? Damn, Kenda, I'm wiser than I thought."

"As I was telling you, or trying to tell you, we may not know the name of Mr. Gardner's killer, but sources say his social circle included a nefarious crew of local drug dealers associated with the Hinojosa family trafficking enterprise. And one of our informants, who is familiar with this crew, told me that a rising star in the family's local drug operation, Manny Mendoza, would likely know who pulled the trigger and under whose orders. I'm going to run Mendoza's name by our friends in Metro Vice and Narcotics Investigations."

"Good idea, let me know what they say."

Walking into the office of this task-force unit was like stepping into a Broadway production of the hippy rock musical *Hair*. The undercover guys had to blend in with the scumbag dealers and dopers that they hunted, so they wore their hair long with full beards. They also favored bell-bottom jeans and T-shirts with tie-dye prints or images of Jimi Hendrix or Frank Zappa, who apparently belonged to a fraternity called Phi Zappa Krappa, according to one of their favorite tees.

"Hey, Kenda, what are you doing here in the doper division? Looking to score some acid?"

"Naw, I'm more into antacids these days . . ."

They liked that I was such a straight arrow. The narcs didn't get to hang out with many of us during working hours.

"I do have a question for you Deadheads, though," I said. "Does the name Manny Mendoza come up in your social circles?"

There were a dozen undercover guys in the room, and every one of them stopped what he was doing and stared at me when I said Mendoza's name.

"Well, well, well, I seem to have rung a bell," I said.

"Why are you interested in that particular dirtbag in our sea of dirtbags?" asked Lt. John Jake, head of the Narcotics unit.

"I've heard that Mr. Mendoza may have intimate knowledge of the Carlos Gardner murder, given that they ran in the same high-society circles," I explained. "I'm hoping to bring him in and see what information I can squeeze out of him."

"Can you wait until tonight to go knock-knock knocking on his door?" Lieutenant Jake asked.

"Sure, I guess. Why?" I said.

"Your timing is impeccable, Detective Kenda. We have learned that Mad Dog Mendoza is moving weight way out of his class these days, and we are about to move on him. He has somehow gotten his grubby hands on thirty keys of cocaine— sixty-six pounds of the devil's own blow—and our task-force team of undercover agents has a million-dollar deal scheduled with him for midnight tonight at his home."

"So you are going in with a million bucks in cash?"

That is the nature of the drug business. Only cash. It is heavy, cumbersome, and awkward, but that's how deals are done. No checks. No plastic. Just dead presidents. Do a warrant search on a dope house and there is cash stashed everywhere. Furnace ducts. Toilet tanks. Freezers. Most of it in plastic-wrapped blocks.

"The buy money is courtesy of our local division of the FBI, which will be sending two of its own undercover guys to make sure their stash does not somehow disappear during our transaction-slash-bust," said Jake.

"You don't mind if I dress down and come along?" I asked. "I only want maybe a half hour with him after you have locked him up. I will offer to be his new best friend and fight for his cause if he helps me find Gardner's killer."

"You are lying about fighting for his cause, of course."

"Oh, hell yes! There is no law against cops lying to scumbags; in fact, we thrive on it."

"Well then, welcome to the party. You will be joining our own Sgt. Ricardo Davies, who has already made one smaller cocaine purchase from Mad Dog to set him up for this deal. You will be accompanied also by the two FBI money minders and a pair of DEA undercover dudes who plan to make a federal case of this because of the quantity of cocaine involved. Our hope is to put the squeeze on Mr. Mendoza to provide us with information that will help us put away the entire Hinojosa family one day."

"I will make sure to leave enough juice in him for you," I said. "Thanks for inviting me to the dance."

We rendezvoused at police headquarters at 11:00 p.m., looking like Sgt. Pepper's Lonely Hearts Club cops. I was the most clean-cut, by far, even though I did my best to dress like a cocaine cowboy.

"We look like carnies who can't find the midway," said Sergeant Davies as we climbed into his beat-up van.

"All except Kenda, who looks like the local minister taking the rest of us to the homeless shelter," said Agent Frank Linden, one of the DEA guys.

"Sorry, I didn't have time to let my freak flag fly," I replied.

"Lieutenant Jake said Mad Dog is so money hungry, he'll be too busy drooling over that mountain of cash to wonder why we brought so many people to his place."

"Don't worry, I told him that I hurt my arm, so I need help carrying all that cash in and all that coke out," Sergeant Davies said.

Upon arriving at the Mendoza residence, we knocked on the door, and our eager host ushered us in.

Lieutenant Jake had nailed it.

The only thing Mad Dog saw when he opened the door was the four gym bags of cash we carried in, which weighed a total of ninety pounds. We put them on his dining room table, and he sat down with his eyes on the prize as we took seats on the couch and chairs behind him.

"Gotta count it before anyone leaves with even an ounce of coke," he said. "And if any of you make any sudden moves, my little puppy in the corner will take you apart limb by limb."

None of us had noticed the massive Rottweiler hiding in a dark corner. He'd been behind the door when we came in. So that is why Mad Dog felt so secure. He had 130 pounds of muscle and teeth as backup.

The dog didn't pay much attention to us, and neither did Mendoza, who immediately focused on counting the $1 million in $100 bills. We let him have a few moments to feed his fantasy of impending wealth. Visions of Ferrari convertibles were dancing in his head.

He continued to count the money without looking up, but he did take time to boast about his guard dog.

"You boys should know I paid two grand for that beast because he's specially trained," he said.

"Really?" said Sergeant Davies. "What's he trained to do?"

"He can sniff a cop from two miles away," Mad Dog said proudly.

Like all the other lawmen in the room, I had to stifle a snicker.

"Well, Mad Dog, considering your present company, maybe you can get a refund on the two grand and the useless mutt," I said.

With that, Mendoza finally looked up at us and into the barrels of our six very large and very powerful handguns. Make that five; one of the DEA agents had his 9mm aimed at the Rottweiler, but there was no need. The beast was sprawled out and snoozing on the floor with a stream of drool flowing down his massive jowls.

Mad Dog quickly turned into a whipped pup. The DEA agents cuffed him while reading his rights and then escorted him to the paddy wagon that had pulled up. The docile Rottweiler was escorted to the puppy wagon by an Animal Control officer, who would take him to the county's shelter for wayward pets.

The FBI agents collected Uncle Sam's cash. I helped Sergeant Davies carry the cocaine stash out to our van. It took a couple trips, but it was worth the effort, knowing that we had taken a good chunk of that shit off the streets.

LET'S MAKE A DEAL

After we returned to police headquarters and our vehicles, I drove to the county jail for my appointment with the newly incarcerated Mad Dog. His jailers brought him into an interview room where I did my best impression of Monty Hall, host of *Let's Make a Deal*.

"Mr. Mendoza, let me first introduce myself. I am Detective Kenda of the Colorado Springs Police Department's homicide division. By that, I mean, I don't give a shit about your cocaine business, tonight's bust, or the case that will be brought against you in federal court."

"Well why are you here then?" he asked.

"I am investigating the murder of Carlos Gardner, who, I'm told, may have run in the same social circle as you, given that he also was dealing in heroin and cocaine as a loyal underling of the Hinojosa family," I said.

"Yeah, I knew that lowlife scumbag. So what?"

"If you have knowledge of who ordered his hit or who pulled the trigger, and you shared that information with me, I am prepared to go to bat for you with the DEA. I would advise them that you cooperated in a murder investigation, and I would expect that maybe, perhaps, they might just go a little easier on you as far as charges and sentencing."

"Can I get that in writing?"

"Oh, hell no," I said. "You know it doesn't work that way. I make my recommendation based on your cooperation, and then your high-priced lawyer on retainer to the Hinojosa family works out the negotiations with the DEA."

Mad Dog was a practical man, and he didn't have anything to lose at that point.

"Look, I know some people with their heads up their asses are saying that Carlos got himself shot because he wasn't paying what he owed the family—and that may have been a factor, but it is only part of the reason they took him out," he said.

"Go on, I am a very good listener," I said.

"You probably know we have a problem here in the Springs

with some people dying after shooting up Mexican brown," he said.

"Yes, I have heard a few rumors of that," I said.

"Well, that is bullshit, because one of the people who OD'ed was that Buck Medina guy, and the press has been all over the story. So I know you know, OK?"

"I'm *still* being a very good listener," I said. "And you still haven't told me anything that will help shine your apple for the mean old DEA."

"Detective, I could give you some bullshit name and send you off on a wild goose chase, but I really don't know who the fuck shot Carlos," he said. "What I do know is that the family gets very concerned when people who buy their product start dying in the streets. It scares away other customers, and it brings too much heat from the media and the cops."

"Again, nothing you've said helps me—or you, Mr. Mendoza."

"I get that. All I can tell you is that the family was sending a message by killing Carlos, instead of just beating the shit out of him or beheading his dog. They are going fucking crazy trying to figure out who is cutting their product with some kinda new shit that is killing people. Maybe they thought Carlos knew and wouldn't tell them, but I don't know that for sure. What I do know is that more people are going to be dying in this city. Some of them may be people who overdose on this bad brown heroin mix. Some of them will be street dealers that the family suspects of using this new mix, or street dealers suspected of even knowing the dealers using the mix."

"Mr. Mendoza, I do appreciate your insight into the

Hinojosa family's local operations, but I need the names of those who killed Carlos."

"I understand. I don't know who did the hit. You and I both know that the order had to come from the very top, but I don't hang out at the family compound in Durango. They never invite me to their parties or their business meetings. I guess what I am telling you, whether it helps me or not, is that your police department better find whoever is cutting the Mexican brown with bad shit before the family finds him or her because they will keep killing people until they can get that shit off the streets."

SHOP TALK

I told Wilson about my meeting with Mad Dog when he and Maggie came over the next day for our monthly Saturday cookout.

"You have to give him credit for not giving you some bull-shit names to chase just to mess with us," Wilson said. "Even if he does know who made the actual hit, I'm sure that guy hightailed it back to Durango right after taking out Carlos. We'd never find him there even if we had a name, and we will have our hands full here at home if he is right about the Hino-josa family's plan to keep killing local dealers until there are no more overdoses."

I poured us both a couple more Maker's Mark and Cokes. We drank soda with our bourbon when socializing but took the Maker's straight up otherwise. The kids were inside, going nuts over something called Pong, an apparently addictive video game played on their Atari console, which was hooked up to the television set.

Don't ask me how the game worked or why they were so

crazy about watching a one-dimensional ping-pong ball bouncing around an otherwise blank television screen. I was hoping this video game fad would pass quickly along with the damn Pet Rocks that I had been stepping on for six months, usually while barefoot.

I was grilling steaks on our back patio, enjoying the peace and fresh air on a beautiful summer day in the foothills of the Rockies. Wilson had downed a couple more drinks than me because he had no grill to tend. I could tell my partner was feeling loose because he launched into another story from his glory days as a performer in a Nashville country rock band. I'd heard it before, of course. Maybe only twenty or thirty times.

This was his tale of the night his band opened for Willie Nelson and the Record Men in a Nashville honky-tonk. This landmark event in his life occurred just a short time before Willie moved to Austin and made it big, leaving Wilson in his dust.

"Ol' Willie favored whiskey more than weed back then, which wasn't a good thing because even Willie admits that he was a mean drunk," Wilson said.

Kathy and Maggie had been in the house prepping side dishes. They wandered back out and stood next to us as Wilson was spinning his yarn. He paused to see if they were impressed, but the two of them were engaged in their own deep conversation on something called "synthetic opiates."

"You girls are a buzzkill," Wilson said. "Joe and I are gonna start trading our gory stories of murder and mayhem if you two don't lay off the medical mumbo jumbo."

That comment was met with twin death stares. Our wives had no problem telling us to clam up when Wilson and I got caught up in cop shoptalk, but they were just as prone to plunge into their world of the sick, the dying, and the dead.

Inevitably, there are times when our worlds intersect. This would turn out to be one of those times.

"Well, Detectives Wilson and Kenda, the topic of our mumbo-jumbo discussion is a new drug that could create more murder and mayhem than your profession can handle in years to come if the general drug-abusing public gets ahold of it," said Kathy.

"What the heck is a synthetic opiate? I mean, I've heard of opiates like heroin and morphine made from poppies, sure. Are they making them out of plastic in a lab now?" Wilson asked.

"Not exactly, stud muffin," Maggie replied, winking at my wife.

"Synthetic opiates aren't made from natural sources like heroin or morphine, which are made from the seedpods of poppies," Kathy chimed in. "Those natural drugs are good at killing pain but also terribly addictive. So for many years drug companies tried to manufacture their own painkillers that weren't as addictive—and were less likely to cause heart problems."

"They didn't have a whole lot of luck achieving that goal, but one of the most powerful synthetic painkillers won FDA approval a few years ago," Maggie said. "It's called fentanyl and sold only by prescription. It is mostly used on patients during surgery and in recovery."

"Anesthesiologists and surgeons love it because, when carefully controlled, it is highly effective," Kathy added. "Our anesthesiologists use it every day on patients as young as newborns and as old as centenarians. We even give it to pregnant women and women in labor. But they use great care in administering fentanyl because it is so powerful and fast-acting. Patients are given weight-appropriate doses, and they are closely monitored. We keep an eye on the oxygen saturation in their blood, heart rates, blood pressure, and breathing rates. If needed, we can give patients oxygen or put them on a ventilator."

"It is also less expensive and easier to make than natural opiates, but red flags are going up already," added Maggie.

"Why the red flags?" I asked, fearing what I was about to hear.

I had not told my wife or Maggie about the warning given to me by Mad Dog Mendoza the night before, but this conversation appeared to be on a similar track. There was some sort of new powerful drug out there with the potential to kill a lot of people if it hit the streets.

"Fentanyl turned out to be highly addictive, too. And a tiny bit of this stuff goes a long, long way," Kathy said. "Just a few milligrams can kill you."

Maggie rose and paced around the backyard. The singing birds, shining sun, and beautiful mountains were lost on her.

"Drug companies aren't concerned about anything but making money. We're already getting warnings about people abusing this drug. When administered by a professional, it is safe and effective. But in the wrong hands, it can be deadly. I read one report that said the risk of overdose from fentanyl is twice as high as heroin and eight times higher than other prescription opioids."

"That's why we say that fentanyl is a good medicine but a bad drug. When drug abusers take it illegally, they aren't taking doses that are adjusted for their weight and other factors. There is no one standing by to monitor their pain levels or give them supplemental oxygen," Maggie said.

"So when this painkiller hits the streets, all bets are off?" I asked.

"There are growing concerns that stolen batches are already out there. Fentanyl is not easy to make in a lab, but the incentives to manufacture it illegally are so strong that it won't be long before the Mexican drug lords, the Mafia, and other major drug traffickers figure it out," said Maggie. "They won't need poppy fields anymore, they'll just need trained chemists, and when it hits the street, there will be hell to pay. I have family still in Mexico, and they live in fear of the drug traffickers who recruit the young men, rape and enslave the young women, and terrorize their communities. They are infiltrating and seizing control of the police, the army, and the government itself. And this new drug is so cheap, powerful, and addictive; it could make them wealthier and more dangerous than ever before."

"We've received a couple national medical bulletins reporting that surgeons, anesthesiologists, and nurses have become addicted to it," Kathy added. "The AMA is also sending out warnings that just absorbing it on your skin or getting a good whiff of the powdered version can put you down."

She and Maggie looked at each other like they had more to say, but weren't sure we wanted to hear it.

"Go ahead, spill it, you have already thoroughly violated our no-shoptalk rule and made me overcook the steaks," I said.

Maggie put down her wineglass and went into medical examiner mode, as if she had just called a press conference.

"I don't have any of the lab tests back yet, but I suspect, and fear, that Buck died of an overdose from brown heroin cut with something as strong as fentanyl," she said. "Your patrol officers saw him go down, and they got him to the ER quickly, but it was already too late. He's a big guy, so he got a lethal dose of something, and usually the heroin sold around here has been cut so much that, by the time it hits the street, it isn't all that potent, relatively speaking.

"I don't think anyone purposely gave him a lethal amount, or at least I have no proof of that, yet," she added. "But if street dealers have somehow gotten access to fentanyl and are using it to cut heroin, we are in for a world of hurt. It only takes about two milligrams of fentanyl to kill someone—and two milligrams of this stuff would fit on the tip of a sharp pencil."

"I thought it was a liquid?" Wilson said. "Doesn't it come in vials?"

"Most of the pharmaceutical fentanyl comes in liquid, but it can be made in powder form too, which means it easily can be pressed into pills or mixed in with heroin."

"Oh shit," Wilson said.

"Yeah, but that's not all," Kathy added, looking at Maggie.

"Suddenly we have two more OD cases besides Buck in just the last week or so. They found an air force guy dead of an OD in his apartment the day after Buck died, but since he was stationed with NORAD in Cheyenne Mountain, the military put a lid on that case. They took his body to their own morgue," Maggie said.

"You already know about the Mountain Vista ski instructor whose body was found in his vehicle. We don't know for sure if fentanyl was involved, but something stronger than heroin likely killed them. I'm worried. What if the Mexican drug lords have figured out that cooking up fentanyl in a lab is a whole lot easier, cheaper, and quicker than growing and harvesting fields of poppies? If local dealers have tapped into a heroin supply cut with deadly doses of fentanyl, we will be finding a lot more bodies."

CAUSE OF DEATH, UNDETERMINED

The report from Maggie and Kathy about fentanyl and all the dangers it posed mirrored what I'd heard from Mad Dog Mendoza. The more I thought about these developments in our illegal drug trade, the more pissed off I got.

"You know, I heard some clueless talking head on television say that drug abuse is a victimless crime. I wanted to kick his ass," I said. "Nearly ninety percent of homicides in this country involve some sort of connection with drugs, so that is just absolute nonsense. Sixty percent of our murder cases are linked to drugs. There is no such thing as a victimless crime when narcotics are involved."

Wilson ticked off the list of drug-related crimes, none of which were victimless.

"Burglaries, armed robberies, assault, homicides, rapes . . . I've had cases where drug users stole the rings off their dead grandmother's fingers so they could score another hit while granny's body was still warm," he said.

"Yeah, the victims pile up quickly in the drug world, where all the addicts can think about is finding the money to score another hit, and all the dealers can think about is getting another sucker hooked," I said.

"There would be no drug cartels slaughtering their own people in Mexico if it wasn't for the huge market for narcotics in the US, which is where eighty-five percent of the world's overdoses occur," Wilson added.

My partner and I had ample reasons for yelling "bullshit"

every time we heard the term "victimless crime" associated with drug dealers and users. When transactions are conducted by heavily armed criminals and addicts, violence is inevitable. Usually, both the seller and the buyer are screwed up on drugs. Most of them can't remember anything from one deal to the next, so we always had cases of dealers shooting the wrong people because they thought they owed them money.

Before I could recount all of the havoc that drug-related crimes had wreaked in just the last few months, my partner reminded me that we were supposed to be relaxing for a change. He raised his cocktail glass and said, "How about those Broncos?"

"Yeah, Joe, how about those Broncos?" said Kathy.

I took the hint. No more shoptalk from me either.

So, I played along, gladly.

"They got off to a good start beating the Raiders in their first home game, but then they lost in overtime to the Vikings. I'm hoping they can get back to winning tomorrow against the Chargers at Mile High."

"Or maybe, instead of sports, we could talk about how the world's first test-tube baby is doing!" said Kathy.

"Oh, good lord, first it's synthetic opiates and now they are making kids in a lab too?" said Wilson. "Where's the fun in that?"

"I think that's why they invented video games like Pong, so future generations wouldn't miss drugs or sex," I offered, scoring a total of three eye rolls in the process.

We relaxed the rest of the night, and Kathy and I focused on the kids on Sunday, but on Monday, back at police headquarters,

Wilson and I mulled over the possibility that a new killer drug might be on the streets of our city.

"There's not much we can do until Maggie gets back the lab results," Wilson said. "And even then, we have no proof that anyone deliberately set out to kill them by adding lethal doses to the heroin."

"Yeah, we need to know what lurks in the bloodstreams of Buck and the Mountain Vista ski instructor, at least," I agreed. "In the meantime, let's contact other medical examiners in the surrounding counties and figure out if they've had an increase in overdoses, too."

WORKING THE CASE

We were on the first steps of the journey known as Homicide 101. At this early juncture, we didn't even know if we had a murder case—or cases. We had suspicions, or rather, our wives who were medical professionals had their suspicions, which they'd graciously shared with us over cocktails and steaks.

In the last few weeks, at least three individuals had died after using drugs. That didn't mean there was any reason Wilson and I should drop everything and open a case file. Heroin users die with some regularity in every city, but that doesn't make them murder victims.

Dying of an overdose is an occupational hazard for drug addicts. For Wilson and me to get involved, there had to be at least some evidence that there was murderous intent, or at least murderous negligence in the preparation and sale of the heroin that killed them.

It was strange that the three victims were in different parts of the city and from distinctly different backgrounds, which made it unlikely, but not impossible, that they'd bought their heroin from the same dealer. Or maybe their dealers had bought the lethal drugs from the same supplier. At this stage, we just didn't know.

Buck Medina's death shook us all because we had no idea he was taking heroin again. The well-heeled parents of young Mountain Vista ski instructor Curtis Whitford claimed they didn't know he was a heroin user, either. Shooting heroin isn't conducive to skiing, or teaching skiing, or even riding the ski lift. True junkies tend to fall and pass out a lot.

"Our son was planning to go to my family's place in Aspen with some friends this weekend, so maybe he was picking it up for them?" suggested Whitford's mother.

"Except that some of it mysteriously ended up being injected into his arm," I noted.

Mom didn't like that. If looks could kill, I would have been glared to death.

"Or maybe he was just testing it before giving it to his pals or selling it to pay for his ski vacation?" Wilson asked.

"Curtis had plenty of money from his trust fund," the mom replied. "He only worked as a ski instructor because he loved the sport and it kept him fit for his trips to Aspen. My husband said Curtis told him that he was planning on moving there soon."

Then, there was Airman Alfonso Peres who hailed from the area's vast military population, which included soldiers from Fort Carson, Peterson Air Force Base, Schriever Air Force Base, the US Air Force Academy, as well as those, like Peres, who were assigned to the Cheyenne Mountain complex.

His death was notable because there is a low tolerance for drug abuse in the military. Soldiers are given random drug tests on a regular basis, especially when they work in top secret sectors like Cheyenne Mountain. So how did he get away with it? Or was this his first dance with drugs? That seemed unlikely. Heroin is not in the drug-user starter kit. Most of the time, it is the final nail in the coffin.

Wilson and I also had to consider whether any of these overdose deaths were connected or just random occurrences. Had they purchased their drugs from the same source? Was there a dealer out there purposely killing customers?

"I mean, street dealers aren't exactly MBA-level businesspeople, but even so, most mopes would know that killing off your buyers might have a negative impact on future sales, right?" Wilson said. "What the hell would the motive be?"

This was not our typical homicide case involving a shooting, a stabbing, a beating, or some other clear example of violence resulting in death. There was nothing cut and dry about this case, other than the heroin, that is.

Wilson and I had a lot to figure out because there were state statutes that put these deaths under our jurisdiction, but only under specific circumstances. In Colorado, if you cause the death of someone by engaging in reckless behavior, you can be charged with manslaughter, which is a felony carrying prison time. A good prosecutor might be able to make a case that a first-degree murder was committed because the drug dealer, or whoever cut the heroin with something lethal, had demonstrated "an extreme indifference to human life."

But any decent defense attorney would likely put up a strong challenge to that claim.

"So what most likely happened to these three?" Wilson asked over coffee in our office the Monday after the cookout.

"Well, given that they found needle marks on all three victims, I would assume that they thought they were just shooting up for a good time, but somewhere along the Mexican brown supply chain, someone cut the heroin with shit that resulted in a fatal overdose. If that happened, then it could be manslaughter because whoever cut it could be charged with recklessly causing a death, though proving that in court would be very difficult."

Wilson agreed.

"Yeah, I doubt that we have any criminal masterminds or cold-blooded killers here. It doesn't make sense that a dealer would want to kill off his customers, does it?"

CHAPTER SIX

BODIES ARE BAD FOR BUSINESS

SEPTEMBER 18, 1978

"*¿Que mierda? ¿Que mierda?* I mean, *Sobrino*, what the hell are you telling me? Do you realize this could get us all killed if the boss finds out?"

Jorge Santos, the Denver HVAC and trucking magnate and Southwest lieutenant in the Hinojosa family drug-trafficking network, was duly alarmed by reports of recent overdoses among Mexican brown heroin users in Colorado Springs.

Lorenzo Martinez, his nephew and *Los Capos* in the network's Denver hub, flinched at Santos's fury. It was his unfortunate duty to report any problems that cropped up in the heroin supply chain, and that was what had brought him to his stern uncle's Littleton office at 7:00 a.m. on a Monday in late September.

"Tío Jorge, I'm just telling you what I'm hearing from our people on the street," Martinez said. "We're getting reports that at least three people have died from overdoses in different parts of the city. Some are saying their doses may have been cut with a new potent drug."

"So you're thinking it wasn't the heroin that killed them but this new drug?" asked Santos.

"I don't know how else to explain it," Martinez said. "We've never had this problem before. And we haven't had reports of OD deaths anywhere else that we distribute."

"Now listen, *Sobrino,* you must keep this quiet, and you must find out the source of this new drug, whatever it is, and shut it down. If it is a competitor, kill him and his family. If it is one of our own people cutting our product with this shit, kill them and their families. No one will buy our Mexican brown if they hear people are dying from it. And the boss in Durango will go apeshit if he learns *anything* or *anyone* is contaminating our product and threatening the river of cash that flows into his coffers.

"You and I will have targets on our backs if he decides this is our fault! I want you to go down there and start busting nuts and cracking heads until you find me the son of a bitch who is cutting with this shit, but before you kill him, find out where he is getting it and how it is made."

"Yes, sir. Do you want me to leave today?"

"Yes, I want you to leave today! Did you have a hot date with one of your stripper girlfriends or something?"

"No, Tío Jorge."

"Okay, go. And listen, Nephew, I may be sending some muscle to help you, so call me tomorrow after you are settled in. These will be guys from outside the Hinojosa family, independent contractors who are professionals."

"Yes, sir. Do they understand they will take orders from me?"

"They will take their orders from *me*, Nephew. But yes, from me, through you. I want to see if you can get your hands dirty for a change."

Lorenzo felt the sting of that comment but knew better than to show his anger and hurt. Once again, he would do his best to prove himself to his demanding uncle, he thought as he headed to his apartment to pack a suitcase.

After getting his things together there, he made a call to Colorado Springs.

"Primo Lula, it is Lorenzo."

"*¿Cómo estás, prima! ¿Qué pasa?*"

"We have some trouble, Cousin," Lorenzo said. "You know about the ODs, right?"

The pause from Lula was all Lorenzo needed to hear.

"Tell me there haven't been any more than three!"

"No, not that I've heard, anyway," Lula said. "Mostly from what I'm hearing, the dealers are afraid to sell, and the buyers are afraid to buy."

"I am heading down there now with orders from the *regio* to find the dealer—or dealers—who sold the Mexican brown to these three people, and then to find out what it was cut with so we can put an end to these deaths, which are already hurting business if your report is correct."

"I will keep my eyes and ears open for you, Lorenzo."

"Yes, do that. I know I can trust you."

Lula Lopez hung up the telephone and collapsed on her apartment's couch.

Did Lorenzo call to warn me? Or to make sure I was home? Or does he really not know that I was the source of the heroin that killed all three?

Either way, I am a dead woman. Sooner or later, they will come for me.

THE SMILING ASSASSIN

Jorge Santos loved and trusted his nephew, but he feared Lorenzo was not the man for this important job—to track down and kill the source of the lethal heroin in Colorado Springs. He needed someone ruthless and experienced. He wanted that person to do the job cleanly and then vanish.

I need a cutthroat who is also willing to torture this dealer if necessary to determine what lethal substance was used and where it came from. I need to know how it is made and whether this is a substance that the family can safely use to cut our product. If that is the case, we might want to manufacture it ourselves. This could be a very lucrative business opportunity for our operation.

After mulling over a long list of experienced hit men, torturers, and homicidal maniacs on the Hinojosa family roster, Santos chose to bring in a man who was more loyal to him than the family itself. He preferred to keep the deaths in Colorado Springs out of their ears for as long as possible.

Miguel will understand that this need not concern the family, for now, anyway.

The day after Lorenzo left for Colorado Springs, Santos called the man he'd chosen: Miguel Diaz, a chief investigator for the Mexican Directorate of Federal Security. His government law enforcement job was merely a cover for Diaz's main source of income as an investigator, enforcer, troubleshooter, and hit man for hire. It was in this sideline business that he had earned a small fortune as well as the nickname *El Asesino Sonriente*, the Smiling Assassin.

Diaz served as an occasional contractor if the Hinojosa family needed to send someone outside its own army of murderous thugs to accomplish a mission, usually to distance themselves from whatever the bloody results might be. Diaz had worked more often for Santos and his Denver operations, both legal and illegal.

In the early days of Santos's trucking company, one of his employees had attempted to bring in a representative of the Teamsters union to sign up all his drivers. Most of them were illegal aliens who worked for far less than union scale. Santos wanted to keep it that way, so he brought in Diaz to slit a few throats and end any talk of unionizing.

The timing was fortuitous since truckers were at war with employers and each other all over the country. A militant group of truckers was conducting a wildcat strike against the Teamsters union and trucking companies, shooting at any truckers on the road who refused to go along with it. Some were comparing them to Middle Eastern terrorists.

Diaz and his thugs used the violent strike as their cover, attacking pro-union drivers in truck stop lots, dragging them out of their rigs, and beating them with tire irons. Others were shot while on the road, or they crashed their rigs because the hoses carrying pressure to the air brakes were slashed.

Within a few weeks, the unionization bid by Santos's truck drivers ended. Diaz and his henchmen returned to Mexico, their pockets stuffed with cash. Two years later, Santos put in another call to Diaz.

"Miguel, I need you to go to the Springs. We have an issue there. Someone is cutting our Mexican brown with shit that is killing our customers," Santos said.

"That is definitely a problem," Diaz agreed. "Does the family know yet?"

"I sure as hell hope not, and I want to keep it that way, so I need you to find out who is poisoning the product down there. Before you kill the fucker, find out what sort of shit this person is adding and where it comes from. We need to get this under control quickly before more people die and the family starts raising hell with me."

"How about the local cops or the DEA? Are they on it yet?"

"The local cops, yes. The DEA, I don't know, but probably. One of the ODs was active military working the NORAD base down there. They don't like their people in top secret posts doing drugs, so they are probably all over it, too. And another one of the OD cases was a local hero and brother to the county medical examiner, whose husband is a damned homicide detective . . ."

"¡*Guau*! You have some shit piling up down there, amigo. I hate to think what could happen if the Hinojosas get wind of this."

"That's why I'm calling you."

"I will be down there tomorrow."

"Okay, one other thing. My nephew Lorenzo is down there. I told him to find the source, but I really don't think he has the stones for this kind of job. I want you to meet up with him, show him the ropes, but keep him safe. He is my nephew, after all."

"Your nephew is a good boy, I'm sure. I will try to give him some training, but I will keep him out of harm's way."

"I appreciate that, but if he slows you down or gets in the way, don't hesitate to send him home—alive, that is."

"Yes, sir. I understand, and, sir . . ."

"Yes?"

"I will bring two of my soldiers—the Dorado brothers, Emilio and Dionisio—to assist me, if that is all right with you. They are professionals and not directly affiliated with any of our friends in Mexico."

"Okay, that is your call. I'm sure they are stone-cold killers like you, right?"

"Yes, they have a lot of experience in these matters."

"Good, I want you to put the fear of God in all the street dealers down there so they know their lives will be very unpleasant until we find the source. And let them know that there is a reward of ten thousand dollars for anyone who leads us to this *hijo de puta*. I don't have to tell you how to do your job, but I *will* tell you, do whatever it takes."

TRACKING THE SOURCE

Aurora Santiago was trolling for drive-by johns at 2:00 a.m. on South Nevada Avenue when she got the heads-up from Rock Hardson, a male prostitute and junkie whose real name was Marcus Lebovitz.

"Aurora, sweetie, there were two giant burrito boys asking a lot of questions down here last night about that ski instructor who crashed and burned on Mexican brown," he said. "They wanted to know where he scored the bad smack. I shook my wang at them until they turned and ran, but they were offering a wad of cash to anyone who gave them a name."

Santiago knew she didn't have much time to get out of the Springs.

That fucking bitch Lula set me up! She knew that shit was deadly, and she used me to unload it on that poor kid just looking to party with his friends. He must have decided to sample it after

I left him in the parking lot. I don't know what Lula cut it with, or where she got it, but that stuff is death in a baggie.

Santiago still had most of the cash Lula had paid her to make that sale and another one she'd made that Lula did not know about. She'd put aside a pinch for herself and then used powdered milk to cut Lula's mix again, creating enough for two sales. After she'd done the deal with the kid at the Overlook Inn, she'd made another sale to one of her regular johns.

She knew him as Al. He'd been bugging her to get him a hit of Mexican brown, always waving a wad of cash at her, so she figured why not make him happy and make some extra dough. She thought cutting it again with the powdered milk would make it safe enough and still provide a rush for the guy. Al was always quoting the Bible and, other than some kinky sex, he seemed like a straight arrow, so he probably wouldn't know the difference between a regular hit and this stuff.

She'd given it to Al a couple days later, after he'd picked her up on South Nevada Avenue and paid her for a blowjob in his car. He seemed even more grateful for the bag of brown than the blowjob.

"Bless you!" he'd said, making her feel only slightly guilty for cutting it so much.

Thanks to those two sales, she had stashed away enough money for bus fare out of town, but where do you go to hide from a drug-trafficking ring that has eyes all over the country? She was in her apartment's bedroom packing and still trying to figure out where to flee when Emilio and Dionisio kicked in the front and back doors.

She had prepared for this worst-case scenario by saving a pinch of Lula's lethal Mexican brown. She was dead anyway, and she'd been tortured enough by life already. She didn't want to face any more of it at the hands of the Hinojosa's henchmen.

Aurora snorted the powder just before the Dorado brothers blasted through her bedroom door, tearing it off its hinges. They stood her up and pinned her hands behind her back, yanking the back of her hair. She didn't cry out in pain because the fentanyl had already kicked in.

Lorenzo Martinez and Miguel Diaz showed up right on cue. Diaz flashed his assassin's grin as he congratulated his "dynamic duo" for tracking her down. Martinez, who had been ordered to watch and learn, retreated to a corner.

"Hello, Miss Aurora. So good to see you with your clothes on. I've heard that you were quite the talented pole dancer in your day," Diaz said. "If you have a moment, I'd like to ask you a few questions about that Mexican brown you sold to the young ski instructor the other day."

As it turned out, Aurora did not have a moment.

She managed only a faint "Fuck you" before her body convulsed and her eyes rolled back in her head. She gasped for breath. Spittle flowed from her mouth in a foamy stream. Then her heart stopped, and her body went limp.

"Dammit, she must have taken a hit of that shit. How did you morons let that happen?"

They were still holding tiny Aurora up by her hair.

"Let her go. She's dead, you brainless curs," said Diaz. "I ought to shoot you both right now. This worthless whore was our connection to whoever is cutting the family's H with this poison. Fuck. Fuck. Fuck."

Diaz ordered his thugs to search the apartment for more heroin, hoping to gather samples for testing to determine what it was cut with. They tore apart the tiny living room and kitchen while Diaz searched the bedroom. An old jewelry box was on the bedstand. He threw out all the cheap costume jewelry and noticed that there was a pathetically obvious false bottom meant to conceal a compartment beneath it.

He tore it off and found Aurora Santiago's leather address book. He put it in his jacket pocket and walked out into the living room. Emilio and Dionisio had found no more heroin, they reported.

Diaz surveyed the destruction and ordered an end to the search.

"What do you want us to do with the body, Boss?" Emilio asked. "Should we just leave it, or do you want us to dump it somewhere?"

"No, I want to use this bitch to send a message to all the other dealers and junkies in town. I want them to know we will not stop searching until we find the source of this bad mix, and none of them will be safe until that happens."

MESSAGE DELIVERED

Wilson and I were heading back to police headquarters after chasing some leads on another case when we hit a traffic jam on North Nevada Avenue south of the I-25 overpass. We were still stuck in traffic a mile south of the interstate overpass when dispatch called on the police radio of our unmarked car.

"What is your ten twenty?"

"We are stuck in a traffic jam on Nevada approaching I-25," I replied.

"Proceed to the I-25 intersection for a possible ten ninety-nine. We have multiple reports of a body hanging from the overpass. Ambulance is en route. The medical examiner has been notified."

Wilson turned on our emergency lights and siren and drove around the traffic jam to that intersection where we saw the horrific cause of the backup. A Hispanic woman's naked body was hanging from the overpass. She had been gutted, causing blood to drip onto the roadway and any vehicles that went under the overpass.

There was a crude sign fastened around her neck and hanging over her chest. The scrawled message was in Spanish and said, "¡*Revelar la fuente*!"

Wilson had taken Spanish lessons after marrying Maggie because she tended to switch over to it when she was mad at him. He translated the sign's message for me: "Give up the source!"

"What do you bet this is connected to our OD cases?" I said.

"Are you thinking the Hinojosa family is looking for the source of the bad mix, and they are sending a message that they will keep killing people until they find it?"

"That thought did pop up in my demented mind. And you know what? Now that I think about it, this woman, whoever she is, matches the description we got from the janitor who saw a chunky Hispanic female get in the car with the ski instructor at the Overlook Inn."

It didn't take long to identify the body once it was removed from the overpass and taken to the morgue. Aurora Santiago, thirty-seven, had an extensive rap sheet, mostly for prostitution, possession of narcotics, and petty theft.

We went to her apartment once we had an address. Her killer or killers had been there, obviously.

"They were probably looking for her heroin stash so they could test it to see what it was cut with," said Wilson.

"I doubt if she was using the same shit that she sold to Whitford; otherwise she'd have been dead before the Hinojosa gang found her," I said.

"Yeah, you are probably right about that. Too bad for her. They probably tortured her for the name of her supplier before they killed her," Wilson said.

"That's a good point, but do you see any blood anywhere in this apartment? They gutted her somewhere, but it wasn't here. And I didn't see any other stab wounds or signs that she was beaten."

"No, I didn't either. I'm sure Maggie will be looking for that when she does the autopsy."

"The only thing I can figure is that maybe she was dead or dying when they got to her," I said. "Maybe she got wind that they were looking for her and took a hit of the bad Mexican brown before they showed up."

"The autopsy would tell us that, too, right?" Wilson said.

"Right. Once again, we should ask Maggie to see if she can get a rush on the lab results. The shit is going to hit the fan if the Hinojosa crew is planning to torture and kill every street dealer in town."

CHAPTER SEVEN

A DEADLY MIX

SEPTEMBER 22, 1978

Springs General is a public hospital owned by the city of Colorado Springs and its taxpayers. Unlike the private hospitals in town, Springs General turns no one away.

"Shouldn't all hospitals treat anyone in need?" asked our teen daughter, Kris, at dinner one night. Kathy had been explaining why she preferred working for public hospitals, despite the lower pay and heavier workload.

"You would think so, honey," I said. "Doctors take an oath to treat all who are in need, but the people who own private hospitals are mostly interested only in treating those who are willing to pay five hundred dollars for a Band-Aid and a bowl of watery apple sauce."

Kathy grumbled an obscenity, got up, and poured herself a glass of wine. I didn't blame her. Nurses have a tough job even on slow shifts, and lately, her shifts were one long gory parade of shootings, knifings, beatings, and overdoses.

Springs General was the catch basin for the city's dregs and derelicts, and Kathy had been working long days in pools of blood, bandages, and body fluids. She was a veteran nurse and knew what the hell she was doing, so the hospital used her as an all-star utility player. She'd step up and fill in wherever she was needed.

The doctors had nicknamed her "Franny Float" because they'd see her working in all departments and wards, whether it was the ER, intensive care, surgery, mental health, obstetrics, pediatrics, or labor and delivery. Kathy could cover every base and the outfield, too. And since she worked in nearly every department but janitorial, my wife knew everyone on the staff. The younger nurses and even many of the physicians confided in her and came to her with questions. They knew she was a caring soul with a wealth of experience who didn't take shit from anyone—especially those doctors and surgeons who thought they walked among the gods.

Kathy enjoyed mentoring the younger members of the hospital staff. She welcomed their questions and was known for handing out regular doses of encouragement to them because she knew the emotional and physical demands of their jobs.

My wife wasn't surprised then when Kayleigh Burkett, a young nurse anesthetist who worked in surgery and recovery, asked her to meet in the hospital cafeteria for coffee and "a private conversation about something concerning."

Kathy had known Kayleigh longer than most of the other hospital staff members. Kayleigh's mother, Mimi Burkett, was a pediatric nurse and friend whom Kathy had worked with for many years. She'd watched her daughter grow into a young woman eager to follow in her mother's footsteps, and beyond.

Kayleigh had gone to nursing school and interned under

Kathy's supervision. After she graduated with her RN degree and worked for four years at Springs General, Kayleigh decided to go for a nurse-anesthetist degree, which required another three years of college and clinical training.

"I'm sure you could do it, but getting accepted into a program can be tough," Kathy had told her.

"I'm already in! They told me that I was their number one pick!" Kayleigh said.

The kid was a star. She graduated at the top of her class and could have worked at any of the private hospitals, but instead chose to join her mother at Springs General. This proved to be a good decision. If any of the anesthesiologists or surgeons gave Kayleigh a hard time, Mimi and Kathy tag-teamed them, pinning them to the mat until they screamed for mercy.

"So, what's up, hon?" Kathy asked Kayleigh after they'd found a quiet corner in the hospital cafeteria. "Are you being harassed by another horny intern?"

"No, thank God. Now that I'm engaged that doesn't happen as much," Kayleigh replied. "This is something troubling that I've observed a couple times lately, but I'm worried about taking it to hospital administrators."

"Are you talking about something in the surgical unit?"

"Yes. In the last month or so, I've had sudden changes in the vital signs of three surgery patients—increased heart rates and blood pressure—indicating that they were in severe pain, even though I'd given them the approved doses of painkillers. So far, I've caught this problem in time, and I've been able to readminister the drug before anything terrible happened, but I'm worried that one of these days something awful could occur."

"Oh, that *is* bad, Kayleigh. I'm so glad you were able to get ahead of it."

"I don't want to have surgeons blackball me because my patients are experiencing pain during their procedures. But I don't want to set off alarms and create a big stink without figuring out why this is happening," Kayleigh said.

Kathy had a couple sips of coffee as she pondered the situation.

"Have you talked to Dr. Moreland about this? He is head of anesthesiology, so he should be made aware of your concerns," she said.

"You are the first person I've shared this with," said Kayleigh. "Honestly, Dr. Moreland makes me nervous on several levels. First off, he is a letch who has said some disgusting things to women on the staff, including me. Secondly, he seems to take a perverse pleasure in hearing about patients in pain. I've heard him laugh about patients who've complained after surgery. And, most concerning, if someone on the staff is stealing from the hospital's supply, he would be at the top of my list of suspects. There is just something off about that creepy guy."

"Why would you suspect him?"

"I probably shouldn't have said that because I do not have any proof," she said. "But he's made comments about envying the 'buzz' patients get from painkillers, and he's said other things like, 'I could use a good buzz myself.' He's just a strange man, and I think he is capable of stealing and even using drugs. But again, I have no proof of that."

This was a serious accusation, and Kathy did her best to assure Kayleigh that she would keep their conversation confidential while making discrete inquiries.

"Is there a way we can get the lab here, or somewhere, to test your drug supply to see if it has somehow been compromised?" she asked the nurse anesthetist.

"Well, I don't think we need to test the entire supply because, in each of these cases, I have administered the same drug. It's that new synthetic opiate: fentanyl."

PARTNERS IN CRIME

Kathy's nursing job and my detective job intersected more often than you might expect given that she worked to save the living and I worked to avenge the dead. We'd had a couple situations where one of her patients or coworkers who'd had dealings or a gripe with me would notice her last name on her hospital ID and figure out she was my wife. Most of those incidents didn't go well.

One involved Rudy, a big lug orderly at Springs General, who got in Kathy's face one day and yelled: "Your fucking husband killed my brother!"

Kathy had no clue what he was talking about, but she wasn't easily intimidated.

"Rudy, you and I have never had a problem, but if you don't get out of my face, we are going to have one, and believe me, my job is a lot more secure than yours!"

Big Rudy backed off.

Kathy had a few questions for me after the kids went to bed that night.

"I'm fairly certain you don't kill anyone without good reason, but someone got in my face today and said you killed his brother," she said as I prepared our cocktails.

"I haven't killed anyone that I know of lately. Or ever. Who got in your face?"

"A giant drooling orderly named Rudy Michaels."

It took me a few minutes to make a connection.

"Oh, he must be the brother of Stanley Michaels," I said. "I didn't have to shoot him because he shot himself. You might have seen it on the news the other night while I was working late. Brother Stanley killed five people while robbing a jewelry store, and then he set it on fire in a lame attempt to cover his tracks.

"We took the SWAT team and half the police force to the apartment where he was hiding, called him on the phone, and invited him to come out and turn himself in. The next thing we heard was the sound of Stanley blowing off the top of his head with a .357. He had decided to pursue another option, which I assume involved burning in hell for all eternity."

Kathy listened to all of this while thinking she should have married an accountant.

"Thanks for the recap. Please do me a favor and try not to arrest or even pursue any more of my coworkers or their family members for the next few months," she'd said.

"I will do my best as long as they refrain from murdering anyone on my watch," I replied, toasting her from across the room and out of her throwing range.

Let it be noted then that Kathy was the one who broke down the wall she'd put up between our jobs when she came to me with the suspicions her coworker had shared about Dr. Moreland.

"If Kayleigh Burkett happened to bring me a vial of fentanyl from the hospital supply that she suspected had been diluted with saline, could you arrange to have it analyzed at the crime lab? You wouldn't need a court order or anything, would you?"

I raised an eyebrow. Maybe two.

"Are *you* asking *me* to use *my* position as a city homicide detective and dedicated public servant to conduct a covert investigation of one of *your* coworkers, my dear?"

"No, you big jerk, I'm giving you a potential clue to a possible thieving anesthesiologist who is suspected of stealing a drug that may be killing people in our fair city," she said. "It's a call to do your damn duty . . . *dear!*"

The lab we used then was forty-five miles south of Colorado Springs in Pueblo. The Colorado Bureau of Investigation Laboratory there served law enforcement agencies in the southern section of the state.

As luck would have it, I just happened to have a contact there by the name of Ivan "Mac" McKinley, who was a supervisor of lab technicians. We had bonded while we were both waiting to testify in one of my homicide cases. Ivan had tested evidence gathered at that crime scene. I had investigated and tracked down the alleged killer, who would be the convicted killer by the end of that two-week trial.

After our victory in the trial, which ended in a life sentence for the killer, Ivan and I had dinner and a drink—or two or three—to celebrate. Over the years after that, Ivan had testified in trials for several of my homicide cases. He was a true expert witness, a PhD forensic chemist, not a poseur or charlatan like those often called by defense lawyers.

I admire competence, especially when the competent individual also enjoys a steak and bourbon dinner now and then.

"Hello, my friend, Detective Kenda here, how are your Bunsen burners burning at the state crime lab?"

"We are burning our Bunsens off around the clock these days, Joe. Hope you are doing well," said McKinley.

"I am doing fine and working a case that may require your

expertise," I said. "If I were to show up at your lab, say, the day after tomorrow, with a vial of a certain painkiller used by hospitals, do you think you could test it to see if it had been diluted with, perhaps, saline?"

"That sounds like an interesting case, Detective Kenda. I gather that some patients must be feeling more pain than they bargained for at a local hospital? No need to explain, I'll be glad to do this one off the books while you wait if you feel it is important."

"In return, I gladly would spring for dinner and drinks next time you are in the Springs," I said.

"Done deal," said my favorite chemist.

LAB RESULTS

The forty-minute drive down I-25 to Pueblo proved to be even more rewarding than I had expected. Mac had the test results on the vial of fentanyl back to me just twenty minutes after I handed it to him in the parking lot of the state crime lab's operation there.

"Your suspicions have been confirmed, Detective Kenda. Someone drained about a third of the fentanyl out of that vial and replaced it with saline solution. If an anesthesiologist or nurse anesthetist had administered that full vial to a patient, expecting it to keep them pain-free during a lengthy surgery, I'd say that a couple people would have been disappointed, including the patient."

"Could someone have died because the vial was diluted?" I asked.

"No, I don't think so. Fentanyl is extremely powerful and even just a drop or two would have kept the patient pain-free for hours, but, depending on the type of surgery, it is possible that a patient could experience significant pain at some point during or right after the surgery because of the dilution level. You should ask an anesthesiologist if you want a more precise answer, but there are a lot of factors that would play into that."

He paused for a few seconds. I could tell something else was bothering him. Finally, he came out with it.

"I'd like to know why anyone on the staff at the hospital would remove a portion of the fentanyl from the vial," Mac said. "That's a dangerous thing to do, and most likely a firing offense."

"We have a couple theories about that," I said. "Maybe the thief is a drug user taking the fentanyl for the buzz. Or maybe the thief is selling it to other users, or to drug dealers who are using it to cut their heroin, so they can make higher profits."

"Interesting," he said. "The world of illicit drugs often seems to have more entrepreneurs than any legitimate business sector. I guess that shouldn't be surprising given the amount of money to be made."

"Yeah, why let Pfizer have all the fun and profits?" I said. "The Hinojosa family just wants their fair share of the market, right?"

"Oh! Glad you said that. It reminded me that I have some other results you can take back to the Springs."

"What do you mean?" I asked.

"We just finished up our lab reports on the three heroin overdose deaths you had up there. Dr. Medina had asked us to make them a priority. I know you are investigating those deaths and working with her, so do you want to be the bearer of bad tidings?"

"And by that you mean . . ."

"Your theory that someone might be stealing the hospital's

fentanyl to sell it to a drug dealer may be exactly what is happening, Joe," Mac said. "We found lethal levels of fentanyl as well as heroin and other substances in the blood of all three of your overdose victims."

"That's what we had feared," I said. "Damn, this could be just the beginning if there is more of that bad mix out there."

"You're right. There could be many more overdoses if more fentanyl hits the streets. It is deadly in the wrong hands," Mac said.

"We have to find the source of this and shut it down," I said.

Mac went silent for a few minutes. I could tell something was troubling him.

"What is it?" I asked.

"I am puzzled about one aspect of this," he said. "The fentanyl from the hospital comes in liquid form so medical staff can add it to an IV tube for patients. But street heroin is mostly in powdered form. Most addicts 'cook' their powdered heroin by heating it on a metal spoon to liquefy it. Then they draw it into a hypodermic syringe and inject it. Some do snort it, but frequent users prefer the faster and more intense high from shooting up. So, if someone is stealing the liquid fentanyl, how are they adding it to the heroin powder before selling it on the street?"

"Could they somehow spray the liquid fentanyl on the heroin powder?" I asked.

"I've never heard of that, and I don't know how the liquid fentanyl would hold up after they cook the heroin," McKinley said. "I'll do some investigating and see what I can come up with. This is such a new drug; we don't know all that much about it, or about how it will be used and abused. The only thing I'm sure of at this point is that a lot more people will be dying."

"Let me know what you find out. I'm heading back to share your lab reports with Wilson and Dr. Medina. Thanks, Mac."

TROUBLING RESULTS

I gave Wilson the lab results to pass on to Maggie that night. Then we met at the medical examiner's office the next day to discuss our next moves.

"Well, Detectives, we may have three homicide cases for you, or we may not, depending on how this shakes out," she said. "The lab reports say there was heroin and fentanyl in the bloodstreams of Buck, Alfonso Peres, and Curtis Whitford. There were also traces of caffeine and ketamine, both of which are often used by street dealers to cut heroin. The lab indicates that there was more than enough fentanyl to kill them."

"Damn, I'm sorry, honey," said Wilson, breaking the family rule about maintaining professional decorum with his wife while both were on duty.

Maggie let it slide this time.

"The fact that all three victims had the same mix of heroin, fentanyl, caffeine, and ketamine in their systems would seem to indicate that their doses came from the same supply source, but we have no proof of that yet," she added.

Wilson and I knew we had to investigate this. It was our duty, but we dreaded the prospect. These overdose cases were always difficult, especially if we were looking at connecting three deaths and proving each of them was a homicide.

We did not have any proof at all that the OD victims had been intentionally killed by whoever had added the fentanyl to the heroin, but under Colorado law at the time, a person could be charged with first-degree murder if a killing resulted from "risky behavior exhibiting extreme indifference to human life."

Cutting heroin with a lethal dose of such a powerful opiate and then selling it to someone certainly would seem to meet that criterion, though I'm sure a defense attorney might beg to differ.

"We have our work cut out for us," I said as Wilson and I rose from our chairs and prepared to leave Maggie's office.

After returning to police headquarters, Wilson and I informed our bosses of Maggie's report. With their approval, we opened a case file and initiated a murder investigation into the death of the three victims we'd identified so far.

Under the line for Suspect, I had to type: "Unknown at this time."

ANOTHER VICTIM

The case file was still on my desk when police dispatch had the audacity to dump another overdose victim in our laps.

"God almighty, our caseload could get out of hand if they keep dropping like this," Wilson said.

There were eight homicide detectives back then. Six of us worked days, 8:00 a.m. to 5:00 p.m. Two others worked the night shift, 6:00 p.m. to 2:00 a.m. But all of us were on call if needed twenty-four hours a day, every day of the week. We also worked all the cases and signed off on all reports, though there was a lead detective assigned to each case who got the ass chewing if the investigation wasn't producing results on a timely basis.

"Maybe this will just be a routine heroin OD case, but I don't think we're that lucky," I said.

"The address makes me think there won't be much routine about this one," said Wilson.

Wilson was driving, so I hadn't paid much attention. I took another look at the address the dispatcher had provided.

"Oh, shit."

"Yeah, Brother Kenda, put on your Sunday shoes, 'cause we are going to church!"

The address was for a storefront church in a strip mall on the West Side called The Upon This Rock I Will Build My Church Church.

We were familiar with it not only because of that ridiculous name but also because, as patrol officers, we had each been sent there to break up fights among the congregation members.

"My fight call there was better than your fight call," I told Wilson.

"I think I've heard this story, but go ahead," my partner said wearily as we sat in heavy traffic.

"Remember? My fight occurred during a funeral. It started when one of the alleged mourners stood up and said, 'That lying bastard deserved to die.' You can imagine that didn't go over well with the grieving family, but it turned out there were others present who voiced similar sentiments. One of them rushed up to the open casket, climbed atop the dearly departed, and began beating him into a bloodless pulp. I had to drag him off and charge him with defiling a corpse. That was a first!"

"Yeah, you win," Wilson said, laughing. "My fight at that church was between the pastor and his girlfriend and his wife. Just a run-of-the-mill, unholy trinity kind of thing."

A billboard just a block away from our destination offered a warning that apparently had gone unnoticed or unheeded: Your Eternity Is at Stake.

Pastor Threesome was our victim. His real name was the

Righteous Reverend Albert Hoskins. The newly widowed Mrs. Hoskins was waiting for us at the front door of the storefront church, which had previously been a Mexican produce market and still had a faint smell of chili peppers.

"Right this way, officers. Thank you for coming."

"It's our . . . job, ma'am," said Wilson, who'd almost said, "Our pleasure" but caught himself and corrected on the fly.

Patrol Sgt. Marvin Manley was once again standing guard over the body.

"No signs of bullet or knife wounds, blood or blunt trauma, but, based on the hypodermic needle marks inside his elbows, I don't think it was a heart attack," he said.

Wilson and I had the same thought, but he said it first after pulling me aside.

"If this pastor has fentanyl in his bloodstream, we will have an OD caseload that is like a cross section of the city: a Native American, a soldier, a ski instructor, and now an evangelist?"

"That's a fair cross section, except of course for the millions of normal, law-abiding Colorado Springs citizens who don't shoot opiates into their bloodstreams with hypodermic needles," I said.

"Good point. Thanks for being my little ray of sunshine, Kenda."

CLOSING IN

Lula Lopez had slept little since the ominous phone call from Lorenzo saying that he was coming to the Springs. She felt like her world was collapsing.

She had not told Dr. B. about the deaths of the three men who had purchased heroin cut with his painkiller drug—two of them had purchased it directly from her and one from poor Aurora who was murdered and hung from the overpass.

If I tell the doctor about the three overdoses, he will probably kill me himself to keep me from telling anyone where the painkiller came from, especially if he finds out that the Hinojosa family has sent Lorenzo to find the source.

Lula had decided to book a flight to Orlando, Florida. She had family there, and some friends from her air force training days lived in nearby Kissimmee. Some of them worked at Disney World, which offered pay and conditions better than those for workers in the Durango poppy fields.

I'm going to need to move my entire emergency stash to pay for my flight and relocation costs, and I have to do it fast.

Lula had an emergency stash, six bricks of uncut Mexican brown, each containing enough for eleven single doses that could be sold on the street. She needed to sell them all at once, so she'd have to find another dealer who had enough cash to pay for that much. She spent the day making calls, putting the word out that she was looking for a buyer.

No one called her back.

CHAPTER EIGHT

THE LAB IN THE WOODS

CUCHARA, COLORADO
SEPTEMBER 1977

Dr. Blair Moreland drove off Highway 12 and up the dirt lane of his Cuchara cabin in his Jeep Wagoneer loaded with more equipment that he'd ordered through the hospital. He saw no sign of his lab assistant, Lester, as he parked.

I hope he's working and not off somewhere in the woods boinking his girlfriend.

Moreland hadn't bought old man Collingsworth's cabin because he liked the scenery or because he wanted to hike in the surrounding Pike and San Isabel National Forests. The remote property was part of the anesthesiologist's ambitious Plan B. He had figured that sooner, rather than later, some of his nosy colleagues would wonder why Springs General's surgery patients were having unusual degrees of pain during surgery. And maybe they would figure out that someone was diluting the hospital's fentanyl supply to feed their own addiction.

I've become too reckless. This painkiller is more addictive and more powerful than I imagined. I can't seem to get enough of it, and there were even more powerful forms of it coming down the pike.

"The new stuff will be five to seven times more powerful than our original fentanyl product," the drug rep had said.

Moreland had taken to ordering fentanyl for the hospital's patients, and for himself. As head of the anesthesiology department, he could order all the drugs he wanted, but they were supposed to be for the patients, not the physicians. Moreland didn't care about the rules. He was addicted, and he was using his job to steal the drug that drove his addiction. Initially, he swiped any leftover or unused fentanyl after surgeries. Then, he began ordering more of the powerful painkiller than was needed, guaranteeing that there would be enough for his own use.

He would sneak off near the end of his shifts, use a shoelace for a torniquet, and inject just twenty-five micrograms at first, but he quickly increased his dosages to one hundred, then five hundred, and as much as a thousand micrograms administered throughout the day, before, during, and after work. He would inject as much as twenty milliliters over the course of a day, which was enough to kill most adults if administered in one dose.

For me, this is like having a glass of fine wine. It takes the edge off and keeps me on top of my game. But I need to find a better source for fentanyl, or I will end up without a job, with a revoked medical license or, even worse, in a prison cell.

The synthetic opiate was available from pharmaceutical companies that sold only to pharmacies and hospitals. Those sales were tracked at both ends. Moreland's addiction was growing, and he knew, if he kept stealing more and more from the hospital, someone would eventually raise alarms.

So Moreland came up with a plan.

If they can make this in a lab, so can I. And if I make enough of it, I'll have a product that I can sell in case I lose my job because of my addiction. I guess all those years studying organic chemistry and working in the lab are finally about to pay off.

Moreland had selected old man Collingsworth's property in Cuchara for its remote location and, even more so, because it already had a large, vented outbuilding with power and water that could be converted easily into his fentanyl lab. Joshua Collingsworth had been a skilled taxidermist. He'd worked on animal carcasses in a large metal building tucked into thick stands of Douglas fir and aspen trees behind his cabin, which was hidden from anyone who drove or walked by on the road.

After buying the property in the fall of 1977, Moreland used his hospital connections—and his department's budget—to order all the lab equipment and chemicals he needed to produce his own fentanyl.

I've jumped all over the hospital's lame-ass number crunchers anytime they've questioned my department budget. They are too intimidated to red-flag my purchases anymore. If they do, I'll just feed them some more bullshit about needing the lab equipment to test the quality of the drugs we use as a safety measure.

Even if the hospital accountants raised alarms about Moreland's spending, he had an ace up his sleeve. Her name was Jennifer Davis Purcell, and she was the wife of Daniel Purcell, the hospital's chief financial officer. Mrs. Purcell was an

avid equestrian who participated in Grand Prix show jump-
ing on Corsair, on her $15,000 Hanoverian gelding, until
her jumper stumbled and dumped her during a competition
in 1974.

Mrs. Purcell, forty-three, had considered herself an Olympic-
level equestrian prior to her accident. After her fall, she felt
doomed to a life of relentless suffering. The fall from her horse
fractured her coccyx at the base of her spine, which left her in
constant blinding pain even after several surgeries.

When Moreland heard that the CFO's wife was in dire need
of relief, he saw an opportunity to take advantage of her suffering. He went to Daniel Purcell's office in the administrative
wing of Springs General Hospital and, posing as a truly caring
medical professional, offered to serve as Jennifer Purcell's pain
manager.

"Daniel, I know Jennifer must be going insane with pain,
and I can provide opiates to relieve her anguish, and yours too,
because I'm sure it isn't easy living with her as she suffers," he'd
told Purcell. "I won't charge for my services, of course. Consider it a professional courtesy. Your poor wife needs someone
who won't be afraid to give her everything she needs to return
to a normal life."

Under Moreland's care, Mrs. Purcell was addicted to fentanyl within a couple months. He provided the drug from the
hospital's supply, helping himself to portions of her dose each
time. As he took control of her care, Moreland also moved to
manipulate her husband.

"Since I'm doing this for you and your wife, I hope you will
protect me from the damned bean counters who keep question-
ing my department's budget," he told the CFO. "I need these

resources to keep Jennifer comfortable and functioning, as well as all of my other patients."

Daniel Purcell agreed to run interference for the head of the anesthesiology department who had saved his wife and his marriage. Later, Moreland took out additional insurance by drugging Mrs. Purcell into a stupor and videotaping her in compromising positions, just in case her husband ever wavered in his support.

Moreland believed he had the CFO in his pocket, but he also knew that hospital administrators come and go, so he proceeded with his plans to create his own fentanyl lab to feed his habit and to provide what he believed would be a substantial secondary income.

Obtaining the formula for manufacturing fentanyl proved to be easier than Moreland had expected. He simply bribed his drug rep for the ingredients, formula, and lab instructions. Thanks to his background in organic chemistry, the physician figured he'd quickly master the complex process known as "the Janssen method" for making fentanyl. He'd also found dozens of legitimate suppliers in the US and abroad where he could buy the cheap precursor chemicals for making the synthetic opiate.

His medical license served as a DEA permit, meaning he could order anything from anybody, including Schedule Two narcotics. Even better, Moreland discovered that the ingredients for making fentanyl were unbelievably cheap. He could buy enough to produce a kilogram of it for under two hundred dollars.

This can be done, but I can't do it by myself and still work at the hospital. I need that job to get the lab up and running.

His final challenge was finding and recruiting an assistant, one qualified to work in the lab, willing to illegally produce a synthetic opiate in a remote area, and not prone to running his mouth off to potential police informants. Dr. Moreland thought this might be an impossible task, but he soon found a promising candidate among the residents of the Rocky Mountain Recovery Center.

I've heard the nurses at Springs General wonder why a heartless bastard like me works as a counselor there, but it's a great way to make connections to the local drug scene without risking my reputation or my medical license.

After reading Lester Sharp's file to prep for a counseling session with him, Dr. Moreland decided the young addict was a needy lost soul who could be manipulated and molded into a perfect assistant for his illegal fentanyl lab. Somehow, he had not fried his brain.

Sharp was living in the center's rooming house because he was in the treatment and recovery program under court order. He'd been busted with a dozen other junkies in a DEA sweep of a Denver shooting gallery.

Unlike the other addicts, Sharp still had functioning brain cells. He'd gone from being a promising grad student to a homeless addict. If he didn't complete the program successfully, he faced revocation of his probation on a felony conviction for possession of heroin.

"Your file says that you were a high school honor student and went on to the honors program at the University of Colorado, where you dropped out just a few hours short of earning a doctorate in organic chemistry? Why did you quit school, Mr. Sharp?" the doctor asked.

"I was bored in high school. I didn't have to study, so I started smoking weed with the other smart bored kids. Then, when I was seventeen, I found a bottle of my mother's Percodan pills from her surgery, and I started popping those. I thought, *This is how I want to feel every minute of every freaking day!*"

"When did you move on to heroin?"

"In college, after quaaludes and cocaine. Heroin was cheaper and the high lasted longer. I thought I could handle it and still go to classes. I made it through my bachelor's degree, but the stress of grad school got to be too much. It was easier to drop out and shoot up. I guess maybe I took that slogan 'Better living through chemistry' personally instead of professionally?"

"Funny, but not very smart for such a smart guy. If you'd completed your degree and landed a job with a pharmaceutical company, you could have afforded even better drugs, right? Instead, you were living here under a court order—and before that, you lived like a stray dog on the streets. You were damned lucky the judge sent you here instead of giving you prison time."

"Yeah, I know," said Sharp, laughing sheepishly. "I fucked up. Big-time."

"So, what are your plans after you get out of here?"

"I'm not sure, Doc. My family has disowned me. I don't have a woman. And until I can get my felony expunged, I doubt if I'll find a decent job or be able to finish my degree."

After their first counseling session, Dr. Moreland did more checking on Sharp's background. He was a loner and not likely to stay drug-free for long even after going through the program, according to his psychological profile. On the other hand, he had been at the top of his class in grad school and had won honors for his work in the organic chemistry lab.

The fact that Lester Sharp had no plan or direction for his life was a plus for Moreland's purposes.

I have a plan for him that is better than anything he could dream up. He needs a job and a place to live and someone to give him direction. I could do all that. The hard part will be keeping him from getting hooked on our product. I'll need to watch him closely and find other ways to keep him busy and engaged so he doesn't go back to drugs.

The anesthesiologist spent two months grooming the vulnerable young addict, building trust, playing father figure and best friend as well as a counselor. Then, just two weeks before Sharp completed the ninety-day recovery program, Moreland invited him to lunch.

"I will sign you out under my supervision, so we can go wherever you want for lunch," he'd said. "What have you been craving, besides heroin?"

"Oh man, I've been dreaming about giant, juicy beef burritos like those at Taco Ted's! I'm so sick of the bland crap they serve here. If I see one more plate of meat loaf, I'm gonna puke."

They both ordered Ted's Ultimate Big as Your Head Beef Burritos and sweet tea—Sharp wanted a beer, but he was not allowed alcohol while in the treatment program. Lester Sharp ate like he'd been starved. Moreland let him gorge until his face was greasy and only traces of taco sauce remained on his plate. Then, after the kid belched his satisfaction, the doctor made his pitch.

"You have two weeks left in the program, so it is make or

break time, Lester. And I'm the guy who makes the final decision on whether you graduate successfully or fail and go to prison for five years."

"C'mon, Doc, I know you wouldn't bust my balls like that. You are more a father to me than my real old man. You get me. He worked in a sawmill and thought the periodic table was about 'female issues.'"

"So your father wasn't in your league mentally. I bet he made fun of you for being a nerd, right?"

"You got that right, Doc. You make being smart seem cool; that's why I dig you and want to make you proud. Haven't I kept my nose clean and done everything you asked?"

"Yes, that's true, Lester. Look, I think you are a talented young guy who deserves a second chance. You've done well here. That is why I want to offer you a new life better than anything you've ever dreamed of."

"What do you mean? Is this part of the program, or something else?"

"No. This is my deal. How would you like to work for me on a new venture I'm starting? You'd be working solo, in a state-of-the-art chem lab, making more money than you could make anywhere else, and living rent-free in one of the most beautiful and unspoiled parts of Colorado."

"Maybe I've got burrito brain fog. Are you really offering this junkie a job and a sweet place to live on top of all that? Did you forget I didn't finish my doctorate?"

"I've come to believe in you, Lester. You've had a rough couple of years, but you and I both know what you are capable of, especially in the lab. You won't need a degree for this job. And, frankly, I need a partner I can trust. This venture won't be registered with the Better Business Bureau, if you get my drift."

"Now you are freaking me out. Is this some sort of character test to see if I'm ready to complete the program? You aren't narcing on me, are you, Doc? I thought we were friends."

"No, I'm not a narc, Lester. In fact, because I trust you and I like you, I will tell you something that you could use to destroy my career and my life if I ever let you down. Do you want to hear it?"

"I don't know, Doc. I've heard other people talking about you. I mean, you are a big-time anesthesiologist and a pillar of the community. Why would you tell me something like that? I'm just worried this is all a trick of some kind and I could end up in prison."

"I will tell you this potentially damaging information for the same reason I offered you the job, a generous salary, and a place to live, Lester. I need help with a new business start-up, and I've decided that with your skills and experience, you are the perfect person to partner with me. Are you interested or not?"

"Well, I find it hard to believe that you see me as a business partner. I mean, I'm facing a felony conviction if I screw up again, so what sort of business are we talking about here? It sure as hell can't be anything legal, right?"

"You are correct there, Les my man. You see, believe it or not, I am an addict, too, and I have the track marks to prove it, just like you."

Moreland rolled up his sleeve and briefly flashed the heavy bruising on his inner elbow where he had injected himself.

"Now I am really freaked out! You shoot dope? How could

that be? How could you work at the hospital or the recovery center?"

"Well, of course no one else knows about this. No one except you. And I'm only telling you because we are so much the same, Lester. We are way smarter than most people. We are like Freud, Miles Davis, Chet Baker, Sherlock fucking Holmes! We can control our shit. It doesn't control us!"

"Man, you are a different dude once you get out of the recovery center. I like the whole Doctor Feelgood vibe!"

"I'm good at counseling addicts because I've been there, done that. Like you, I started out with pot and amphetamines, then coke, before I graduated to heroin, but there is some new synthetic shit developed for controlling pain during surgeries that I'm really into now, both professionally and personally. You probably haven't even heard about it because it is so new."

Lester pushed his chair away from the table and stood up again. For a split second, Moreland feared he would bolt out the door, which would have been problematic. Instead, Lester Sharp paced around their table releasing nervous energy before he sat down again.

"Oh man, you're talking about fentanyl, aren't you? I've heard about it from other residents in the program. They say it is more powerful than anything out there. That is some illegal shit you are talking about now, Doc. You're right. You could lose your medical license for using, making, and dealing anything like that. So if you are telling me, you trust me, and you must be serious about this package deal. And if you are serious, I'm in . . . Hey, you aren't wearing a wire or anything are you?"

"Ha! Son, if I was wearing a wire, then I just incriminated myself and destroyed my fucking life."

Lester Sharp recognized that as bullshit, thinking, *Narcs lie all the time when they are trying to trap you.* But he let it go and decided to go along for the ride while looking for better opportunities down the road.

I don't have a lot of other options, and he knows that. And if I say no, this fucker could make sure I never complete the program, and then I'd go to prison where my chances of survival are zero to none.

At least if I play along, I will have time to save up some money and figure out my own plan. And who knows? If this deal turns out to be as sweet as Doc makes it sound, I may even enjoy working in his fancy-ass lab, living out in the boondocks, and getting high.

CUCHARA INITIATION

Upon completing the program at the recovery center in early October of 1977, Lester had a court hearing. The judge notified him that he'd have to keep clean for three years before his felony conviction would be expunged from his record. Dr. Moreland testified on his behalf as a character witness.

"Your Honor, I have been counseling this young man throughout the program, and I have the utmost faith that he can stay clean, get his life on track, and become a productive member of society."

The hearing ended and, after a celebratory lunch, they packed up his meager belongings and drove in Doc's Wagoneer to Cuchara.

They stopped in Cuchara Village to pick up supplies at the Country Store.

"Before we go to the cabin, let's get a beer and dinner to celebrate your freedom," Moreland said.

"I haven't had a beer since I got busted!" said Lester.

They were walking to the Wagon Wheel Grill restaurant and bar when Lester froze, pointed down the dirt street, and said, "What the hell is that?"

"Looks like a young bear lost its mama, or maybe she told him it was time to go find his own place," said Moreland. "Get used to it. They won't bother you unless you do something stupid like feed them or corner them. And don't ever get between a mama bear and her cubs. That's really the only time these black bears get aggressive."

Both men did a quick scan around them to make sure there was no mother bear between them and the young bear.

"I think we're clear. Now we really need a beer," said Moreland. "C'mon, Lester. If the bear comes after us, you only have to run faster than me."

"Ha! I will keep that in mind, Doc."

"Yeah, the bears are faster than they look, but not as fast as the mountain lions."

"Mountain lions? You're kidding, right?"

"Naw, but don't worry, they wouldn't want a scrawny kid like you when they have so many deer and cattle to eat."

The Wagon Wheel Grill was in a log building that fit into the rustic and compact downtown area known for years as Cuchara Camps. In its early days, it was little more than a few cabins, tents, and log buildings. It sat on a dirt road just off Highway 12, known as the Highway of Legends, a scenic byway that served for centuries as the rugged region's primary trail for Native Americans, Spanish conquistadors, pioneers, miners, trappers, and ranchers.

The doctor and his apprentice took a table at the back of the dining room surrounded with knotty pine paneling, near a river-rock fireplace and a large picture window that sat below the highway, so most of what they would see were the bottoms of vehicles and tires flying by. Wagon wheels and fading photographs of people eating in the restaurant surrounded the bar and lunch counter.

"I don't recognize any of those people in the photographs," Lester said. "Are they celebrities or locals?"

"Most of them are moldy oldies celebs who've passed through over the years. The only one I recognize is Lawrence Welk, who is every grandmother's favorite bandleader on late-night television reruns, but my guess is you are more likely to watch the rockers on *The Midnight Special*, right?"

"Yeah, right!" said Lester.

"I'm afraid there isn't much TV reception out here in the boondocks, and besides, I doubt that you'll be staying up late anyway," said Moreland.

"Oh yeah, why's that? I am kind of a night owl," said Lester.

Moreland had decided that it was time to ease out of his extended period of playing the benevolent mentor and father figure. Now that the kid was dependent on him for a job and a place to live, he wanted to clarify their roles. He may have pitched the arrangement to Lester as a partnership, but that was not how this was going to work.

"I will help you get settled in the cabin this weekend, and then I have to go back to work in the Springs for a couple weeks. I will return at the end of the month, and we will begin training in the lab," he told Lester after they'd ordered the chicken fried steak specials from their waitress, Daisy.

"I have three weeks off, so we will be working from early in the morning until late at night to perfect our processes. I want to start making our product and getting it out to dealers as soon as possible."

"Geez, Doc. It's been a while since I've been in a lab. Do you really think I can get back up to speed that fast?"

"I've prepared a lot of material for you to read while I'm gone, so that should help," Moreland said. "I will return with all the equipment, ingredients, and supplies we'll need for the next six months, and when we need more, I will order them through the hospital. Once we get the lab up and running and I'm confident that you have mastered the Janssen method, I'll return to work at the hospital while you crank out the product. But you can call me if you need anything at all. I have an account at the Cuchara Country Store downtown, and I'll leave a credit card in your name, but I will monitor your charges, so don't get crazy with it. Are we clear?"

Moreland could see that Lester had picked up on his change of tone and was mulling over his response.

"Funny, you suddenly sound more like a boss than a friend and business partner," he said.

"I may have given you the wrong impression about that, so let's get it straight. You work for me. I am paying you more money than you'd ever make anywhere else given your lack of an advanced degree and the felony conviction that is still on your record. You burned all your bridges when you became addicted and lived on the street. I'm giving you a lifeline. And I'm telling you that you'd better not fuck this up.

"That means you make the fentanyl, but you do not even think about trying a taste—ever! No fentanyl, no heroin. No opiates at all. I don't care if you drink alcohol or smoke weed, but if I catch you heading down that dark road again, I will make sure you go to prison where you will spend the rest of your life giving blow jobs to gang chiefs."

"Wow, this is a new vibe, man. I thought you were cool; now you just sound like a mean boss, or worse, my old man."

"Lester, you don't want to fuck this up. I have the power to revoke your deal with the courts if I tell them you are using again. I can send you to prison, or I can be the guy who helps you salvage your life from the train wreck it had become. You will be living in paradise, doing something you are really good at, and making tons of money."

"Yeah, well, it all sounds good, except that part about sending me to prison if I piss you off, Doc."

"Son, you and I both know that this lab is an illegal operation, so we must be careful, or we will both end up in prison. For that reason, I want you to promise me that you will not start using this shit, because it will kill you. Maybe not right away because you are a smart guy, and you and I both know that opiates take over your mind and soul and eventually destroy your body."

"But you told me you do it, Doc, and look at you, fit as a fiddle."

"I am an experienced anesthesiologist, Lester. I know what I'm doing. I monitor my vitals and measure my doses carefully each and every time—and yes, even I could fall prey to this shit if I slip up. I just don't want that to happen to you. OK?"

Daisy stopped by to check on their progress. The young waitress had been watching their table from across the large, high-ceilinged dining room. She could not hear their conversation, but she could tell that the older guy, Doc, had been berating the nerdy but cute younger guy. She thought maybe he needed a break.

"Can I get you anything else to drink? A beer maybe?" she said to Lester, holding the eye contact for a couple extra bats of her lashes.

Lester was not accustomed to young women paying attention to him. He didn't have a clue she was flirting.

"Yeah, I could use a beer. Coors, please!"

Dr. Moreland had picked up on Daisy's attempt to connect with Lester beyond the usual banter. He made a note to speak to her later. It might be good for Lester to have a local girlfriend to keep him company while also keeping an eye on him for Moreland.

"I'll have a Coors, too, Daisy. Your parents are the owners, aren't they? Larry and Christine Palmer?" Moreland asked.

"Yes, they are," she said. "Are you new to the area or just vacationing?"

"I bought the old Collingsworth place just down the road, the one with a taxidermy shop," Moreland said. "Lester here is going to help me fix it up and keep an eye on things when I'm back in the Springs working."

"Oh yeah, that was sad about him dying. Joshua, right? I think he did some of the stuffed animals mounted in the bar. We have so many that the locals call it the Dead Critter Bar," Daisy said.

"So you're like a caretaker for the property?" she asked Lester.

"Yeah, kinda. I'll be living and working there full time," he said.

"Cool! I mean, there isn't a lot to do here like in the Springs, but if you love nature, we have a lot of it!" she said before going to get their drinks.

"Cute girl. I think she likes you, Lester. You should ask her out sometime."

"I thought you wanted me in the lab twenty-four seven, Doc. Isn't that what you just said?"

"Now, Lester, don't get all pouty on me. I do want you working at least ten hours a day as we master the processes, but I think having someone your own age to hang out with after I'm gone might be good for you. Nothing like sex in the woods to keep the creative juices flowing, right?"

"Oh man . . . she's probably got a lumberjack boyfriend in town. Look at her!" said Lester. "Girls like that don't go for chem nerds like me."

GOING NATIVE

The day after Moreland returned to Colorado Springs, Lester hopped in the Jeep four-by-four the doctor kept at the cabin and returned to the Wagon Wheel Grill for another chicken fried steak. And a side helping of Daisy.

"You're back! Where's the doc?" she asked.

"He had to go save more lives in the Springs, so I'm on my own for a couple weeks until he comes back."

"You two aren't *together* together or anything, are you?"

"Oh no, nothing like that. We're business partners. I'm helping him with a project, a new sort of painkiller he is developing. He is a really smart guy and interested in helping his patients avoid suffering," said Lester, giving the story that Moreland had provided in case anyone poked around.

"Interesting," said Daisy. "He seems intense."

"Yeah, I'm finding that out," Lester said.

Daisy waited until he'd had two Coors and devoured his chicken fried steak before handing him the dessert menu and a proposition.

"If you're going to be here all by yourself for a couple weeks, would you like me to show you around a little on my days off?"

"I'll have the Wagon Wheel Grill Mud Pie . . . and all the time with you I can get!" said Lester.

He was so proud of himself for coming up with that line that Daisy just had to give him a double scoop of ice cream. And then she offered to take him on "the Dike Hike."

"I'm sorry? What is that? They have dikes in the forest. Like dikes on a river or lake?"

"You'll see. I'll come by your place early tomorrow morning before it gets too hot. One of the trails starts just up from the doc's property."

Daisy showed up at 8:00 a.m. in a Wagon Wheel Grill T-shirt, hiking boots, and a pair of highly distracting cutoff shorts. They found the trail in the woods above Doc's cabin and followed switchbacks up a steep hill through towering spruce trees and oak brush. After a mile or so, they paused on a rock outcropping that offered views of the cabin and Highway 12 below.

"That's Trinchera Peak, which is a tougher climb," said Daisy, pointing to a mountain that rose from a long ridge to the south. "But we can take your Jeep partway up there to see the elk herd some other day."

"Is that where the dike is?" asked Lester.

"No, just keep walking!"

They hiked for another mile and found a connector trail

that took them out of the forest and across a rugged section of huge boulders and loose gravel. There, they had views of a strange, jagged wall of rock, like a stone necklace rising from the base of the mountain.

"What the heck is that?"

"That's one of the dikes. There are about five hundred of them in this area. Some are longer than others. They were formed from molten rock from ancient volcanic activity, same as the mountains, more than twenty million years ago. Aren't they wild looking? They are like a smaller version of the Great Wall of China, only made by Mother Nature instead of some emperor's slaves."

"These are so cool. How do you know so much about them?"

"Well, I grew up here, and the tourists always ask about them in the restaurant. I had to figure out how to answer their questions, so I majored in geology at the Colorado School of Mines. I can give you a lot more technical explanation if you want, but I didn't want your brain to explode on our first date."

"This is a date? I thought it was a hike?"

"Okay, you can consider this just a hike, but on our next trip, I will take you to the dike that is known as Lover's Leap over on the East Spanish Peak, and that will have to be a date."

"Does that mean we will have to leap from it?"

"Not exactly. There will be no leaping involved, but there may be other physical activity required," Daisy said, offering a sly smile.

Lester thought, *If she smiles like that at me again, it won't be my brain that bursts.*

Later that night, after a three-course dinner at the Wagon Wheel Grill with Lester and a long first kiss goodnight in the parking lot, Daisy went to her room in her parents' cabin and called the number Dr. Moreland had given her.

"Hi, it's Daisy, calling like you asked me to."

"Thanks for checking in. How's Lester doing? Are you keeping him busy?"

"Yeah, we did Dike Trail today, and I think he's probably already passed out at your cabin, poor scrawny guy. I bought him a big dinner, so he won't starve on my watch."

"Okay, well keep an eye on him for me. He's a city kid, so he isn't used to living in such a remote place, and I don't want him to get lonely, lost, or bored. I need that big brain of his for our project."

"Yeah, he told me you are working on some sort of experimental drug in the lab you built in Joshua Collingsworth's taxidermy studio. It must have taken a year to clean all the critter parts and chemicals out of that dump. I'll have to ask Lester to show me what you did to it."

"He won't do that, I'm afraid, Daisy. We can't let anyone in there due to regulations about keeping the working environment sterile and free of any contaminants. That's why Lester has to wear that big protective suit."

"No problem, Doc. I do want to tell you though, I'm happy to keep Lester company and show him around for the next couple weeks, but I'm not real comfortable with taking any more money from you to do that."

"Why is that, Daisy?"

"To tell you the truth, I really like him, and not just as a friend, if you get my drift. He's so much smarter than any of the other guys around here, and a gentleman, and cute in his own Mr. Wizard way. I think we may even start dating like a couple, so you can keep the money. Maybe *I* should pay *you* for introducing us."

"That won't be necessary, Daisy. I'm glad you two are getting along. Just let me know if you think he needs anything, or if you think he is unhappy for any reason, OK?"

"Sure, Doc, no problem."

After she'd hung up, Moreland poured himself a shot of Bushmills single malt.

No problem? I hope you won't be a problem, dear Daisy. I want my boy to be happy down there, but I don't want him too distracted. And I certainly don't want you or anyone else nosing around our lab. I may need to remind Lester of that before all his blood drains from his brain into his pecker.

CHAPTER NINE

INTERESTED PARTIES

OCTOBER 2, 1978

Wilson and I appreciated that our police chief had managed to downplay any connection between the three August overdose deaths whenever local reporters nosed around about them. He also had squelched any media inquiries asking if drug traffickers might be responsible for the September murder of the prostitute Aurora Santiago, who was found hanging off an I-25 overpass.

"Sorry, we can't talk about ongoing investigations," was our usual dodge.

But with the bodies piling up, it was getting more and more difficult to keep the lid on our twenty-four seven scramble to find the source of the fentanyl that was killing local heroin users.

By early October, the barbarians were storming our gates. The first pain in the ass to show up on that Monday was Rick Becker, the ace reporter and columnist from the *Rocky Mountain High Times*.

He walked into police headquarters at 9:00 a.m. like he owned the place.

"Morning, Mooney. You up for some darts on Friday at the pub?" he said to the desk sergeant.

"Sure, I'm always glad to take your money," Sergeant Mooney replied before hitting the buzzer that allowed pesky reporters into a small office where members of the media, ambulance-chasing lawyers, and nosy citizens who liked to play cop were allowed to read the daily police logs.

The entries in the log were considered public record, which is why we made them as brief and unhelpful as possible. Even a multiple homicide might be described as "Officers dispatched to report of shots fired."

Experienced reporters knew all our tricks, so they weren't thrown off the trail easily. If they smelled a story, they'd pester the desk sergeant, peppering him with questions and whining when he rebuffed them. He'd tell them they needed to talk to the chief of detectives, or the chief of police, and then the walls would go up. We avoided revealing more details until it was conducive to the investigation or politically expedient.

I kept most members of the media at arm's length. Talking to them on or off the record was seldom to my benefit. On those rare occasions when I wanted to alert the public to a danger or enlist their assistance in a case, I'd tell the chief, and he would hold a press conference or hand it off to his public information officer, or maybe the chief detective overseeing the case. Later, I became the chief of homicide and violent crimes, so I had to talk to them, unfortunately.

I usually ignored reporters at crime scenes until that happened. We'd keep the media hordes behind barricades where they shouted questions like baying hounds. I respected those who were professional and dedicated to reporting the truth, but I did not hide my distaste for the hacks and sensationalists who stirred up bullshit and served it to their readers as news.

Television reporters, especially, were known for grandstanding on camera to impress their bosses and viewing audiences. They screamed questions and accusations, and as soon as the cameras were off, they'd sit in their news vans sipping espresso and checking the stock market. Their main interest was building up a video demo reel in hopes of becoming the next Geraldo Rivera or Barbara Walters. Most of them just wanted to get the hell out of Colorado Springs and land a high-paying gig with a big-market television station in Denver or LA.

Some of the newspaper reporters were just as bad, or worse. I often wanted to strangle a certain print reporter because she never got anything right in her stories. You could hand her a press release printed in large type, and she'd somehow screw that up. We had a murder case where a guy was shot, and she wrote that he was stabbed.

"Is there another homicide that we somehow missed?" I asked her.

She once arrived at a crime scene wearing snakeskin boots. I looked at them and then looked her in the eye and said, "How appropriate!"

Miss Misinformation didn't get the message. She wasn't that bright.

Most of the print reporters I dealt with were more tolerable, except for one lazy-ass guy who would call me up from his desk chair and just say, "Anything going on?" Like I was just

supposed to hand-feed the moron stories over the phone. After
that happened a couple times, I said, "As a matter of fact, there
is something significant. Do you have a pencil handy?"

I could hear the numb nuts scrambling to find one before
he said, "Okay, what do you have?"

"We arrested a little guy with a mustache at a bus stop today,
and we have identified him as Adolph Hitler," I said. "We hav-
en't told the *New York Times* yet, so if you report that, you will
win a Pulitzer Prize."

And, to my astonishment, the moron said, "Really?"

Even with idiots like that working at the *Gazette*, I have
to say the worst of all was a reporter from a big Denver television news station who yelled at me across the police barricades
at a murder scene where two little kids and a woman had been
butchered:

"Hey, Detective Kenda, we need a body shot before the next
news broadcast, when are you bringing at least one of them out?"

I have never fired my pistol at a member of the media, but
I was sorely tempted in that moment. Instead, I calmly said,
"Why don't you and your cameraman step on this side of the
barricade and I will gladly give you a sound bite."

I waited for them to set up, trying not to let him see my
fangs before I struck.

"Okay, we are ready to roll," the jerkwad yelled.

I looked into their camera and said, "I have more respect
for a pack of hyenas than I do for you, Mister Channel 7. You
are a blithering idiot, you bloodthirsty bastard. Now get back
on the other side of the barricades before I shove that camera
up your ass."

"You can't talk to me like that," the reporter said.

The Channel 7 hair helmet called the police chief and complained, but when I told the chief that he had demanded bodies for his next newscast, he said, "Fuck that guy!"

MEDIA RELATIONS

I talked to Becker more than most media types, mostly because we enjoyed insulting each other, and we were good at it. Our conversations usually started out like this:

"What do you want this time, P. Rick Becker?"

"Fuck you, Kenda."

"Careful or I'll stake out your favorite watering hole and bust your ass."

That shot stung more than most, given the fact that Becker had left his higher profile job at the *Denver Post* after taking heat from its editors for his DUI bust at MacCallister's.

Becker was a cantankerous sort who did not suffer liars or fools, even when they were his bosses. The *Post* had served one up to him on a platter in the form of Chance Paisley. The guy was a midlevel editor, an officious bootlicker who always carried a clipboard because he thought it made him look like management material. He also wore bow ties and a remarkably bad toupee.

Every morning upon arriving in the newsroom, Becker walked by the sad sap's desk and said, "Good morning, wig head." The daily taunting drove Paisley insane. He complained to his bosses, to HR, and to the Society of Professional Journalists, all to no avail. So when Becker was arrested for a DUI and a small bag of weed was found in his car, Paisley saw it as his opportunity for revenge.

He launched a campaign to have the star columnist fired or demoted to a suburban beat, claiming his arrest had destroyed

Becker's credibility and damaged the newspaper's reputation. The *Post*'s top management spurned Paisley's efforts and refused to fire Becker because his columns were so popular.

But when Becker heard the bosses were considering a pay cut or a demotion, he walked.

"Fuck this place; I'm outta here!"

His sudden departure triggered a massive outcry from his fans. Thousands of readers canceled their subscriptions in protest. Becker packed up and moved to Colorado Springs, where he cranked out exposés and sardonic columns, stirring the pot at every opportunity.

I preferred my pot unstirred, and I let Becker know that when he showed up early into our investigation of the OD deaths.

"I liked you better when you were nagging the Denver cops, P. Rick," I said.

The *Rocky Mountain High Times*, previously known mostly for its drug paraphernalia reviews and hooker-for-hire classified ad section, was smart to hire Becker because he was a pit bull, and no one questioned his ethics. He gave the rag some legitimacy.

Once he had his teeth into a story and wanted more information, your only recourse was to shoot him. I often had to remind myself that was not an acceptable course of action, even in his case.

"You might have made a good cop if you weren't such a subversive and belligerent asshole," I said after I'd let him buy me a beer one night at his favorite dart bar.

"What do you expect? I was an army brat. While my dad hunted Nazis in Germany, I was drinking and whoring with other army brats all over Europe," he'd said. "Then they sent him to Thailand and got him killed, so I had to return to the USA where the drinking age was higher—much to my disgust."

Becker had learned to play darts in British and Irish pubs. His skills were substantial, but they often peaked after three or four beers. Once he'd had more than that, he tended to throw the darts at other customers in the bar, or those working behind the bar, or just innocents walking by the bar.

He had a mean streak, which is why I called him "P. Rick Becker." He secretly enjoyed that nickname, and in return, he fondly called me, "Fuck You Kenda."

I tolerated his responses because he always said it with a smile or a smirk—and usually only after I'd called him "P. Rick."

We both enjoyed snappy repartee. However, I did not enjoy it when the punk reporter showed up at police headquarters that Monday and demanded to talk to me—and only me.

"Hey, Kenda, what can you tell me about these OD deaths? And was the hooker hanging from the bridge connected to them in any way?" Becker asked when I made the mistake of not ignoring his presence at the front desk.

"Sorry, P. Rick, I am not authorized to speak to the media today, especially since you threw a dart at me the last time I saw you in public."

"If I'd wanted to hit you with that dart, I would have nailed you. So, what's with the three people overdosing in the last few weeks, anyway? I knew Buck. I was shocked to hear he was using heroin again. You may remember I did a profile of him as my first column for the *High Times*. We got to be friends after that. He was a great guy. Did his family know he was using again?"

"I don't know, Becker. I'm not a vice cop. Go talk to the narcs or, better yet, ask your favorite dealer."

"Fuck you, Kenda. I'm just getting started with this story, and the next time I come in here, I'll be grilling your chief on how this could happen in your city on *your* watch."

"OK, you do that, and have a nice day!"

He strutted out the door like a banty rooster, smiling and waving a one-finger salute.

"You ever notice that he walks like he thinks he's a rock star?" said Wilson.

"Yeah, he does have a cocky walk, but if he's feeling that cocky I'm wondering where he heard about our other OD victims and how much he knows already," I replied. "If he puts it all together and writes about a contaminated heroin supply before we can track and shut down the source of that fentanyl, we will have an even tougher time getting people to talk so we can make charges stick."

MILITARY INVESTIGATION

I was still at the front desk waving a not so fond farewell to P. Rick when an air force investigator I'd worked with, Capt. Max McAleavy, came through the door.

"Hey, Max. What brings you in?"

"Hello, Detective Kenda. Have you got a minute?"

Captain Max and I had a good working relationship. The city police department lacked jurisdiction on most of the military bases in town and the military's law enforcement officers had no jurisdiction in the city. But criminals and crimes, and murderers and murder victims tended to cross over between our turfs. So we played well together.

Captain Max and I had worked together but not as often as I'd worked with some of the other local military cops. In fact,

I worked on so many investigations with the army CSI team at Fort Carson near Cheyenne Mountain that they made me an honorary member of their Officer's Club.

We didn't have nearly as many cases with the Air Force OSI team, but they were top-notch folks. They must have liked me, too. After I worked a murder case at Peterson Air Force Base on the east side of town, one of their four-star generals invited me to take a guided tour of the top secret NORAD base inside the bunker beneath Cheyenne Mountain.

I felt like Dorothy entering Oz—if the Emerald City had been stashed inside a man-made cave inside a massive mountain. The self-contained military base within the bunker has its own sources of water, fuel, and filtered air. There are fifteen three-story office buildings stuffed inside the mountain and each is built on giant springs to help them withstand a thirty-megaton nuclear explosion. There are also dining halls, dormitories, and a hospital. Everything is encased in granite, offering those inside a limited and close-up mountain view.

"I have to admit, after a couple hours in there, I just wanted to get the hell out, breathe clean mountain air, and bask in the sunshine," I told Air Force OSI Captain Max McAleavy as we sat down to talk that day.

"I know how you felt since I spend many hours encased in that mountain myself. Sometimes I think that confined environment, as amazing as the place is, can put stress on our personnel and incite them to do things they might never do if they lived and worked under normal conditions," he said. "For example, I'm here to talk with you about Airman Alfonso Peres, a member of our Cheyenne Mountain team, who allegedly overdosed on heroin at his apartment in your jurisdiction on September eighth."

"Yes, I can share the autopsy and coroner's report with you, if you'd like," I offered.

"That would be great. You must suspect his death was the result of some skulduggery or you wouldn't be involved, but whether it is a homicide or not is your business," he said. "We are mostly interested in learning if this airman had a history of drug use. As you probably know, we do regular random drug tests of our personnel at Cheyenne Mountain, and somehow, for some reason, during his three years there, he was never tested, according to our records. That set off alarms and brought me knocking on your door."

"Interesting. I can tell you that your airman had a lot of needle marks on his body, and the medical examiner seemed to think he was a regular user, but you can get all of that from Dr. Medina," I said.

"Great, Dr. Medina is my next stop. So, between you and me, I'm hearing that there have been an unusual number of overdoses in the Springs lately, and there is talk that the local Mexican brown is being cut with something lethal. Is that true?"

"That's what we are trying to figure out," I replied. "Like you said, we aren't even sure if these are homicides or accidental deaths at this point, but if you hear anything else, let us know."

After Captain Max left the station, Wilson and I grabbed a cup of coffee in the break room.

"Looks like we need to get out in front of the overdose deaths if Becker and the US Air Force are sniffing around," I told my partner. "What do you think? Should we have the chief do a press conference saying we are in the early stages of looking into these deaths, but so far have no proof that they are connected or that they were anything other than accidental?"

"Yeah, that is probably a good idea, but before you go to

the chief, you should know there is another guy nosing around," Wilson said. "I don't know if it's related to the overdoses, but the timing is odd."

"Who is it? What's going on?"

"While you were shooting the shit with Becker and the air force investigator, I got a call from a Mexican government guy, Miguel Diaz, who said he was with DFS, Mexico's Directorate of Federal Security, which he said is like the CIA, FBI, and DEA, all rolled into one. He wants to talk with us about reports that people are dying here because someone is cutting Mexican brown heroin with a mysterious new substance that is more powerful than morphine."

"Good god, yet another interested party? From Mexico? And we still don't know if we're looking at any homicides here, so what are we doing, Wilson?"

"Our jobs, pardner. Our dang jobs!"

THE FEDERALES

Wilson and I had never dealt with anyone from Mexico's Directorate of Federal Security, but we'd heard enough bad things that we called our friend, John Vicars, the agent in charge of the FBI office in Colorado Springs.

"Vic, we're wondering if we can trust this DFS guy who wants to talk to us, so we're interested in your thoughts," I said.

"I'd be careful what I share with him," he said. "I don't know anything about Agent Diaz, specifically. I can check to see if our Mexican mob experts have him on a watch list for those with proven ties to their drug lords, but the DFS is notorious for conducting assassinations, torture, and illegal detentions of anyone who opposes their government."

"So the DFS is pretty much like our CIA," said Wilson.

"Let the record show that you said that, Detective Wilson, not me," Agent Vicars said. "Sarcasm aside, I'm sure you've heard about Mexico's ongoing 'Dirty War' against government agitators. The United Nations has received hundreds of complaints about the DFS's activities in that mess, but that's not the most important thing you need to keep in mind when talking to this guy about your case."

"What do you mean?" I asked.

"Our experts on Mexico say that members of DFS are just as likely to join the drug lords and their criminal enterprises as investigate them—and often they play both sides," Agent Vicars said. "In some cases, former DFS agents have started their own criminal operations including drug trafficking, kidnapping, murder-for-hire, and car-theft rings."

"So it's like the revolving door in this country? The one that allows federal prosecutors who work for a few years putting mobsters in jail to jump ship and change sides so they can make tons more money as private defense lawyers who get those same mobsters out of jail?" Wilson said.

"Again, let the record show that you said that, not me," the FBI agent said. "No country has a monopoly on corruption and greed. We all know that. I'm just telling you that you should be careful what you share with this guy coming to see you—and anyone claiming to be from Mexico's DFS."

Miguel Diaz, special investigator for that organization, came knocking a couple days later. He was well-dressed and wore a Rolex that was not government issue. Maybe it was a knockoff, but more likely a payoff from the Mexican mob. My initial urge was to throw him in a cell, but I suppressed it.

He showed us his fancy badge, which Wilson inspected like a raw diamond, making a show of it, as if he was a jeweler deciding how to cut it.

Diaz noticed Wilson's scrutiny and likely figured we were not about to hand him the keys to the city, or our case files.

"I know you are wary of sharing information with a government official from another country, Detectives, but I am here only to learn as much as I can about this mysterious new substance," he said. "Apparently someone is using it to cut heroin and putting it out on the street. Several people have died, according to our sources. My government is fearful that this unknown drug, or whatever it is, will find its way into the hands of our drug lords who will find a way to make it themselves and ship it around the world. If that happens, many, many more people may die.

"We are just trying to get ahead of that scenario," Diaz added. "As it stands right now, we know nothing about this new substance, where it comes from, or even if it has a legitimate use. We have heard some rumors that it might be a new painkiller. Can you at least confirm that for me?"

Wilson and I had prepared for the meeting. We had discussed what we would or would not share with Diaz. Neither of us believed his contention that Mexican authorities did not know anything about fentanyl.

It is a common gambit among detectives, lawyers, and newspaper reporters as well, to pretend they don't know something basic in hopes of getting someone to open up and start talking. The idea is that the person will blather on and on, sharing information that the detectives, lawyers, or reporters do not know.

Diaz was fishing. He was hoping we would be sucked in by

his show of ignorance and then overshare and give him specifics about our victims and our investigation.

Instead, we took him to dinner at a nice steakhouse, bought him a few beers and maybe a few shots—all on our department expense accounts—and bullshitted with him for a couple hours. We never mentioned the word *fentanyl*, nor did we acknowledge that we were investigating several heroin overdose deaths.

I suppose Diaz thought he was playing us, just as we thought we were playing him.

"Please understand that we are homicide detectives, not vice detectives, so we know very little about your drug lords and drug traffickers and their operations in our area," I told Diaz after a three-beer, one-shot warm-up. "Maybe you can help us understand more so we can share it with our vice investigators."

Diaz was no dummy. He knew that we were stonewalling him, but he played along and offered the information that rival drug lords with relatively small gangs and well-defined turfs were slowly giving way to more ambitious, aggressive, and ruthless drug operations with international aspirations.

"Think of it this way, Detectives, I have family and friends who have immigrated to many areas of the United States. They tell me that until recently, they would buy their children toys from small, independent stores in downtown areas, but now their kids all want to go to Toys 'R' Us, which has big warehouse stores popping up everywhere in your country and, I'm told, they are expanding around the world as well.

"The same thing is happening in my country with the sale of illegal drugs like marijuana, heroin, and cocaine. Big operators in Mexico are taking out the smaller operators, consolidating and controlling everything from poppy production to drug manufacturing and distribution on a global basis. Call it 'Drugs 'R' Us,' if you want. And when that happens, the drug lords will become more powerful than governments and their countries. They will have their own armies, and they will destroy anyone who opposes them."

We listened attentively. The beer and steaks were free, after all. At the end of our evening, we drove the well-lubricated Mr. Diaz back to his hotel, helped him find the elevator, and all but tucked him in. Wilson and I compared notes on the way home.

"He put on a good show, you gotta admit," Wilson said.

"He put on a good act, but I bet he'd slit our throats in a heartbeat."

"I agree," Wilson said. "Did you get the feeling that he has already chosen sides in the battle between his country and the drug lords?"

"Yeah, I think he is on Team Drugs 'R' Us all the way, and that his real reason for visiting us was to help the drug lords figure out if they need to expand into the fentanyl business now or later," I said.

CHAPTER TEN

COOKING IN CUCHARA

Lester Sharp's hazmat suit was three sizes too big for his scrawny frame, which made it a challenge for him to walk from Doc Moreland's cabin to the lab hidden in the woods. The hazmat suit wasn't Lester's only problem. He was struggling also under the weight of a bulky box of lab beakers, Bunsen burners, glass tubes, and funnels—nearly ten thousand dollars' worth of equipment—that his partner in crime had billed to Springs General Hospital.

"I don't know how you've managed to destroy so much lab gear already . . . Is your girlfriend driving you to distraction? Whatever it is, you need to cut back on the breakage, fumble-fingers," Moreland had complained on his last visit.

Can I help it if this stuff is so fragile?

Thanks to Doc Moreland's lecture, Sharp was so nervous about avoiding disaster that he had his eyes fixed on the rutted path. He was about halfway to the metal building two hundred yards from the cabin when his peripheral vision caught movement at the edge of the tree line.

He froze.

A light-brown bear as big as Lester's Jeep ambled out of the trees and into a clearing. Peering over the top of the box, Lester saw the bear stand up on its hind legs and sniff the air while staring at him.

Why didn't I put on that bear whistle that Daisy gave me before she left this morning? It's still on the table next to my bed, along with the can of bear spray, of course.

Doc Moreland had warned him about the bear that stopped by every few days in search of garbage, discarded fish carcasses, bird seed, or handouts. In his later years, old man Collingsworth had become so addled that he sometimes forgot all the local rules designed to keep the beasts from thinking of humans as food sources. He'd often put out his garbage cans overnight instead of on the morning of the scheduled county trash pickup, which meant the bears could stop by for late night snacks. This made the normally wary creatures think of the cabin as a friendly feeding spot, which was not a good thing.

"Don't feed the bears and they won't bother you, unless they have cubs, then steer clear because, even though you are a large pain in my ass, I really don't want to have to find another assistant," Doc had cautioned him before handing Sharp the can of bear spray and a "Be Bear Aware" pamphlet from the Colorado Parks & Wildlife service.

Lester had read the pamphlet, but, in his fear, he couldn't remember whether he was supposed to run, stand still, or hit the ground and play dead when a bear stood up and sniffed him.

I know it depends on whether it's a grizzly or a black or brown bear—and they say there aren't any grizzly bears left in Colorado— but damn that fur looks golden, or at least light brown, isn't it? Or maybe it's just the way the sun is hitting it. I know that, around here, some of the black and brown bears have lighter-colored fur that makes them look like grizzlies, so what the hell do I do?

Run? Stand still? Lie down? Shit!

Just then, the bear dropped to all fours and, still sniffing the air, walked away from him, following the dirt path toward the lab building another hundred feet back in the woods.

Lester's relief at the bear's departure lasted only a few seconds.

Oh shit, I left a big metal vat of freshly made fentanyl out in the sun so it would dry into powder. If the bear gets close and starts sniffing that shit, it could either go berserk or die.

Without even thinking about it, Lester yelled out: "Stop! Shoo! Get outta here, bear!"

The bear turned toward him.

Well, that wasn't the response I'd hoped for.

Lester's fight-or-flight alarms were shrieking, and fighting was not an option. He dropped the box of lab supplies, shattering the big glass beakers and tubes, and turned and broke the world's 100-yard dash record for chem majors being chased by bears.

Now, in truth, the bear was not interested in chasing Lester, especially after hearing the loud crash and seeing broken beaker glass all over the path. Instead, the bear turned and lumbered back into the woods, in search of sweet grasses, juicy beetles, mushrooms, and berries.

Lester didn't notice that the threat was over until he'd run up the front porch steps of the cabin and dashed inside. Only then did he look back through the windows.

The bear was not in sight, but Lester realized he now had another problem, a threat from an even more terrifying beast.

I'm not sure what's worse, facing that bear, or having to tell Doc that I just broke ten thousand dollars' worth of lab equipment.

When he called Dr. Moreland back in Colorado Springs, his response was much calmer than Lester had feared.

"I can always buy more lab equipment through the hospital, but if that bear had destroyed an entire batch of fentanyl, I would have been seriously pissed off, Lester," the anesthesiologist said. "Do you know how much that shit is worth on the street? Not to mention losing my own supply."

It bothered Lester that Doc didn't care whether the bear died from exposure to the fentanyl they were making. *Then again, I'm a hypocrite for worrying more about what this stuff would do to a bear than what it does to the humans who are buying it. What the fuck is wrong with me? What am I doing out here in these godforsaken woods and mountains?*

Then, he remembered.

Oh yeah, I'm trying to stay out of prison. And then there is Daisy. I'd be an idiot to give up the greatest—and the only—sex I've ever had with another human, especially one that hot.

With those warm thoughts, Lester Sharp headed back to the lab to cook up another batch of fentanyl.

LAB WORK

The process for making a synthetic opiate wasn't as simple as most of his organic chemistry assignments in college, but Lester knew his way around a lab, and Doc's instructions had given him a good foundation.

"I called a sales rep for one of the hospital's drug suppliers and told them I needed to know exactly how they made fentanyl before I could put in another order as head of the anesthesiology department," Dr. Moreland had told his assistant. "They bought it and had one of their pharmaceutical scientists send me a list of the ingredients and their step-by-step manufacturing method. He even offered to send me a few free samples."

"How cool was that?" Lester said.

"Yeah, you'd think they'd be more careful giving out that information considering how powerful and addictive this pain-killer is, but drug companies only care about making money, and my hospital buys a lot of their products," Moreland said.

The anesthesiologist had spent a week working through the formula with Lester before they made their first batch more than a year ago. One of their biggest challenges was performing even simple tasks while wearing the bulky hazmat suits, along with protective gloves.

"You are a clumsy bastard, aren't you, Lester?" Moreland said. "I thought you'd know what you are doing, but so far all you've produced are spillage and breakage. Maybe I should have just hired a chimpanzee and trained it instead."

"Take it out of my wages if you want," replied Lester. "Can we just focus on getting the formula and the process right in-stead of you riding my ass all the time? It only makes me more nervous anyway."

Moreland was not a patient man, but Lester was too valuable to strangle. Instead, he walked him through the process again.

"Pay attention this time: The benzylfentanyl is converted into norfentanyl in one chemical reaction. Norfentanyl is then subjected to another simple chemical reaction to complete the synthesis of fentanyl," he explained. "I'll teach you the Janssen method, which should be no problem if you are the chemistry wiz you claim to be."

Back in those days, before fentanyl became widely abused and created a national crisis, Moreland could have purchased the painkiller in liquid form from many legitimate suppliers in the US and across the border in Mexico. But he was one of the first to grasp the potential profits from illegal manufacturing of fentanyl in powdered form, which was easier for street dealers to use when cutting heroin and for distributing in pill form.

"I can make truckloads of cash selling just to the dealers I've met at the recovery center, and since fentanyl is so potent and cheap, they can increase the potency of their product and increase their profits at the same time. This stuff is so addictive, their customers will be craving it more and more—just like me."

Moreland also stressed the dangers of exposure to it in the lab.

"Working five days a week, you should be able to make enough fentanyl powder for hundreds of thousands of doses once you master the process," he told Sharp. "But this is an especially lethal drug, which is why I spent so much money on improving the ventilation and air filtration systems as well as the hazmat suits and special gloves."

He also explained the risk of the fentanyl powder getting airborne.

"It is such a fine powder that you could die in minutes after inhaling it, ingesting it, or getting it in your eyes—or even on your skin," he explained.

Lester had listened carefully but finally had to ask the question that dogged him.

"Doc, I gotta ask, why not just order enough fentanyl for the hospital to keep yourself supplied too? Or does someone else monitor the hospital's drug inventory?"

"Like I said, we want the powdered form, which the hospital does not keep in stock, so we'll have to make it ourselves. And I could probably get away with ordering the liquid stuff at the hospital for a while longer since the hospital's monitoring system isn't all that sophisticated, but I want to make enough to start selling this shit, too."

Becoming a supplier to street dealers around town was part of Moreland's backup plan if the hospital caught on to his addiction and theft, he explained.

"I need a Plan B in case the tight asses who run Springs General figure out I've been helping myself to their drug cabinets, fire me, and maybe yank my medical license," he said. "With your help, I can manufacture enough of the powdered fentanyl to make a shit ton of money."

Lester looked like a third grader who wanted to raise his hand and ask a question.

"What is your problem, chem brain?" Moreland asked.

"I'm just wondering how we can make sure the dealers who buy this powerful shit don't get greedy and use too much of it when cutting their heroin with it," Lester said. "Because if they do that, people are gonna die."

The arrogant anesthesiologist shot back angrily: "I didn't realize you were such a caring citizen, kid. Yeah, I will tell the dealers to be careful, and I'll tell them how much fentanyl is safe to use in cutting their heroin, but we aren't exactly dealing with mental giants here, you know. And between you and me, I don't really give a shit what happens to their junkie customers. Most of them are practicing slow suicide anyway.

"Still, I don't need the kind of attention from law enforcement and the media that a bunch of overdoses might bring.

That's why I put the lab out here in the boonies where they can never find us."

THE WRONG PATH

Jack Yost and his grandson Buddy began fishing for rainbow, brown, and brook trout in the Cucharas River and nearby mountain lakes as soon as the boy was old enough to hold a rod. The river turns narrow and becomes more of a rocky brook or shallow creek where it runs through their property, just steps from their log home.

"But we call it a river just the same because it flows year-round," Jack told his grandson. "Only the tourists call it a creek."

Since both of Buddy's parents worked, the elderly man and the boy spent most of their days together, especially after Jack's wife died and he moved in with Buddy and his parents, Joe and Dahlia.

Buddy was ten years old when Jack, at eighty-four, began suffering the early stages of dementia. His symptoms were mild at first. He often forgot where he'd put things, and every now and then, he became disoriented and did not know where he was or what he had been doing. Slowly, he became more dependent on the boy to organize and lead their fishing sorties. Buddy's job was to carry the gear—their ultralight spinning poles and their cooler—and to put the worms or salmon eggs on the hooks, as well as remove the fish they caught.

Over time, they cut back on the range of their fishing expeditions, no longer wandering for miles along the river or taking the four-wheel-drive pickup to the more remote mountain lakes, Blue Lake and Bear Lake, where the trout were more abundant.

Jack fished from his camping chair once his hips got too

bad for standing or wading. He walked with the help of a hand-carved stick that bore the image of a haggard face on the knob, that of an old, bearded man.

"The face on your stick looks more and more like you as you get older, Grandpa," Buddy told him.

"I think you are right, my boy," Jack said. "The years are wearing on me and my walking stick."

By the late fall of 1978, Grandpa Yost was more likely to take a nap than go fishing, especially as the temperatures dropped into the sixties by day and the thirties at night. On Thursday, October 5, though, the sun warmed the riverbanks by noon and Jack joined Buddy on the Cuchara at a spot just a quarter-mile south of the cabin while Joe and Dahlia went to town for hardware supplies and groceries.

"I'll just sit in this camp chair and watch you, Buddy," the grandfather said. "My old brain is a little foggy, and the trout are probably too smart for me today."

After an hour or so, Jack told his grandson that he was heading back into the house to take a nap.

"Do you want me to leave this chair for you, son?"

"Yes, leave it," Buddy said. "I want to stay and catch a few more fish for dinner, Grandpa."

"You do that, Buddy. Those trout don't stand a chance with you on their tails."

After another hour of fishing, Buddy returned to the cabin with four large trout in his cooler. He meant to come back for his grandfather's camp chair but never made it. He went to his grandfather's bedroom to check on him and found it empty. Buddy searched the house and the basement, calling for his grandfather.

There was no response. Then, he noticed that Jack's walking stick was not in its usual place near the front door.

Maybe Grandpa went for a walk, but he hasn't done that in a while, especially by himself. He couldn't have gone far, not with his bad hips. He must have walked upriver; otherwise I would have seen him when I was fishing.

Buddy followed the river up toward La Veta, searching for his grandfather on their usual path. The boy called out for him but heard only the sound of the river flowing and the screeching calls of eagles, hawks, wild turkeys, and crows.

After walking a half mile or so, Buddy came to an A-frame cabin on the river. He knew this cabin well because, until a year earlier, his grandfather's best friend, Joshua Collingsworth, had lived there. Joshua had died at the age of eighty-seven, apparently of old age, though he had seemed to be doing fine up until the moment he just keeled over in his kitchen.

Jack Yost had taken his friend's death hard. He'd fallen into a depression, which seemed to have triggered his descent into early-stage dementia.

"Grandpa hasn't been the same since Joshua died," Buddy had told his parents.

Buddy had not been back to Joshua's cabin since the funeral because it had been sold to a doctor from Colorado Springs. As far as he knew, his grandfather had not been back either, but Buddy suspected that, if the elderly man had awakened and become disoriented, he might have headed up the river to his friend's former cabin where he'd spent many happy days.

His theory proved correct. The boy found his grandfather, still carrying his walking stick, wandering near the edge of the woods behind the A-frame cabin.

"Grandpa, are you okay?"

"Joshua? Is that you? I have missed you, old friend."

Buddy's parents had warned him that his grandfather's mental condition might take a turn for the worse if he became stressed. They called this "an episode."

"Grandpa, it's me, Buddy. Come on, let's go home before it gets dark and cold."

"Buddy? I'm looking for Joshua. Help me find my friend."

With that, the old man walked away, wielding his walking stick with surprising speed. Buddy followed as his grandfather entered the tall pines at the edge of the thick woods. The grandson caught up as Jack stopped behind the metal building that had been Joshua's taxidermy shop.

"What is this place, Grandpa?" Buddy asked.

"This is where Joshua did his taxidermy. It looks all cleaned up now, but we never let you come back here because it was always a bloody mess with dead animals and their parts everywhere. We did not want to scare you," his grandfather replied. "And Joshua also had all sorts of dangerous chemicals stored back here for his hobby."

Jack spoke slowly, his speech was slurred. He stared at his grandson as if he did not recognize him, and then staggered toward the back of the metal building. Buddy followed and they both walked into an area behind the building that had been fenced off recently but still lacked a gate. Postholes had been dug for it and the ground was freshly turned.

Buddy reached for his grandfather's arm to lead him back to the path along the river to their home, but Jack pulled away and staggered up to a large metal vat on a table. His grandson ran to him, begging him to return home. As he again reached out for his grandfather's arm, Jack stuck his hand into the vat and grabbed a fistful of a white, powdery substance. He held it up to his face for just a second, examining it, and then collapsed to the ground.

A cloud of powder from Jack's hand flew into Buddy's face as his grandfather fell, and within seconds, the boy went down, too, landing beside the old man, with Jack's walking stick under his back.

Buddy's last thought was that the carved face on the knob of the stick now looked like a dead man.

MISSING

Shadows had given way to darkness by the time Joe and Dahlia Yost returned to their river cabin from their daylong shopping trip.

"I love living out here, but it sure would be nice if we had a grocery store closer," Dahlia said as they carried the first load into the house.

"Buddy, come help us with the groceries, honey!" said Dahlia, figuring the boy was in his bedroom either napping or playing his favorite new video arcade game, *Space Invaders.*

Buddy did not respond, and after carrying in a second load, Dahlia checked his room. Then she checked his grandfather's room.

"Joe, neither of them are here!"

Her husband grabbed a flashlight from a kitchen drawer and did a quick search up and down the riverfront, a couple hundred yards in each direction.

"That's odd, Dad's camp chair is sitting on the riverbank

near their favorite fishing spot, but there is no sign of either one of them. He never leaves that old chair outside."

"I'm worried. What if your father wandered off and Buddy is looking for him? I've been afraid something like that might happen."

"Dad could not have made it far with his bad hips, but I did just check, and his walking stick is gone. I hate to raise a fuss, but maybe I should call the office and get a search party out."

"Huerfano County Sheriff's Department, how can I help you?"

"Hi, Stephanie, it's Deputy Yost."

"Oh hi, Detective. Aren't you off today?"

"Yes, I am, but we have a problem out at our cabin near Cuchara. My wife and I just got home from shopping, and our son and my father are missing. My father has some dementia, and I'm afraid he wandered off. I'm thinking Buddy, who is only ten, went looking for him. I hate to bother anyone, but do you think you could put the call out for volunteers to help search for him? My father is eighty-four and has bad hips, so he couldn't have gotten far, but, as you know, the terrain out here is dangerous. We need to find him before he runs into a mountain lion or bear, or some other trouble."

The sheriff's communications officer said she would send out a telephone alert to area residents and contact every group and individual she could think of to mount a search party.

"I will have them assemble at your cabin, Deputy Yost, so it may take an hour or more to get a group together. It's going to get cold tonight, below freezing, I think, so that's another reason to get this rolling as quickly as possible," Stephanie said.

"Yes. My wife will stay at the cabin and direct the search, and I will keep looking, but please hurry!"

LOCAL PROBLEMS

Lester Sharp had to drive twenty-five miles north to Walsenburg on Saturday afternoon to find a hardware store that had a gate for the fence he was building to keep bears and other animals out of the area where he put the vats of powdered fentanyl in the sunlight to dry out.

"The fence and gate alone won't really stop raccoons, bears, or mountain lions, but I'll hang some electric wire out there, too. That will give them a good zap if they touch the metal fence or gate, which should keep them out of there," he told Dr. Moreland from a pay phone in Walsenburg before driving back to the cabin around 6:00 p.m.

When he arrived at the cabin around 6:45, Lester unloaded the gate and electric fencing from his Jeep and carried it all into the woods to the lab building.

"What the fuck!"

Lester went down. He had tripped over the body of Jack Yost and landed between him and his grandson. Both were dead.

Lester recognized them as locals but did not know their names. He had seen them fishing near a large log cabin just downriver. As he clambered back to his feet, something caught in his throat and made him cough and feel dizzy. Then he saw the white powder on the old man's hands and in the grass around the bodies.

"Oh my god, how did they get into that vat? And why?"

He went to the cabin and called Dr. Moreland.

"Are you fucking kidding me?"

He had not expected the heartless physician to express any remorse for the deaths caused by their drug-lab product. Yet he was surprised at the second thing that the doctor said.

"You have to drag them into the woods and bury them somewhere," he said.

The only detectable emotion in his voice was anger, and it was directed at the two victims.

"What the hell were they doing on my property? And why did they mess with that powder? What were they looking for?"

"Doc?" Lester said.

"What?"

"Maybe we should clear out the lab and get the fuck out of this place before the cops come searching for these two."

"Hell no, Lester! I'm paying you more than you've ever made in your worthless life, so just do what I tell you and do not panic. If you bury them like I said, they will never find them. They will come by and ask questions, sure, but just tell them you never saw these two because you were gone all day, which your receipts from the hardware store will prove.

"The cops will keep looking, but after a few weeks, they will have to assume that the bears or mountain lions dragged them off and devoured them, or they fell into the river and drowned, and their bodies were carried down into the lakes."

"I don't know, Doc. I have a bad feeling about this. I mean, an old guy and a little kid just died because of us," said Lester, breaking down.

Moreland had no tolerance for whining.

"Listen, Lester, you are not a fucking moron. You are a smart guy who does not want to go to prison, right? If you run, they will think you are guilty and track you down—and you suck at lying so that means I will have to kill you myself before they find you. So stop freaking out and go to the garage and get the shovel and the big wheel barrel to haul their bodies into the woods. You will need the grub axe, too. That rocky soil up there is a bitch to break up."

Around 11:30 that same night, the phone rang in Moreland's home in the foothills near Cheyenne Mountain in Colorado Springs.

"Hello?" he said.

"Dr. Moreland, this is Deputy Joe Yost with the Huerfano County Sheriff's Department."

"Yes, what is it? It's nearly midnight. Why are you calling me?"

"Doctor, we are conducting a search for two missing people from the Cuchara area near your property. I'm calling to secure your permission to search there, just in case they may have wandered onto your land. Can I get your verbal permission, sir?"

"No. I do not want anyone tramping around my property, do you understand? I have no way of knowing if you are really a sheriff's deputy or not, and either way, you are not granted permission to step foot on that property!"

Moreland slammed the receiver down before the deputy could explain that it was his own son and father who had gone missing.

CHAPTER ELEVEN

THE PRICKLY DOCTOR

OCTOBER 6, 1978

As if Wilson and I didn't have enough on our hands with the four OD victims and the crew of "interested parties" asking questions about them, the next week brought another unwelcomed distraction.

"Detective Kenda, I'm Deputy Joe Yost. I'm with the Huerfano County Sheriff's Department."

It took my mind a minute to put a location on that county. It was a couple hours south, down in one of the state's more remote and sparsely populated areas.

"What can I do for you, Deputy?"

"I'm working on a case with two missing persons, who happen to be my eighty-four-year-old father and my ten-year-old son," Deputy Yost said.

Up to that point, I'd been planning to keep this conversation short and sweet. I don't mind helping other cops, but we were up to our eyebrows in our own investigations. So I had nearly declined to take the call from this deputy. But any inclination to blow him off ended the moment he said his son and his father were missing.

Despite my crusty exterior, I still had some traces of human compassion, believe it or not.

"Oh geez, Deputy, how long have they been missing, and what can we do from up here to help you find them?" I said.

"We have been searching for them since late last night when they disappeared from our home near Cuchara. My old man has been having mental lapses lately, and my son, as young as he is, feels responsible for him.

"We are surrounded by forest lands, so there is no telling where they might have gone. I've been out with search parties since they went missing," he said. "I'm hoping you can help me with a property owner from your area who has been a pain in the ass. And if it sounds like I'm getting desperate, I am."

The deputy's voice cracked, and he had to take a minute.

At that point, I was ready to jump in a helicopter, fly down there, and join the search. To hell with our OD cases, this poor guy was trying to find his son and his father.

"Sorry, Detective Kenda. Are you still there?"

"Yes, of course, I'm here," I said.

"I'm calling you because a doctor from Colorado Springs owns a cabin and ten acres just down the river from our place. It's probably just his weekend getaway, but when I called him up there and asked if we could search his place, the asshole said no."

"What's his name?"

"Dr. Blair Moreland."

"Oh yeah, I know that name."

"You do?"

"Yes, he works at the same hospital as my wife, who is a nurse. Springs General. He's head of the anesthesiology department there. She's told me he is very competent but hard to get along with. To put it succinctly, he is a notorious asshole."

"Yeah, I'm finding that out."

"Can you get a warrant? I mean, a missing persons search probably doesn't qualify as a life-or-death situation, but his refusal might be enough to piss off a judge, especially given that it is two members of your family, and a child is involved."

"I was hoping to avoid asking for a warrant because it takes time, and I don't have any evidence that they are on his property, but it did once belong to my grandfather's best friend, and he went there to visit him often. I'm thinking maybe he got confused and headed over there with my son. The fact that the doctor won't let us even look around seems strange, but maybe that's just him being an asshole."

"Do you want me to put the squeeze on him? Maybe visit him at the hospital and appeal to his humanity, or point out the lack of it?"

"Thanks, but you made a good point about the warrant. There is a judge down here who I've had some good dealings with, if I can track him down. He goes fishing a lot, when he isn't at his favorite bar."

"Okay, Deputy. Good luck. I hope you find them soon. If I don't hear back from you, I'll check up on you in a few days."

"Thanks, Detective."

Wilson, who was antsy to get to work on our own cases, had been eavesdropping from his desk across from mine.

"What was that about? You went from zero interest to hot and bothered in about three seconds flat."

"A deputy down in Cuchara. His son and father are missing. They are on the fourth day of searching, but they are dealing with millions of acres of surrounding forest and a prick who owns the property next door but lives in Colorado Springs and won't let them on his property."

"So, he wants you to do what?"

"He was thinking maybe we could pressure the guy to let them search his property, but get this: the prick neighbor is Dr. Moreland, the head of anesthesiology at Springs General."

"Oh geez, the same guy that Kathy's nurse friend suspects is stealing fentanyl from the hospital?"

"Yes! Kathy says he's the only anesthesiologist she knows who seems to enjoy seeing his patients suffer. Her nurse friend thinks he might be using fentanyl to get a high."

"It makes you wonder what he's up to down in Cuchara, doesn't it?" Wilson said.

"Yeah, if he was stashing drugs down there, that might explain why he doesn't want anyone on the property."

"Maybe we could go stomp on this doctor's toes a little and see what happens?" Wilson said.

"I'm tempted. Not just for our case, either. I didn't say anything about what we've heard about Moreland to the deputy. He has enough on his mind right now. He sounded frantic, and I don't blame him. The thought of your elderly father and young son being lost out there in that wilderness . . ."

"No, I can't either, especially in that area, which is rugged as hell," Wilson said. "Last time I was down there for a fishing trip, I stopped in Walsenburg for groceries, and damn if there wasn't a dead mountain lion in the back of a big pickup parked next to my car. Some local guy had shot it because it was prowling around his cattle, and the game warden was standing there checking out this huge cat. He was pulling one of its big incisors to get an age estimate, and he told me it was more than eight feet long and weighed just over one hundred fifty pounds."

INSIDE INFORMATION

Early in my career as a homicide detective, I developed a ritual for the end of my workdays and worknights—whenever they ended, and if they ended.

I'd drive home, park the car in the garage, and, before going inside the house, I would take out the garbage. Not just the real garbage, but also whatever horrible crap had happened that day and lodged inside my brain.

I would consciously clear my mind, if not my soul, of any horrors that followed me home from the preceding twenty-four hours, whether it was a mutilated corpse, a stomach-turning crime scene, or, always the worst, the death of a child.

I created this ritual of mental cleansing because I did not want the worst part of my job to ruin the best part of my life— my family time with Kathy and the kids.

Now, as a nurse, Kathy saw her share of horrors. She knew that there were some experiences that we could not wipe away because they were simply too corrosive; like acid, they could eat us up from the inside out.

After the kids were in bed, she'd say, "Let's have a drink and talk." And we would do our best to talk through the worst experiences, with the hope of at least being able to clear out enough garbage so we could sleep through the night.

And so, once we'd tucked in the kids, she and I sat down over cocktails that night, and I told her about the anguished call from Deputy Yost whose father and son were missing in the vast wilderness around Cuchara.

"That's awful, but why would that deputy call you?"

"Because your friend Dr. Moreland owns a ten-acre property next door to the deputy's home, and he has refused to let them search it for the missing father and son," I explained.

Kathy shot up out of her chair and stood hovering over me.

"There's something up with this guy, Joe," she said. "As brilliant as he is, Moreland just seems shady to me."

I knew what she was thinking. It had hit me on the way home. I'd made a mental note to check into Dr. Moreland after Mac at the state crime lab in Pueblo confirmed that the fentanyl sample vial from Springs General had been diluted with saline. But then I'd been distracted by the preacher's overdose death and all the interested parties who kept showing up asking questions, including the shady Mexican *federal*, Diaz.

"Why would Dr. Moreland have a place way down there? He seems more like a guy who'd have a Las Vegas penthouse than a remote cabin in the national forest," Kathy said.

"It does seem strange," I said.

"You know who you should talk to? Nurse Behr," Kathy said.

"Nurse Bear?"

"No, her name is spelled B-E-H-R, and she takes a lot of crap anyway because her first name is Claire, so it's Claire Behr."

"Well, what does she have to do with Moreland?"

"She dated him for quite a while. She's told me stories about the creep. They were engaged for a short time before she wised up and broke it off. Thank God. She had to threaten him with a restraining order after they split."

"Interesting. Can you get me her phone number?"

"Jesus, Joe, do you want me to solve the whole damn case for you, too?"

She said that with a smile.

"I admit it, dear," I said, "you would make a much better detective than I would make a nurse."

"Oh, I know that, baby. I sure as hell know that!"

NURSING A GRUDGE

The next morning, I filled Wilson in on what Kathy had told me about Nurse Behr and her relationship with Dr. Moreland.

"What do you think she's got on him?" Wilson asked. "I mean, do we really care that he doesn't brush his teeth before going to bed and snores like an old Labrador?"

"You are a knucklehead sometimes," I said. "She dated this guy and was engaged to him before they had a big meltdown. Now she hates him. Maybe she can give us some insights and help us figure out if he's the one tapping the hospital's fentanyl supply and maybe, just maybe, selling it to local heroin dealers."

"Wow, you are taking this and running with it—and I like it!" Wilson said. "But is Moreland the type who'd be hanging out with lowlife street dealers? Most doctors stick to the country club bar. If he is the source of the stuff on the street, he must have some sort of intermediary selling it for him, don't you think?"

"The same questions occurred to me. And that is why you and I have a breakfast date in a half hour with Nurse Claire Behr."

"Denny's I hope! I have a hankering for a Grand Slam," said Wilson.

We met at the Denny's a block from Springs General Hospital. Nurse Behr had just finished working back-to-back shifts, but she walked in looking like she could run a marathon. A table of geezers near the entrance fell silent to watch her walk to our table.

She iced them out, greeting us curtly with, "Good morning, Detectives." She then took one long sip from the cup of black coffee I had ordered for her before unleashing an impressive barrage of epithets aimed at her former fiancé.

"So what do you want to know about the sociopathic, psychotic, sadomasochistic asshole I almost made the mistake of marrying?"

"Well, first of all, we'd like to know how you *really* feel about Dr. Moreland?" I responded.

She managed a slight smile at that, but Wilson flinched when she reached for her coffee cup again. I didn't blame him. This was one pissed-off woman.

Kathy once told me pediatric nurses were typically strong-willed because they deal with suffering children and distraught parents day in and day out. "Most of them have big hearts, but they learn to lock them in steel vaults when they go to work," my wife said. "Otherwise, they wouldn't last more than a week."

Nurse Behr fit the description. She was an attractive young woman and obviously took no crap from anyone. Kathy had described her as "a steel magnolia."

"How long did you date Dr. Moreland?" asked Wilson, who seemed afraid to make eye contact with her.

"Nearly two years. He hid his Dr. Evil side for a long time; mostly because for the first year and a half all we did was have sex in his office at the hospital, at his home in the foothills, and nearly everywhere in between. There wasn't much talking, but the more I got to know him, the more I feared him."

"Why did you fear him?" I asked, just as her egg whites and unbuttered toast, along with Wilson's mountainous Grand Slam, arrived. I stuck with just coffee.

"I'm sure Kathy has told you about his reputation at the hospital. He terrorizes everyone, even his bosses. I was warned about him by the other nurses but didn't have much contact with him until he approached me in the hospital cafeteria one day. He turned on the charm. I couldn't figure out why everyone thought he was such a monster. I was new in town, working constantly to pay the rent, and quite lonely. I fended him off at first, but then he asked me to volunteer one day at the soup kitchen downtown, and I saw a different side of him there, or so I thought at the time.

"You mean the one at Springs Rescue Mission?" I asked.

"Yes, it's near the hospital, though I don't know if they are affiliated. He has been volunteering there for several years now. He seemed to know everyone, including the homeless people, and they all appeared to be very fond of him. I've seen him hand out cash to some of them outside the mission."

"So that's how he won you over? Taking you to the soup kitchen and acting like Mother Teresa?"

"I mean, I'd never seen that side of him. I thought maybe he was misunderstood at the hospital because he was such a perfectionist at work. It made me want to get to know him better. And, let's face it, he's a very successful guy who is not exactly repulsive to look at."

"Noted: he's a sociopath but also a stud muffin," grumbled Wilson, who was spewing hash browns all over the table in his feeding frenzy.

"Do you know he also volunteers every week as a counselor at the treatment center for drug addicts?" said Nurse Behr. "That impressed me too."

"Which place are you talking about?" I asked.

"The Rocky Mountain Recovery Center. I went to their annual fundraiser with him, and it was the same story there. Everyone loved him. Apparently, he's a big donor as well as a volunteer. All these recovering addicts kept coming up to me all night, telling me how he'd changed their lives and what a great mentor he'd been to them."

That information was especially interesting because of Kathy's suspicions that Moreland was stealing fentanyl from the hospital. Wilson picked up on that, too.

"Did you ever get the feeling that there was anything predatory about his relationship with the people in that program?" he asked.

"In what way?"

"Like maybe they were addicts whom he not only counseled but also secretly sold drugs to?"

"That seems like a stretch, don't you think?" she said. "Then again, I wouldn't put anything past this guy. And, well, now that I think about it . . . there was one person who seemed to be closer to him than most; she was a former mental health nurse at the NORAD base at Cheyenne Mountain. She had been through the program at Rocky Mountain Recovery Center and then became a paid counselor there. She would call Moreland at all hours, and he'd always make sure I couldn't hear their conversations."

Wilson and I exchanged glances at the mention of the woman's connection to Cheyenne Mountain, given that one of our overdose victims, Alfonso Peres, had been stationed there.

"What was her name?" I asked.

"Lula Lopez."

Wilson put down his fork long enough to scribble down the name.

"And she worked at the recovery center, too, right?"

"Yes, at least back when I was dating Dr. Dickhead," said Nurse Behr. "It's been a while. I've cut off all contact with him because he got pretty nasty after the breakup, threatening me and spreading rumors about me at the hospital."

"Do you think he has a violent side?" Wilson asked. "You'd think a guy whose job it is to relieve people of pain wouldn't be capable of violence, or is that just me being a simple-minded civil servant?"

"I have given that a lot of thought, actually," she said. "Yes, I think Blair Moreland is capable of violence. He is known for his mood swings, and, as I'm sure you have been told, there are many who suspect he is addicted to the very painkillers that he uses on his patients. I never saw him strike anyone, but one of the reasons I ended our relationship was because he was pushing me toward the sort of sex that borders on violence—and that is not my thing."

Wilson and I didn't push for more details on that revelation.

"We appreciate your taking the time to meet with us, especially after working a double shift," I said. "Please don't share any of what was discussed with anyone. We will be checking out this Lula woman and don't want her to be tipped off."

"That's fine. I hope that I've been helpful. I would like to see that bastard burn in hell, along with the choke collar he tried to put on me after he drugged me one night," she said.

"You know, Miss Behr, if you wanted to press charges on that . . ."

"No, I have something else for you that might help put that asshole away for a much longer time than that," she said.

She reached down and searched inside a large rolling bag like the one Kathy took to work at the hospital, which usually held extra scrubs, a lab coat, a change of clothes, comfortable shoes, snacks, and highly caffeinated sodas. Nurse Behr pulled out a small sheet of paper that proved to be from Dr. Moreland's prescription pad.

"The asshole had me so enraptured in the early days that I was even doing his laundry for him," she explained.

Her face was flushed red. I figured it was more from anger than embarrassment.

"I found this in one of his pants pockets and put it in a drawer, thinking I'd return it, but he never asked about it, and I forgot about it until just the other day when I looked in the same drawer for something else."

She handed it to me.

It appeared to be a list of chemicals or drugs, but I had no idea what they were or what they would be used for.

1-Benzy-4-Piperdone
1-Benzyl-4-Phenyliminopiperidine
1-Benzyl-4-Anilinopiperidine
Benzylfentanyl
Norfentanyl

"I managed to pass high school chemistry, barely, but I can't make anything of this list except that the last two things end in fentanyl," I said.

"No problem, Detective. I looked them up last night after Kathy called and asked me to meet with you," Nurse Behr said. "I believe they are the ingredients used in manufacturing fentanyl."

Wilson put his head in his hands and then stared up at the ceiling as if he were thinking, "Thank you, Lord, for finally giving us a lead!"

This information made me think of another question I wanted to ask.

"Did Dr. Moreland ever take you to his cabin down near Cuchara?"

"No, he never mentioned having a cabin anywhere. I can't imagine him doing something like that. He is not the outdoorsy type. He freaked out if he got so much as a mosquito bite."

CHASING LEADS

Wilson and I could hardly contain ourselves from dancing atop the Denny's lunch counter because of the information Nurse

Behr had provided us. We thanked her, paid the check, and all but sprinted to our unmarked car.

"Now that really was a true Grand Slam of a breakfast, Kenda my boy," Wilson said before issuing a prolonged belch.

"No kidding," I said. "For the first time in my life, I am grateful that hell hath no fury like a woman scorned."

"Is that from a John Wayne movie?" asked Wilson.

"No, I think it might have been a Clint Eastwood line in *Play Misty for Me.* Or maybe Shakespeare."

"You are such a smart-ass college boy, but I love you just the same. That pissed-off little lady gave us a few interesting strings to follow. So what's our first order of business? This is a test to see just how much you've learned from me."

"I'd say we do a deep dive on the background and any criminal records of this Lula Lopez and then go have a talk with her," I suggested. "I doubt that our air force investigator friend, Captain McAleavy, can help us access her military records. I'm sure the Pentagon wants to keep a lid on any report that says soldiers inside that base are using drugs—but maybe someone in our department has a contact inside the NORAD base that we can reach out to."

"I'll ask around. It seems like I've heard that one of our guys in Vice or Narcotics has a confidential informant there," Wilson said. "I also think we need to put in a call ASAP to that sheriff's deputy down in Cuchara. Have you heard anything about his search for his kid and his father?"

"No, we've been so damned busy, I haven't checked in with him."

"I don't want to bother him if he's still looking for them, or if he's dealing with something even worse after finding them, but I'm really curious about what Dr. Moreland might be doing down there now that we know he has a list of ingredients for manufacturing fentanyl," Wilson said. "It's not like you can cook that stuff up in an Easy-Bake Oven. I gotta wonder if he's set up his own lab down there. And is he just making it for his own use, or is the son of a bitch selling it, too? Why would a doctor making a big salary take that risk?"

"One explanation might be that the guy is more addicted to this shit than anyone realizes," I said. "And he probably knows that if he keeps stealing it from the hospital, sooner or later someone will figure it out, and they'll file charges and fire his ass."

CHAPTER TWELVE

THE LONG GAME

Dr. Blair Moreland had nothing but contempt for the media, its liberal biases, and its general ignorance of medical sciences. Besides, he simply did not have time to follow local news. His days were packed with administrative work and covering his patients while also volunteering at the Rescue Mission soup kitchen and the Rocky Mountain Recovery Center.

With all of that going on—not to mention feeding his growing drug addiction and supervising his illegal fentanyl laboratory down in Cuchara—he had only heard snippets of conversations about the overdose death of Buck Medina, which had sounded like suicide to him.

He seemed to do good work around town and at the recovery center, but you never know what haunts veterans—or anyone for that matter.

Moreland had also heard hospital staff talking about some hooker found hanging from an I-25 overpass near downtown. He hadn't given much thought to either of those events, and he certainly had not made any connection between them. But that was about to change.

While driving to the Rocky Mountain Recovery Center for a counseling session, Dr. Moreland reminded himself to check and see if Lula Lopez was in her office.

I'm surprised I haven't heard from her. She must have unloaded that first batch of powdered fentanyl by now. I hope she followed my directions on how much to use when cutting her heroin. Why hasn't she called me? I'll go to her office after this next meeting and see if she is in. I think she works today, but I can't keep up with her schedule and mine too.

Moreland had come in early to prepare for his first session with a new and quite unusual patient at the recovery center. She had been given an alias upon admission because of her background. None of the other patients knew her true story, which was included in her file for Moreland's eyes only.

The woman admitted under the alias "Jenna Jenavi" was a former DEA undercover narcotics agent who'd been assigned to Operation Trizo. The goal of that operation was to locate and eradicate poppy fields tended by Mexican drug-trafficking rings in the states of Durango, Sinaloa, and Chihuahua—and to identify and arrest members of those rings.

The young agent was a natural for this operation, according to her file. Her Israeli father was a member of the Mossad intelligence agency, who'd met her mother, a Mexican lawyer and human rights activist, while he was serving as the Mexico City station chief. Jenna had joined the DEA after college because she feared the violent drug lords and their murderous henchmen were destroying her native country.

Upon completing her training in covert investigations,

Jenna was assigned to infiltrate the Hinojosa family trafficking ring in Durango. She was successful, and for more than a year, she provided intelligence to the DEA on the ring's members and the location of their poppy fields.

Her work came to an abrupt halt when she was recognized by one of her childhood schoolmates from Mexico City, who was a *sicario* for the Hinojosa operation. Things did not go well from there. She was abducted, tortured for weeks, and forcibly given heroin each day.

By the time she was rescued by a US Special Forces team, Agent Jenavi was near death. She was hospitalized for months while undergoing detox and withdrawal and recovering from her many injuries. She was then admitted to the recovery center in Colorado Springs for addiction therapy and counseling.

After reading her file prior to their first session, Dr. Moreland made a mental note to be especially cautious. *This is a very smart, well-trained intelligence agent who obviously knows much more about drug trafficking than me. I will have to be careful around her. She can probably spot another addict from miles away.*

"Good morning, Dr. Moreland. I am here for my first session."

A slender woman with light blond hair and the bearing of a ballerina walked into the room and took a seat across from Moreland.

Back straight. Chin raised slightly. Her dark brown eyes bore into his own.

This formidable woman does not look in any way like a drug addict, or a torture victim, Moreland thought.

"Hello, Miss Jenavi, you appear to be well along in your recovery," he said.

"Yes, thank you, Doctor. I pride myself on my resilience

and, as you have probably already learned from my file, I come from strong stock."

"I have no doubt about that! You seem to have done great work for the DEA. I see that you have received many commendations and honors there."

In fact, Operation Trizo had resulted in the eradication of more than 22,000 acres of poppy fields. The DEA had also arrested more than 4,000 members of Mexico's drug-trafficking rings.

"I see it says you were involved in Operation Trizo," said Moreland.

"Yes, I think we made a dent, but only a dent. It will be interesting to see how the drug lords respond to the loss of those poppy fields," she said. "They may be cutting their heroin more than ever to stretch out their supply. And we've heard they are already looking for ways to diversify their criminal enterprises."

"Sounds like you've kept up with things during your recovery," Moreland said.

"I have indeed. In fact, some of my fellow residents have been sharing copies of the *Rocky Mountain High Times*. They have an investigative reporter there, Rick Becker, who seems to be working on a series about overdose deaths caused by some kind of powerful opiate that is being used by local dealers to cut their Mexican brown. I checked with my DEA contacts here, and they confirmed that they've been hearing the same reports on the street."

"Oh, is that right? You seem to be better informed than me on the local drug trade. I had not heard that."

Moreland tried to remain calm at this information, but his mind was struggling to process what it meant, or might mean, for him.

She said several people had died because of their heroin being cut with something deadly? Why haven't I heard this? Was Buck Medina one of them? Why hasn't Lula told me about this? Surely she would know.

He could feel sweat forming on his face under the intense gaze of the DEA agent. She had picked up on his anxiety and wondered about its source as Moreland stumbled through their thirty-minute introductory session.

He could not get her out the door quickly enough.

After watching Miss Jenavi walk down the hallway toward the patients' quarters, Moreland went to the office Lula used when she was counseling her own patients. She was not there.

He returned to his office and dialed Lula's home number. She did not pick up.

A RECKONING

It had taken longer to find a buyer for her Mexican brown than Lula expected. The local market had dried up because of the string of overdose deaths in Colorado Springs. So far, no one had connected her to those deaths, but she'd had to set up a deal to sell her uncut stash at a discount to a strip club owner who kept his dancers high so they'd work longer hours just for tips. Finally, she would have enough cash to get the hell out of town. She just needed to make the handoff and collect her money.

Everything was crashing around her. Friends had reported that surly strangers were hanging out at her favorite bars and asking about her. She couldn't sleep. She felt sure either the cops, the crazy doctor, or the Mexican mob would get to her soon. She was packing up her rental house, located in a rough block wedged between railroad tracks and I-25, when the call came.

"You have maybe ten minutes to get the hell out of there. They are coming for you now," said Lorenzo Martinez before hanging up and leaving his hotel room. Outside, he stopped and pretended to tie his shoe, hoping to buy Lula a little more time while the *federal* and the Dorado brothers waited for him.

"Lorenzo, come on. Get your ass in the truck. We got someone to talk to!" Miguel Diaz yelled.

Neither Diaz nor the Dorado brothers were aware that Lorenzo Martinez was a friend and relative of the woman they intended to torture and kill. If they'd known, they never would have called and told him to meet them at Diaz's Chevrolet Suburban in the hotel parking lot.

They had found Lula's address in Aurora Santiago's address book. They'd asked around and discovered that Lula worked as an addiction recovery counselor while selling drugs on the side.

"The brothers kicked some asses last night and learned that this Lula Lopez may be the source of the bad Mexican brown," Diaz had told him just before Lorenzo called Lula to warn her.

Lula had participated in many emergency alert simulations while serving at the NORAD base in Cheyenne Mountain. She could scramble when scrambling was called for. She shoved the six bricks into a gym bag and headed out the front door with her car keys in the other hand.

If only Lorenzo had taken a few minutes longer to tie his shoes, he might have bought her enough time. But he did not.

Diaz spotted her coming out of the tiny house as he parked the Suburban a few houses down the block. She matched the description that his soldiers had beaten out of two junkies the night before. And she appeared to be in a real hurry.

"That must be our Lula. Take her down before she can

drive away. Then get her back in the house. Lorenzo and I will meet you there."

Emilio and Dionisio moved fast for big men. Emilio pinned Lula against the driver's door of her Impala and muffled her screams with his hand while Dionisio searched the gym bag he'd snatched from her hands.

"Lookee, lookee here, Emilio bro! The little lady Lula was rushing out the door with six bricks of Mexican brown!"

"Careful with that, brother. If she already cut it, you don't want to get any of it on your hands or up your nose."

While they dragged Lula into her house, Diaz and Lorenzo sat in the Suburban watching.

"Ready to go in?" Lorenzo asked.

"Not just yet. I want to ask you something first," Diaz said.

"What is it?"

"Lula was on the run with that bag full of heroin bricks. Someone must have tipped her off that we were coming for her. It wasn't you, was it?"

Lorenzo's stomach churned.

"Why would I do that? I was sent to find the source of the bad mix and to bring her back to the *regio*. Your two thugs beat up half the dealers and dopers in the Springs trying to get to her. One of them probably tipped her off."

Diaz decided to drop it for now.

I still think there is some connection there. He seemed concerned when the brothers were roughing her up. Maybe he's just soft. Even so, he is the second-in-command for the Denver operation, and the nephew of Jorge Santos, who is one of my best-paying patrons . . .

"Lorenzo, I need you to stay in the SUV with the engine

running. Keep an eye out in case the cops show up. She was making a lot of noise. Some nosy neighbor may have heard or seen the brothers nab her. If you see any signs of the law, honk the horn three times. Got it?"

"Yes, I will keep watch, but don't be too long, and don't kill her if you can help it. The *regio* wants to know her supplier, and how this powerful shit is made, whatever it is."

Diaz entered the house where the Dorado brothers had Lula strapped to a kitchen chair and gagged with duct tape.

Emilio was slapping a ball peen hammer into his open palm while standing in front of their terrified captive. Diaz ripped the duct tape from her mouth and slapped her, just to set the tone of this meeting.

"So, Miss Lopez, we don't have time to fuck around here," he said. "We have already learned that you were the source of the killer heroin that has cost the Hinojosa family at least three customers already. You are screwing with their business, and they don't like that. So now we need to know who supplies you with this deadly shit. And we want to know where it is made and how it is made. Do not make me ask you again!"

Lula knew her fate was sealed, no matter what she said. She was also pissed off that Moreland had set her up by giving her the killer drug to cut her heroin product, so she didn't mind giving him up.

"I can tell you the name of my supplier; it is Dr. Blair Moreland. He's chief of anesthesiology at Springs General Hospital."

"He's a fucking doctor? An anesthesiologist? What the goddam hell?"

"He's a fucking junkie doctor!" said Lula. "He sold me the powder to cut my heroin, but the son of a bitch didn't tell me it was lethal. I had no idea until people started dying, believe me. I gave it to a couple of my friends, and it fucking killed them!" Lula said.

She was playing the victim, hoping to get some sympathy from her torturer.

It wasn't working.

"What is this drug? Where does this doctor get it? Does he steal it from the hospital?" Diaz asked.

Emilio was looming behind Lula's chair, still with the hammer in hand.

"Probably. I don't know, really, but that makes sense. It's some new painkiller, he said. He wouldn't tell me where he gets it, but he did brag that he controls the manufacturing process from start to finish, so maybe he is making it himself. I don't know. I really do not know."

"One more time, Lula baby: What is the name of this drug, and where does the doctor get it?"

"Probably the hospital. I mean, he's head of his department. But I don't know much else. I would tell you if I did. I already gave you the name of the damned doctor, didn't I? He set me up, and his drug killed my friends. Why would I do that?"

Emilio was still standing behind her chair, so Lula did not see him raise the hammer and slam it into her left hand, shattering every bone in it. Dionisio stepped in with perfect timing just as the hammer came down and wrapped a towel around her face to muffle her screams.

"Emilio, bring me one of the bricks of Mexican brown out of her bag," Diaz said.

Lula was slumped in the chair, head down, nearly passed out from the pain. Emilio opened the packaging and handed the brick to Diaz, who scooped a small bit of powder out of the brick and rubbed it under Lula's nose.

"Here you go, honey. This will either help with the pain or kill you, depending on whether or not you already cut it with the Doc's killer drug."

Emilio was behind the chair again.

"Pull her head back," Diaz said.

Emilio grabbed Lula's hair and yanked her head back, exposing her neck.

"Now, I'm giving you one last chance to tell me where the Doc gets this stuff that killed your friends," he said, flashing a box cutter he'd pulled from his back pocket.

Lula made a muffled moan; her eyes rolled back in her head.

Diaz pressed the box cutter blade to her neck only hard enough to draw a thin line of blood.

Lula moaned again.

And then Lorenzo came through the door and shot Diaz in the back of the head with a Colt Python .357.

Lula was showered in Diaz's blood and brain matter, but by then the heroin had kicked in and she was passed out.

"Don't either of you fuckers move!" Lorenzo said, pointing the pistol back and forth between the Dorado brothers. They instinctively began to move apart, but Lorenzo froze them by putting a shot into the floor a half-inch from Dionisio's left foot.

"Here's the deal. You work for me now. You are officially on the payroll of the Hinojosa family, and you will be set for life if this goes down the way I'm planning."

"We're listening," said Emilio.

Lorenzo had been plotting this move ever since he realized Lula was in danger. His uncle would be pissed that he killed

Diaz, but he planned to tell him that Diaz had bragged that he was planning on taking the doctor to the Hinojosa brothers for a bigger paycheck.

Lorenzo had also figured that the Dorado brothers were mercenaries with no allegiance to Diaz or anyone else. They worked for the highest bidder, and he had a strong bid for them.

"With Lula's help, we are going to set a trap for this junkie doctor. We will take him down, and we will find out where he is getting this lethal shit. We will be heroes to my uncle and the Hinojosa family. I am sure they will reward us, especially if we bring them the name of this drug."

Both Emilio and Dionisio were splattered with Diaz's blood and brain matter, which seemed to take most of the fight out of them. The lethal Python in Lorenzo's hand kept them open to discussion.

"How's she gonna help set up the doc, if she even wakes up? She insisted she didn't know where he got this shit, and I don't think she'd lie about that after I threatened to smash her other hand into a bloody pulp, too," said Emilio.

"She doesn't have to know anything. We're going to dump her on the doctor's doorstep at the hospital. He will see she has been tortured, figure she ratted him out, and panic. I think it is a safe bet that he will head to the source of his stash, so he can either protect it or destroy it before the Hinojosa family, or the cops, catch up to him. But we won't let that happen, will we?"

"I like this plan," said Dionisio. "What do you think, bro?"

"Hell, if nothing else, we can take all of this Mexican brown and sell it ourselves, right?" said Emilio.

"That might work, too," said Lorenzo. "But I think your life spans will be longer if you make nice with the Hinojosa family instead of pissing them off, don't you? You gotta play the long game, man, because anything short-term has a big downside."

SETTING THE TRAP

Lorenzo called Dr. Moreland's office at Springs General Hospital to make sure he was working that day.

"Yes, Dr. Moreland is in, but he is preparing for surgery. Could I take your number and have him call you when he has time?"

"Yes, please. Tell him that Miss Lopez needs to speak with him as soon as possible," said Lorenzo before hanging up.

"That should get his attention. Now, let's get her to the hospital," he said to the Dorado brothers.

They made sure to place Lula's purse, which contained her driver's license, in her lap when they wheeled her up to the admitting desk of the ER. Emilio, who had cleaned himself up, stood and watched Lula until the receptionist saw that she was unconscious and splattered with blood and brain bits. Her battered and broken hand was wrapped in a bloody towel.

"Nurse! Let's get this woman into the ER *now!*"

An hour later, Dr. Moreland saw Lula's name on a list of patients admitted from the ER. She had been moved to the trauma unit. He found her there. She had been cleaned up. She was unconscious and on a respirator, with an IV in her arm.

"Lula. Lula. It's Dr. B. What happened?"

Lula moaned slightly.

He examined the knife slice wound on her throat, then removed the bandages that had been placed on her hand in the ER. He could tell that most of the bones in the hand had been broken.

Someone got to her and tortured her. It was probably the Hinojosa family. They figured out she was the source of the heroin sold to the OD victims. They tortured her trying to find out where she got the opiate used to cut their product. They didn't kill her, so she must have given them my name. They'll be coming after me next. I've got to shut down the lab and get to Lester before they do.

Before he left for Cuchara, he went to his department's supply room and took a vial of liquid fentanyl. He extracted a small amount into a hypodermic needle and injected it in his inner elbow. He then took another vial and extracted a smaller amount into another hypodermic syringe. He taped the red cap back on that vial and put it in his pocket, saving it for his own use.

He returned to Lula's bedside with the second syringe.

This should be just enough to put you down without raising suspicion. Now, little Lula, you will be among the blessed few to experience death without pain.

As he left Lula's room, the charge nurse sitting at a desk doing charts looked up at him. He passed a security officer approaching in the hallway and watched him place a chair outside Lula's room and sit down in it.

Moreland stopped in his office and told his secretary to reassign all his surgeries for the next three days. "I'll be out of town," he told her.

CHAPTER THIRTEEN

THE VICTIMLESS CRIME VICTIMS

I called Captain McAleavy, the air force investigator I'd talked to about Airman Peres's overdose, and asked if he could provide us the records on mental health nurse Lt. Lula Lopez and her time inside Cheyenne Mountain's NORAD base.

He hemmed. He hawed. Finally, he apologized because he owed me a favor or two or three, and we always tried to cooperate with our military counterparts. But when it boiled down to it, Captain McAleavy said, "Sorry, but those military records are confidential."

He could only confirm the period that Lopez served on the base. Then I asked him about Airman Alfonso Peres. Again, he could only give me his time on the base, which included the period served by Lieutenant Lopez.

"Sorry, Detective Kenda, the brass would ship me to outer Mongolia if I gave you that information, especially on a case as sensitive as Lopez," Captain McAleavy said.

"Oh really? How sensitive is the information on Lieutenant Lopez?" I asked.

McAleavy was trying to help me without seeming to help me.

"Always nice talking with you, Detective Kenda," he said.

So my only takeaway from that conversation was that Lopez and Peres had served on the NORAD base at the same time, and that the air force felt that Lopez's file contained "sensitive" information. In other words, Lula Lopez got into some kind of trouble while serving in the top secret base—the kind of trouble that the air force wanted to keep quiet.

That could be a lot of things, but given what we'd been hearing about Lopez, my guess was that she'd either been caught using drugs or selling drugs on the base, or maybe both. That would explain why she entered civilian life and a drug recovery center at the same time.

The air force probably booted her out and agreed not to file charges against her if she completed a recovery program. They would do that because they did not want the news media to get word that drugs were a problem at NORAD.

All of that was my speculation, of course, which wasn't worth a damn thing in a homicide investigation. Fortunately, Wilson had better luck when he made another visit to Metro Vice and Narcotics, which was made up of detectives from all area police departments.

A couple of the VNI members, detectives Herb Miller and Mike Robertson, had already been helping us in the overdose investigations by talking to their drug-world informants around town.

I'd just hung up on the mostly unhelpful air force investigator when Wilson walked into our office with his report on that meeting.

"Joe, I talked to Detective Robertson over in VNI, and he has a confidential informant, a former air force guy who was stationed at the NORAD base when Lopez and Peres were there. He checked in with the guy as a favor to me. The CI said Lopez and Peres were tight. Always talking in the cafeteria and hanging out after hours. Some people thought they were dating or maybe just bunk buddies. When Lopez became a civilian, there were rumors that she was quietly sent packing for using or selling drugs inside. He said that was a shock since Lopez, as the base's mental health nurse, oversaw its random drug-testing program, including keeping the list of those to be tested."

Wilson paused while we both mulled over all that new information.

"So now we know that Lula Lopez and our OD victim Peres served at Cheyenne Mountain at the same time and that they were at least friends—and that Lopez may have been involved with drugs while serving there," he said. "If Lopez was in charge of the random drug-testing program, she could have protected Peres and any of her other drug clients by keeping them off the list—and, of course, she was never tested either."

"Well, this explains a lot," I said. "Lopez becomes a civilian, and shortly after that, Peres goes down from an overdose of heroin cut with fentanyl. We know from the doctor's pissed-off ex-fiancée, Nurse Behr, that Lopez was tight with Moreland, who had a ready supply of fentanyl he could tap as head of the anesthesiology department at Springs General."

Wilson was hopping around like an overgrown kid with a story to tell. The shit-eating grin on his face was another clue that he had some hot info to share.

"Okay, spit it out, you big country hick."

"Robinson came up with another gem from one of his druggie sources. This guy told him that he'd been to Narcotics Anonymous meetings with both Lula Lopez and Buck Medina—and both had ended up doing counseling work at Rocky Mountain Recovery Center, where Dr. Moreland volunteers."

"So now we have Lopez securely tied to two OD victims—Buck Medina and Airman Peres—as well as to the ass-wipe anesthesiologist from hell," I said. "Who do you want to have a friendly chat with first? The funky doctor or the junkie nurse?"

"Let's go put the squeeze on Lula and see if she'll throw doctor gas passer under the bus," said Wilson.

"Sounds good! I'll even let you drive since you've been such a good boy today."

LATE TO LULA'S

It's never a good sign when we pull up to a suspect's house and the front door is wide open. The trail of blood running from inside the house all the way to the curb was also problematic.

Wilson hadn't even put our unmarked car in park before he started with the *oh shits*, *oh damns*, and *oh fucking shit damns*.

We went in with guns drawn, fully expecting to find Lula sliced and diced with body parts dispersed all over the tiny wood-frame house. Instead, we came upon the corpse of the shifty *federal* investigator, Miguel Diaz, sprawled on the floor with the back of his head blown off.

Next to him was a blood-splattered kitchen chair with strips of duct tape still stuck on it. There was a box cutter with a bloodied blade on the floor next to Diaz.

It didn't take *all* my powers of deduction to come up with a likely scenario to fit this crime scene.

"If I had to hazard a guess, I'd say someone strongly objected to Mr. Diaz torturing Ms. Lopez, introduced him to the power of a large caliber handgun, and then freed Lopez from the torture chair and took her away."

"I'll radio headquarters and have dispatch check all the ERs," said Wilson, heading out to our car.

"You might alert our crime scene team and your favorite medical examiner, too."

"On it!" Wilson yelled from the porch.

Wilson first requested police dispatch to call the emergency rooms at all local hospitals to see if they had Lula Lopez or any Hispanic woman matching her description who appeared to have been severely beaten or cut. He also asked dispatch to send a crime scene team to the house.

"Thanks, and would you now put me through to the medical examiner's office, please?"

"El Paso County Medical Examiner's Office," said Maggie's assistant Amy Henning.

"Please put my wife on the phone, thanks."

"Oh, okay, Detective."

"Hello, Lee. Why are you calling me at work?"

"Maggie, we are at the home of the former air force mental health nurse we told you about, Lula Lopez. We suspect she was the source of the heroin sold to your brother and the other OD victims. She isn't here, but it looks like she was tortured here and then taken away."

"Oh, my lord."

"That's not all, baby. From what we can tell at this point, it also appears that someone came into the house while Lopez was being tortured and blew the head off the guy torturing her, so we have one body at the scene for you to certify and take to the morgue. Oh, and the dead guy is that Mexican federal investigator, Diaz, whom we suspected of working for the Hinojosa family."

"So you think that whoever shot Diaz was rescuing Lopez?"

"That would be one likely scenario," Wilson said. "We are checking with all the ERs in town to see if she was brought in. There is blood all over the house and a trail of it out to the street."

"What a mess this is. And you think it is all tied in with the OD cases?"

"Dr. Medina, don't you know that drug abuse is a victimless crime?"

"Oh, shut up, you big jerk. You're talking to a medical examiner here. I am not that naive. This certainly does sound like the sort of violence that follows Mexican drug traffickers everywhere they go. Oh, by the way, the lab results are back on Hoskins, the preacher. He had the same mix of heroin and fentanyl in his system, so now we have four OD victims, along with the poor woman hung off the overpass, and now another woman being tortured, and a Mexican federal investigator shot in her house."

"The body count just keeps growing. Now, you'd better get over here, declare this guy officially dead, and have his body hauled to the morgue in your carcass carrier."

"What's the address?" Dr. Medina said.

"The address is 303 Railyard Court."

"Oh, that's not far. I'm on my way," his wife said.

Wilson returned to the house. He and I were still processing the scene when the CSPD techs arrived to take blood samples and gather other evidence. Maggie showed up a few minutes later. She was usually very composed and professional in these situations, but she looked anxious.

"Joe, Kathy called me right before I left the office. She said Nurse Behr had just informed her that Lula Lopez was dropped off at Springs General ER. She appeared to be drugged and comatose. She'd also been badly beaten, and her neck was slit, though not deeply. And on top of that, she was covered in blood and what looked like brain matter."

"We need to go to the hospital and see if we can get any information from her," I said to Wilson.

The two of us were headed to our car parked in front of Lula's house when a beat-up four-door Mercedes, circa 1960, came clunking up the street and parked behind our vehicle. There was a large Press sticker on the windshield.

Rick Becker jumped out with a notepad in hand, looking overheated.

"Did something happen to Lula?" he asked.

"We're in a hurry, paper boy. And what the hell are you doing here, anyway?" Wilson said.

"Just tell me, is she dead?"

"Not as far as we know. We are headed to the hospital right now."

"Can I come with you?"

"No and hell no, and you still haven't told us why you showed up here."

"I've been talking to addicts, dealers, and other sources on the street. Word is out that Lopez sold the bad heroin mix to Buck Medina and one of the other OD victims, too," the reporter said. "I remembered she was at Buck's wake, and she made some comments that maybe he'd overdosed on purpose. I'm writing a series on all the recent OD deaths, and I was hoping to interview her."

"I'll make sure that doesn't happen—at least not until we've talked to her first," I said.

"So she's still alive?" Becker said.

"Yeah, knucklehead, last time I heard."

"One other thing, Detective," Becker said.

"Damn it, boy, didn't I tell you that we were in a hurry?" Wilson roared.

Becker did not back down.

"There's also talk on the street that Lula was cutting her heroin with some lethal shit that she was getting from a doctor she was screwing," he said. "Have you heard anything like that?"

"No comment, and you can quote me on that," I said. "Careful we don't run over you."

Wilson and I headed to the hospital, leaving Becker at the curb.

"If word is all over the street that Lula Lopez was the source of the killer heroin, then it is no surprise the Hinojosa family sent Diaz after her," I said as Wilson drove. "Let's hope she can tell us who killed Diaz and then dropped her off at the ER."

"It would be nice to know what she told Diaz, if anything, before he got plugged," Wilson said. "And if Diaz was working for the Hinojosa family, who killed him? I mean, it looked like one of their hits, but why would they kill one of their own while he was trying to find the source of the fentanyl?"

"Maybe it was a rival drug-trafficking ring that wanted that information, too," I said. "Maybe that's why they took Lopez, to question her themselves. But why didn't they just kill her instead of taking her to the ER?"

Our discussion triggered another thought. Maybe Lula was still in danger. If another drug-trafficking ring was involved, they might be afraid she'd die before they could get the information they wanted, so they took her to the hospital with plans to snatch her once she had been treated.

Then something else hit me. Moreland might try to kill her himself to keep her from talking, or to punish her if she'd already given him up. I called police dispatch on the car's radio: "Dispatch, notify security at Springs General to put a guard in the room with patient Lula Lopez until we can get someone over there from CSPD. And tell security not to let Dr. Moreland anywhere near her."

"Are you thinking Moreland might try to take her out?" asked Wilson.

"Let's say maybe Dr. Evil was providing fentanyl to Lopez to cut her heroin. He wouldn't be happy that she was using too much of it and killing her customers. And he'd be even more concerned that she might rat him out—either to us or to the Hinojosa family, right?"

"Your ability to think like a sociopath sometimes concerns me, pardner."

"I will take that as a compliment, sir."

After arriving at Springs General, we went to Lula's room

in the trauma center and met outside with Dr. Sarah Spahn, the doctor attending to her.

"Any chance we can talk to her?" I asked, knowing that the odds were slim.

"No, she is unconscious and on a respirator. I don't think she will make it. The wounds to her neck and hands are not the major concern. The drug or drugs they gave her are the problem. Her blood test showed heroin in her system. She's barely hanging on. I'm surprised she's made it this long, frankly."

Fred Jones, the chief of hospital security, came out of the elevator and walked over as Dr. Spahn returned to Lula's room. Jones had joined the hospital security team after retiring from CSPD where he'd risen to head the vice and narcotics units over his twenty-five-year career.

"Hey, Joe, what's the word on Dr. Moreland? Why did you want him kept away from this patient?" Jones asked.

"He's a person of interest in a case that involves this woman," I said. "Is he here?"

"No, I just checked. The charge nurse said he visited this patient's room right after she was cleaned up and placed there. Then he handed off all his surgeries to another anesthesiologist and rushed out the door."

CUCHARA CALLS

Wilson and I headed back to headquarters to talk to the chief and figure out our next move. On the way, we discussed our options.

"We need to find Moreland before the Mexicans get to him," I said.

"Or that fucking Becker, who seems hot on his trail, too,"

said Wilson. "We don't want him tipping off Moreland that he is a suspect."

"Do we need to get a search warrant for Moreland's home here in the Springs? Or do you think he's using the place in Cuchara as the base of his fentanyl operation?"

"My bet is on Cuchara. Whatever he's up to, if that smart bastard figures the Mexicans are on to him and maybe the cops too, he'll try to destroy any evidence linking him to the fentanyl."

"He'll be in deep shit if the Mexicans get to him first. Not that I feel sorry for him."

We arrived at police headquarters and had just walked into the chief's office when the desk sergeant knocked on the door and said he had an urgent call for me from a sheriff's deputy down in Huerfano County.

I took it at my desk.

"Detective Kenda here."

"Detective, it's Deputy Joe Yost."

From the quaver in his voice, I knew I should tread lightly.

"I've been meaning to check in with you, Deputy. I hope your search for your son and father ended well."

"No, sir, I'm sorry to report that the outcome was the absolute worst-case scenario."

Again, his voice cracked, and I could tell he was fighting a breakdown.

"I am so sorry, son. Is there anything we can do for you?"

"I wanted to bring you up to speed because I'm beginning to think your Dr. Moreland played a role in this, somehow."

He explained that a few days into their search for Deputy Yost's father and son, their team was joined by members of the Denver Police Department's search and rescue team. They brought with them two specially trained canine units: Scruffy, a bloodhound tracking dog; and Molly, a Belgian Malinois cadaver dog.

"We started with the bloodhound at my house, giving it pieces of clothing from my father and son to establish their scents. Scruffy took us straight up the road from my place to the property owned by your Dr. Moreland," Deputy Yost said to me on the phone.

"Now that is interesting," I said.

"Since we couldn't go onto his property, we walked the back perimeter of his land, which borders the national forest. There is a big metal building back there that the previous owner used for his taxidermy shop. It looks like the doctor has fixed it up and added a fence and gate behind it. We heard someone banging around in there, but I saw no sign of the doctor's Wagoneer. I know he has some younger guy living there, probably as a renter or caretaker.

"Anyway, Scruffy picked up the scent again out there on the perimeter near the metal building and took us deep into the national forest. In bare patches of dirt, we could see what looked like wheelbarrow tracks. They were pretty deep in places, like there was a heavy load in the wheelbarrow."

I knew where this story was headed and braced for it. He paused to keep his composure, taking deep breaths before continuing. I almost told him he didn't need to go into such depth, but then I thought maybe it was helping him process it all.

The deputy continued: "We got a couple hundred yards into the woods, and Scruffy was having difficulty tracking the scents. We had to wander around for a while, but then Molly the cadaver dog alerted. She'd picked up on something.

"She led us into a little clearing and, well, it was the worst thing I'd ever seen. Something I will never be able to get out of my head."

He was sobbing at that point. I didn't really need to hear any more, but I waited in case he needed to go on with it, the poor guy.

"At first, we only saw two shallow graves. There was nothing in them but scraps of clothing. Something had dug them up. Maybe a mountain lion. Molly got all worked up and led us deeper into the woods where we found just bits and pieces, bones, and more clothing . . . all that was left of my son and my father . . ."

I could hear him in the background, raging with grief and pain, unhuman sounds I have heard all too often in my career, the echoes that accompany my sleepless nights. I waited on the phone for a while, worried about leaving him alone in such a vulnerable state. Suicide is not uncommon among the families of murder victims, especially those with easy access to firearms and even more so for men who feel they have failed as protectors and guardians.

I wanted, in that moment, to give the deputy a different focus—a purpose, something to get him through the next few days, at least.

"Son, with your help, we will find whoever is responsible for this," I said. "You have more than enough evidence now to get a warrant to search Moreland's property. We think he may be headed down there now, so I'd suggest you take some other deputies as backup. And there is something else going on with this guy that you and I have not discussed because we are still piecing it all together."

"Sir?"

"We think this doctor is a drug addict. We think he has been stealing a powerful new painkiller from the hospital where he works and using it."

"Okay, but . . ."

"There's more. We just received evidence that suggests Dr. Moreland has been gathering the ingredients for manufacturing this drug himself—maybe down in Cuchara in that metal building you described . . ."

"What the heck? You really think that's possible? Why would he need to make it himself when he can steal it from the hospital?"

"This drug is highly addictive, fast-acting, and powerful. We have more evidence that he may be selling it to street dealers up here who have used it to cut their Mexican brown heroin. It is much cheaper than heroin, and more addictive, so the dealers make more profit and get their customers even more hooked— if it doesn't kill them."

"This guy is evil," said Deputy Yost.

"It gets worse. In recent months, we have had at least four overdose deaths in Colorado Springs, and the lab tests show that each of the victims had both heroin and this new drug— it's called fentanyl—in their systems. So these OD cases may be homicides if we can prove that Moreland and the street dealers knowingly sold lethal quantities of this substance."

"You know, if it is Moreland and he's making it down here in that old taxidermy shop, I think he may have someone helping him," said Deputy Yost. "We heard someone in that building while we were conducting our search. Maybe it was that young caretaker or whatever he is. I've seen the same guy eating at the Wagon Wheel Grill in town."

If nothing else, I seemed to have succeeded in giving Deputy Yost a purpose to distract him, at least temporarily, from his grief. I wanted to find some temporary relief from his pain by focusing on finding out whether Moreland was somehow connected to their deaths or whether he was making or distributing fentanyl from that property. We had no jurisdiction outside the Springs, so we couldn't conduct the search ourselves.

"Maybe you will find the wheelbarrow or something else linking either of them to the deaths of your father and son. Or maybe you will find a stash of fentanyl—or even a fentanyl lab in that metal building. I'm hoping you find enough to link them to at least one or both investigations, yours and mine. Make sure you put Moreland and the young guy in separate cells so we can come down and question them in our cases. Does that work for you?"

"Yes, sir, the more we have on them, the better."

Deputy Yost was sounding stronger.

"Be careful, this doctor is smart. And be especially careful around that lab. From what we have learned, it only takes a pinch of this drug to kill you. My advice would be to secure it and then get the DEA or another agency to go inside in protective gear. Besides, I wouldn't put it past this guy to put booby traps around it."

"I hadn't thought of that. We will be careful. Thanks."

I wanted to believe that Deputy Yost was finding strength despite his suffering. I couldn't be sure. You can never be sure how anyone will respond to such a devastating loss. I did not want to contemplate how I would handle it.

"Deputy Yost."

"Yes, sir."

"I have no doubt this doctor and his lethal drug have killed others, probably some we have not yet found. We need to shut him down. But please be careful."

"Yes, sir, don't worry. Message received. I will let you know how it goes."

CHAPTER FOURTEEN

BURNED

The eight-ounce Mason jar next to Lester's bed was Daisy's idea. She brought it from the Wagon Wheel Grill after their first romp at the cabin and placed it on the nightstand.

"I want you to put a quarter in it every time we have sex," she'd told him.

Lester had never had a girlfriend or even a friend with benefits, so he wasn't sure if this was normal, but it didn't seem normal.

"That's just weird, sort of like I'm paying you for sex like a hooker, and besides, from what I experienced last night, you are worth a lot more than a quarter," he teased. "I'd be willing to go at least a buck fifty."

"Ok, a buck fifty, but you aren't paying me for sex, silly boy, you are investing in our future," Daisy said. "This way, the more we do it, the more money we will have for our honeymoon on the coast of Spain!"

Daisy's favorite novel was *The Drifters* by James Michener, which is about a group of adventurous, pot-smoking, hashish-loving hippies cavorting across Spain, Portugal, Morocco, and other exotic locations. Her dream was to follow their path on her honeymoon one day.

Lester had not read the book, but he was game.

The jar filled up fast.

"Have you got four quarters for a dollar? Or can I start throwing dollar bills in there, too." Lester had said that morning after Daisy woke him at 5:00 a.m. by rubbing her naked body against his.

"Sure, I have some tip money in my jeans," she said before adding another $1.50 to the glass jar now labeled *Honeymoon Fun(d) #1*.

"Looks like we're gonna need another Mason jar pretty soon. I'll bring one home tonight."

"Bring more quarters, too," said Lester, who was entranced watching Daisy perform a runway model strut across his loft bedroom on her way to shower.

Lester had never had it so good, even if he was basically Doc Moreland's indentured servant. In fact, he'd never had it at all until the waitress daughter of the Wagon Wheel Grill owners had taken him into her welcoming arms, not to mention other places he'd never gone before.

My life would be perfect right now if the old guy and kid hadn't wandered over and stuck their noses into the vat of fentanyl powder I put outside to dry.

He had not told Daisy about finding their bodies behind the lab and then, under Doc's orders, hauling them in the wheelbarrow deep into the forest and burying them. She still didn't have any idea what Lester did in the lab, other than a vague concept that he was helping Dr. Moreland develop a new painkiller of some kind.

The nightmares were a problem, though. Daisy had asked why he groaned and moaned and bolted up nearly every night.

"I keep dreaming about that bear showing up again, chasing me into the woods, dragging me down, and devouring me," he'd told her.

This wasn't entirely a lie. Lester's nightmares came with visions of a bear or mountain lion dragging the bodies of the old man and the boy from their graves and devouring them.

I was so freaked out and exhausted from finding them and hauling them into the forest, I didn't dig the graves deep enough. But Doc, being the heartless asshole he was, said it wasn't so bad that something dug them up and hauled off their remains because now no one will ever find out how they really died.

It wasn't like I intentionally tried to kill anyone. It was an accident. I have to keep telling myself that. And I can't slip up and tell Daisy.

Lester had nearly spilled the beans after they'd downed a couple bottles of Boone's Farm Strawberry Hill. Daisy had taken his face in her hands, leaned in nose to nose, and said, "Are you okay, baby? You seem sad sometimes."

He'd choked up but managed to keep from telling her the truth, which made him feel even shittier since she was so loving and trusting and kind to him.

"I'm okay, Daisy. I'm not sad, really. I just want our thing to last forever, and I worry that someday a studly geologist will walk into the Wagon Wheel and steal you away to some exotic rock garden somewhere."

In truth, Lester's main worry was that Daisy would figure out what he was really doing in the lab, cranking out millions of dollars' worth of an illegal and dangerous substance—the drug that had killed the old man and the kid.

I mean, it is a painkiller, so that's a good thing. If Doc and his dealers are using it to cut heroin and selling it to junkies who overdose, well, that's on them. I'm just the cook. Besides, where would I find another job given my checkered past and lack of a degree? And now that Daisy is in my life, I can put up with my maniacal boss.

"Okay, gotta go make the bacon, babe!" Daisy said after emerging from the bathroom showered and dressed in her work uniform: a denim blouse, jeans, and tennis shoes.

He kissed Daisy goodbye and watched out the bedroom window as she departed in her bright-orange Scout with black racing stripes.

Then, Lester showered, dressed, and donned his hazmat suit for another day in the lab.

EXIT PLAN

Blair Moreland had a lot to think about on his drive down to Cuchara. It was likely that the Hinojosa family, which dominated the Colorado Springs heroin trade, had sent one of its *sicarios* to torture and kill Lula Lopez. They'd figured out that she was the source of the cut heroin that had killed several of her customers.

They didn't kill her right away because they were after the name of whoever supplied her with the fentanyl. Of course, they probably don't know it is fentanyl, the morons. They just know it is some drug that is killing people and hurting their business. And they will probably want to know where to get it or how to make it for their own use once they fully understand how powerful and addictive it is.

The overdose deaths in Colorado Springs were a problem for Moreland. Two of the victims, Buck Medina and Alfonso Peres, had traceable ties to Lula, and that's probably how the Hinojosa family tagged her as the source of the bad Mexican brown.

If they looked at Lula hard enough, it wouldn't take them long to connect her to me since we both work at the recovery center. That would be an obvious place to nose around. They do good work there at the center. They have saved hundreds of people from addiction. But I'm sure everyone in the drug world understands that treatment centers, like prisons, serve as institutions of higher learning for criminals and addicts.

Some people get changed for the better during treatment programs, but many others come out of them more hardened and better educated on the ways of the underworld. I've had patients at the recovery center tell me they learned more about finding drugs, using drugs, and feeding their addictions from other patients at the recovery center than they ever would have learned on the streets.

Moreland did not blame Lula for giving him up to her torturer.

Why wouldn't she? She was probably pissed that the fentanyl I gave her was responsible for the deaths of her customers—even though I told her to be precise in measuring it because it was so powerful. So if she gave me up, they will be coming after me next. And even if she didn't give me up, the police will eventually make the same connections that the sicario did.

Either way, I'm fucked unless I get down there, destroy the lab, and disappear.

Maybe I could blame it on Lester. I could say I felt sorry for him and gave him a place to live so he could recover, and he began manufacturing fentanyl on his own, but they'd figure out that was a lie because he never had the financial resources to build that lab. I may have to just blow up the whole operation with Lester in it and then move to St. Martin, or Costa Rica, or somewhere else that doesn't yet have an extradition treaty with the US. I kept the rest of that vial of fentanyl from the hospital in case I need a fix on the way down there, but it might come in handy if Lester doesn't cooperate.

AN AMBITIOUS PLAN

After Lorenzo shot Diaz and convinced the Dorado brothers to work with him, they told him that Lula had identified Dr. Moreland as her supplier.

"At least the *federal* got your lady friend to tell us who gave her the drugs that killed her customers," Dionisio said. "It was the doctor who works at the recovery center, Moreland. She said he's addicted to the stuff. It's some kind of new painkiller."

"Did she give you the name of it?"

"Well, Diaz was working on that when you blew his brains out."

Martinez had proven to be more ruthless and more diabolical than anyone expected. He had even come up with a plan to capture Moreland and take him directly to the Hinojosa family's headquarters in Durango, Mexico.

"If they can learn from the doctor how to manufacture this potent drug, the family can make millions," Lorenzo said to Emilio and Dionisio as they tailed the unsuspecting Dr. Moreland out of town and south toward Cuchara in his Range Rover.

"We will deliver the doctor and his secrets to them, and we will be heroes in the eyes of the entire family," he added. "My friends, you and I will be kingpins in the family's new product division."

Dionisio, the more politically astute brother, processed this for a few miles before asking, "What will your Uncle Jorge in Denver have to say about that? Are you sure we shouldn't take the doctor to him first, since he sent you down here to figure out what was going on? Won't he be pissed off if you cut him out?" said Dionisio.

"I will handle my uncle, don't worry about it," Lorenzo said. "Why should he get all the glory if we do all the work and take all the risks? He might want to kill me at first, but he won't because I'm blood. And once he sees me rising in the Hinojosa operation, he will be glad to have a family member on the inside who can serve as his eyes and ears."

"Well, you do have this all figured out, don't you?" said Emilio. "Let's just hope it all goes according to plan. Kidnappings and torture jobs can get messy, as we all know."

"True, brother," said Dionisio. "As our great-grandfather Arturo Villanueva used to say, 'Every caballero has a plan, until he is thrown from his horse.'"

CLOSING IN

Daisy was surprised to see Deputy Yost enter the Wagon Wheel Grill just after noon. Like everyone else in town, she had heard the horrible story about his son and father going missing and then, a few days later, the discovery of their remains scattered in the national forest.

The Yost family members were all regulars at the restaurant. They were good people. The grandfather and grandson had such a special bond. She remembered them teasing each other and laughing over the restaurant's Black Cow root beer floats.

Daisy had been wondering when their memorial service would be, but decided it was not a good time to ask the deputy, who seemed to be looking for someone.

"Hi, Deputy Yost. I'm so sorry for your loss. I loved those two guys," she said. "How's Dahlia doing?"

"Thank you, Daisy. As you can imagine, she is grieving. We are all grieving. I'm trying to stay focused on work, so I don't just sit around crying all day, to tell you the truth."

"Oh, I'm so sorry. Can I give you a hug?"

"Sure, thanks. You are a sweetheart. Buddy and Jack loved you, too. Everyone loves you and your folks."

After a brief hug and a few tears, the deputy asked Daisy, "Have you seen Judge Spenser today? I checked at the courthouse, and they said he was taking the day off to do some fly-fishing up at Blue Lake."

"Oh yeah, he caught some beauties and then came in for a late breakfast," Daisy said. "I think he's still in the bar with some of his buddies, playing euchre and swapping lies as always."

Daisy watched as the deputy walked into the dark bar at the back of the restaurant off the dining area. She noticed that he squared his shoulders and tensed up as he entered the bar.

Something's up, she thought.

From the doorway, she saw Deputy Yost approach Judge Marcus Spenser at a table where he was sharing a pitcher of Bloody Marys with three friends, all retired attorneys. They greeted each other—the locals all knew each other in this small town—and then she saw Deputy Yost ask the judge to speak with him privately. They went to an opposite corner and sat down in a booth.

Their discussion seemed intense. Deputy Yost did most of the talking initially. Then the judge, who had a booming voice, asked a few questions, which the deputy responded to.

After only fifteen minutes, they stood up and shook hands. The deputy thanked the judge. Deputy Yost then walked out, went to his patrol car, and drove off. The judge went to the bar and paid his bill, then he waved to his table of friends, saying, "Gotta go back to the courthouse. The deputy needs a search warrant signed on the old Collingsworth place that the doctor from Colorado Springs bought."

The judge then left the restaurant and drove off toward Walsenburg, the county seat thirty-five miles to the northeast.

That's Doc's place he's talking about, thought Daisy. *Why would they want to search there? I should tell Lester about this. I left my bag of weed in his night table. What if they find that?*

She went to the restaurant office and called the cabin phone, but there was no answer. Lester had told her there was no phone in the lab. Daisy went to her father who was carving up a big pork roast in the kitchen.

"Dad, I need to run an errand for Lester, so I'm taking my break now, okay?"

"Have you asked your mom to cover your tables for you?"

"I will right now."

"If she can do that, then it is fine with me, but don't be gone too long."

Daisy drove the fifteen minutes down County Road 12 to Dr. Moreland's cabin on the Cucharas River. She noticed that his Wagoneer was parked in the driveway. He must have arrived after she'd left for work. It was unusual for him to come down from the Springs during the week because he worked a heavy schedule at the hospital.

For a moment, Daisy wondered if she should turn around and go back to the restaurant. Dr. Moreland was intimidating, even scary. He'd acted friendly when he first asked her to show Lester around the area and keep an eye on him, but Lester had told her that the doctor could be mean and domineering. She'd also caught him staring at her in a way that made her uncomfortable. Like he was leering at her. Lester said he often bragged about all the nurses he'd slept with.

"Yeah, the more I am around him, the more he seems like a perv," she'd told Lester.

"That may be one of the nicest things a woman has ever said about him," her boyfriend said. "He can put on the charm at first—he even had me convinced he was a good guy for a while, but he has a mean streak. Believe me, he's ripped into me plenty of times."

Daisy was torn between her fear of Moreland and her desire to warn Lester about the deputy's search warrant. She walked up to the front door of the cabin but then heard muffled voices coming from the lab back in the woods. She could tell that the doctor and her boyfriend were arguing.

She walked around, hoping to make out what they were saying but still not sure if she wanted to deliver her news with Moreland there. When she could hear them better, she realized they were standing just outside the building in the fenced-off area. She heard Moreland shout, "Lester, I'm telling you, we need to burn this damn place down, now!"

Daisy turned, ran back to her Scout, and drove away.

"Good decision, little hottie, you don't want to be part of

what's coming down here," muttered Lorenzo Martinez from his hiding place in the forest behind the lab.

LAB RAID

When Daisy drove up, Lorenzo had been monitoring the conversation between the doctor and the guy in the protective suit from behind a thick stand of aspen. Emilio and Dionisio were with him.

Lorenzo had figured correctly that once Moreland saw Lula Lopez with her neck cut and hand broken in the ER, the doctor would assume she'd given him up and make a run for it. They had not counted on following him more than 130 miles south to this remote cabin outside of Cuchara.

After watching him park his Wagoneer at the cabin, they'd driven a mile up the road to the Spring Creek Trailhead and parked in a small lot there. They then hiked back, staying in the trees to avoid being seen, and surveyed the doctor's property from the woods.

Like Daisy, they had heard voices coming from the fenced-off area outside the building behind the cabin. They moved closer to hear what was being said. They'd only been there a few minutes when Daisy pulled up.

After she left, Dionisio said quietly to Lorenzo, "I've seen my share of illegal drug labs in Mexico, and with all those roof vents, the painted and barred windows, and the guy in the protective suit, I'd say that's what we're looking at here. It also looks like they have a vat of some kinda powder drying in that fenced area."

"I think you are right. We still don't know what sort of shit he is cooking, but this must be where he makes it," Lorenzo said. "They are going inside. The doc was talking about burning the place down, so we'd better move on him now."

The three of them moved forward with their weapons ready. Lorenzo had his Colt Python revolver. The Dorado brothers were both packing AK-47s with thirty-round magazines.

Emilio was preparing to kick in the door when a car horn blasted repeatedly from the driveway of the cabin.

Daisy had changed her mind and returned to warn Lester.

I have to do something before Lester gets in serious trouble.

She had walked again toward the building in the woods when she saw three big Mexican guys carrying weapons and moving from the forest toward the building. She didn't want them to shoot her, so she ran back to her Scout, honked the horn like crazy, and then drove off.

"That little bitch," said Dionisio.

Emilio stepped up and kicked in the lab door. The faint smell of vinegar took them by surprise, as did the bright lights and sophisticated setup of the laboratory inside the rusting old building. A guy in a hazmat suit was standing at the other end of the lab next to a vat of something. They moved toward him.

Moreland, who was wearing a surgical mask, had been standing behind the door, so when it flew open, he went down. When the three Mexicans entered, he saw them moving toward Lester and quickly got to his feet, then sprinted out the door before his would-be captors could see him.

Lorenzo and Emilio heard him running into the forest, turned, and gave chase.

Dionisio already had Lester pinned against a wall. The thug for hire was yelling at him and trying to rip off the head cover of the hazmat suit when Lester reached out with a gloved hand,

grabbed a fistful of fentanyl powder from the vat, and threw it
in his face.

His attacker went down, hacking and coughing, rubbing
his eyes and screaming. Within seconds, Dionisio lost control
of his limbs, which were flailing wildly. His skin turned blue.
He gasped for air and then lost consciousness.

Lester ran out of the lab and tore off his hazmat suit. He
could hear the two other guys screaming at Moreland to stop
as he ran through the forest. The doctor had been preparing to
pour gasoline on the floor of the lab to blow it up when the three
guys came through the door. Lester now saw that as a good idea.

He went back inside the lab, quickly poured a long stream
of gasoline on the floor, grabbed a flint striker used to ignite
Bunsen burners, lit a wad of paper, threw it into the gas puddle,
and dashed out the door.

Lester didn't have his car keys on him, but he knew Moreland always left the keys to his Wagoneer in a pocket on the
driver's door. He jumped inside, started it, and tore off toward
Cuchara, trying to figure out his next move, hoping Daisy would
go with him, wherever he went.

As Lester drove off, the fire in the lab spread rapidly and
triggered a series of explosions. The lab's propane gas tanks were
blowing up, rocketing through the building and out the roof
and walls. Some of them rained down and crashed through the
roof of the old A-frame cabin, demolishing part of it, too.

INTO THE ARMS OF THE LAW

Dr. Moreland was no woodsman, but he had hiked around the
forest behind his property many times, planning an escape route
in anticipation of a day like this. He knew the sloping terrain,

and he was more acclimated to the higher elevations, so he had managed to put a good distance between him and his pursuers who were thrashing around, stumbling, and cursing the loose rocks that made it difficult for them to gain any ground.

Moreland had a vague plan to lead them up and away from his cabin, and then to double back so he could return to his Wagoneer and escape.

Smart as he was, the doctor had not counted on running directly into Deputy Yost and two other members of the sheriff's department on ATVs. They were following a hiking trail toward his property, hoping to surprise him with their search warrant.

"Hold up right there," said Deputy Yost, aiming his 9mm pistol at the doctor's chest. Moreland could only drop to his knees in exhaustion and defeat.

"What are you charging me with?" Moreland said between gasps. "Running like a madman in the woods?"

"Are you Dr. Blair Moreland?" asked Deputy Yost.

"Yes."

"I have a search warrant for your property. From the smoke I see coming from that direction, I'm assuming it is on fire, which would make you an arson suspect. How is that for starters?" Deputy Yost said.

Moreland glared at him.

"We can talk more about that, and other things—like why you were running through the woods—when we get you tucked into a cell at the county jail and conduct a full search of your place."

The two other deputies approached Moreland and patted him down for a weapon as a precaution before cuffing him.

"Deputy Yost, this was in his pocket," said Deputy Len Smythe.

"What is it, Smitty?" Deputy Yost asked.

Deputy Smythe held up a small vial that contained a clear liquid. The vial was slightly less than full, as if a small amount had already been taken.

"The label has a lot of medical mumbo jumbo on it. 'Fentanyl Citrate Injection USP.' Bunch of numbers, and then it says discard unused portion. 'Rx only.' More numbers. 'Hospital use only. Intravenous or Intramuscular.'"

"What is this, Dr. Moreland, and why do you have it?"

"I'm an anesthesiologist. I came here from the hospital. I must have put this in my pocket for a patient and then forgot about it in my rush to get down here," Moreland said. "I am licensed to have this. It's a common painkiller used on surgical patients."

"Interesting," said Deputy Yost. "We'll just hang on to that for now."

Lorenzo and Emilio, who'd finally caught up to their quarry, watched from deep in the trees as deputies handcuffed Moreland, placed him on the back of one of the ATVs, and drove off.

"Your plan just fell off its horse, caballero," Emilio said to Lorenzo.

"No shit," replied Lorenzo. "And I don't like the smoke and explosions back at the doctor's place either. It looks like someone torched the lab or the cabin or both, which makes me wonder what happened to your brother and the guy in the hazmat suit.

"Damn, we gotta go back there, man. That looks fucked up," said Emilio.

They were still more than one hundred yards from Moreland's place when they saw the metal building in flames. Emilio started to run toward it, screaming for his brother, when Lorenzo grabbed him.

"You can't help him now if he is in there, and I don't think you want to get anywhere near the fumes from whatever they were making. The guy was wearing a safety suit for a reason."

Emilio tore away from him, ripped off his T-shirt and wrapped it around his face. He saw his brother's body, covered in burning debris, and moved toward him. A series of explosions and intense heat drove him back.

He dropped to his knees. Lorenzo put a hand on his shoulder.

"That fucker will pay for this, I promise you," Lorenzo said. "We will get to him one way or another."

CHAPTER FIFTEEN

CONFRONTATION IN CUCHARA

Rick Becker pulled off Highway 12 and parked his Mercedes junker in front of the Wagon Wheel Grill in Cuchara as two firetrucks and an ambulance from the volunteer fire department blasted south toward Dr. Moreland's place.

You could say it was our fault that the reporter made his way to Cuchara. Wilson and I had made the mistake of telling Becker we were going to Springs General to check on Lula before we left him standing in front of her blood-washed house. Becker had driven to the hospital, too. He'd seen a security guard outside Lula's room, so instead of trying to get past him, Becker flagged down a passing nurse.

It happened to be Dr. Moreland's ex-fiancée, Nurse Behr, who had been checking on Lula.

"Excuse me, how is Lula doing?" Becker asked, hoping to be taken for a concerned friend or family member.

"I recognize you from your column picture in the *High Times*," said the nurse. "You're Rick Becker, right? I love your columns."

"Thanks, I appreciate that," said Becker, feigning modesty as best he could.

"Hey, I'm writing about the string of recent OD deaths in town. One of the guys who died, Buck Medina, was my friend. My sources have told me that Lula was the dealer who sold the heroin to him and at least one other guy who died from it. So I'm wondering what happened to her today. Is she going to live?"

"I shouldn't give you any information, but I don't think she's going to make it. She's in a coma. It looks like someone tortured her. They slit her neck and smashed her hand, breaking every bone in it."

"No kidding? That sounds like the Mexican mob figured out the same thing I did and sent one of their *sicarios* after her," Becker said.

He studied Nurse Behr's face. She hadn't told him to fuck off, which is what he'd expected. She seemed to want to tell him more. Sometimes having your face on a newspaper column meant drunk guys in bars threw punches at you, but, sometimes, it paid off if the person liked your work.

"I heard something else about Miss Lopez. Can I run it past you?" he asked.

Nurse Behr hesitated. She could be fired for talking about a patient with a reporter.

"Tell you what, I'm about to take my break," she said. "Can we talk outside? Maybe in your car where none of my supervisors can see us?"

"Oh yeah, sure. It's the old gray Mercedes in the second row of visitor parking, I'll meet you there," Becker said.

"Ok, meet you there in ten minutes," she said.

Wow, this shit doesn't happen very often, Becker thought as he left the hospital and walked to his car. *Usually, they throw my ass out of hospitals as soon as I pull out my notepad, or they sic their media relations bullshit artist on me. This nurse seems to have some sort of stake in this story. Why else would she agree to talk to me?*

He watched Nurse Behr come out of the hospital, survey the parking lot, and then walk to his car. She'd thrown on a hooded jacket to hide her identity from anyone watching.

"Sorry, but the hospital gestapo frowns on the staff talking to the press," she said with a smile. "Now, what was it you wanted to ask me about Lula Lopez?"

"One of my sources told me that word on the street was that Lula was cutting her heroin with some new drug she was getting from a doctor friend," Becker said. "I wondered if you had heard anything like that and if you knew who the doctor might be?"

"Strange that you would ask *me* that," she said, staring at him with suspicion.

"Well, I just ran into you in the hallway, and you seemed to know something . . . I just thought I'd run it by you. I don't have many sources in the medical community."

Becker could tell she was still wrestling with what she should tell him.

"Look, we can go off the record," he said. "That means I won't use your name in the story or tell anyone where the information came from, even if they threaten to put me in jail."

"You mean like Woodward and Bernstein and Watergate?"

"Well, not quite like that, but yeah, they did protect their sources to get information on Nixon."

"Okay, Mr. Becker, investigative reporter, I'm going to trust you, so don't let me down," Nurse Behr said.

"You have my word," he said.

"First of all, the drug we are talking about here is called fentanyl. It was developed just a few years ago and billed as a great new painkiller, much more powerful and fast-acting even than morphine," she said.

"How do you spell that?"

"F-e-n-t-a-n-y-l. But what the drug makers didn't say is that this drug is highly addictive and even more powerful than anyone expected," the nurse said. "We are already getting reports of medical staff becoming addicted to it, and some overdosing and dying—even though when properly administered, controlled, and monitored, we can even use it on expectant mothers and infants safely."

"But when it is used by street dealers to cut their heroin, it is proving deadly, right?"

"Right. The alarms are already sounding, and many are predicting that abuse of this drug will get a lot worse," she said.

"Do you know who was supplying Lula Lopez with this fentanyl?"

"I do not know for sure, meaning I do not have direct information on that exact question, but here is what I do know: Dr. Moreland, the head of the anesthesiology department here at Springs General, had a close relationship with Lula Lopez. They both worked as counselors at the Rocky Mountain Recovery Center. I also know that some hospital staff suspected Dr. Moreland was an addict and that he was stealing fentanyl from the hospital for his own use.

"And again," she continued, "those are only rumors, and this is all off the record, right?"

"Right, no problem," Becker assured her. "So you don't know for sure that he was providing it to Lopez?"

"No, I do not know that for sure, those are dots you, or the police, will have to connect."

"The police have this information?"

"We are still off the record, right?"

"Yes."

"They do. I spoke with detectives Kenda and Wilson myself."

"And as far as you know, Moreland was just stealing it from the hospital for his own use?"

"I said he was suspected of doing that, yes, but I think that is still under investigation," she said. "I can tell you also that those detectives suspect Dr. Moreland may be manufacturing fentanyl in powder form, which you can't get in the hospital supply room."

"How do they know that, I wonder?" Becker said.

"Let's just say they discussed that possibility with me."

"Did they say anything about where he might be making it?"

"Not exactly, but they did ask me if Dr. Moreland had ever told me about his cabin down in Cuchara," she said.

Becker paused and processed that information.

"Did you have a personal relationship with this guy?" he asked.

"Yes, I did, and let's just say, it did not end well. He's an asshole."

So she does have a stake in the game, and I will need to be careful in checking out her information before using any of it in a story.

"Did you know about him having a place in Cuchara?"

"No, that must have happened after I broke up with him, or, at least, he never talked about it."

"Would Dr. Moreland have the skills and training to make

this stuff in a lab by himself? Or would he have the money to build and equip his own lab?"

"My understanding is that fentanyl is not easy to manufacture, but Dr. Moreland would certainly have the training and probably the money to do it—if he was willing to risk his medical license and going to jail."

"Do you think he would take that kind of risk?"

"Mr. Becker, you and I both know that drug addiction will make even the smartest people do dumb and self-destructive things. Dr. Moreland is smart, but his addiction seems to have taken over his life. And, as I said, he is a ruthless asshole as well."

SHOWDOWN AT THE WAGON WHEEL GRILL

As soon as Nurse Behr said goodbye and left his car, Becker had checked a Colorado state map for the best route to Cuchara. He had driven down from the Springs and arrived a half hour after the Mexicans raided Dr. Moreland's property a few miles south of town.

Becker pulled into Cuchara, saw the sign for the Wagon Wheel Grill, and figured the only restaurant in town would be a good place to start asking around about the drug-making doctor from Colorado Springs.

"What's with the fire trucks and ambulance?" he asked the Wagon Wheel hostess.

"We just heard there was a fire and explosions a few miles down the road," said Daisy's mother, Christine, who was filling in as hostess that day.

Becker noticed that she looked stressed out but didn't say anything. As she walked him to a table, he heard loud voices coming from behind a door marked Office, Employees Only.

Inside, Daisy was frantically explaining to her father, Larry, what she'd seen at Doc Moreland's place.

"Dad, I have to go back and see what happened to Lester! He could be in trouble. Maybe he's hurt. Will you go with me?"

"No! And you are not going anywhere near that place—or Lester—ever again. I will call the sheriff's office and report what you've told me about the Mexican guys with guns. We need to warn them that the volunteer firemen and ambulance drivers may be headed into a gunfight."

Becker could only hear bits and pieces of their conversation with the office door shut. Christine noticed him trying to eavesdrop, so she put a quarter in the jukebox and played "Stayin' Alive" by the Bee Gees.

Becker nodded and gave her a thumbs-up. He hated the Bee Gees.

Then, Lester came stumbling in the front door of the restaurant, looking like a man who'd just escaped death, or at least a raging fire. He reeked of smoke and gasoline. His face and arms were smudged. His clothing had burn holes in it.

He scanned the restaurant looking for Daisy.

"Where is she? We gotta get out of town," he said to her mother.

Christine ran to the office door, banged on it, and said, "Larry, Lester is out here!"

Becker watched intently as Daisy rushed out and flew into Lester's arms.

"Oh my god, oh my god, I was afraid they'd killed you!" she cried.

Becker wondered, *What the hell is that beautiful girl doing with that scrawny geek?*

Oblivious, Lester was hugging Daisy and sobbing into her hair.

"We gotta go, they still might! I think one of them is dead. They'll be looking for me."

Daisy's father came out of the office with a shotgun, pulled Daisy out of Lester's arms, and said, "Go! Get out of here, now! She is not coming with you, and if you don't leave now, I will shoot you myself."

Daisy crumpled to the floor, crying.

"I don't know what the hell you and the doctor were doing out there, but if the Mexican drug lords are sending their henchmen after you, it can't be anything legal," Larry said. "If you care about my daughter, you will not drag her into this. I will not let that happen."

Daisy, who still had no idea what Lester was making in the lab, knew that her father was right.

"Lester, you'd better do what Daddy says. Go, get out of here before they come and kill you. Go and hide. I will find you. This isn't the end for us. Just go!"

Her father had the barrel of the shotgun planted in Lester's chest, pushing him toward the front door. Lester stumbled and fell, scrambled to his feet, and ran out to the Wagoneer.

There, he encountered Emilio sitting on the hood with his AK-47, which he pointed at Lester.

Lester froze.

Lorenzo came up behind Lester, pressed the barrel of the Colt Python to his head, and said, "You'd better come with us now, lab rat, or my partner here will shoot you in the street. That was his brother you left behind to burn."

Becker watched from the front door of the Wagon Wheel as

the two men forced Lester into the back of their Range Rover at gunpoint. The larger guy joined Lester in the back seat, jabbing their captive's rib cage with the barrel of the AK-47.

The Range Rover pulled out with Lorenzo behind the wheel. Becker stepped out of the restaurant and scribbled down the license plate number on his notepad. Emilio gave Becker a death stare from the back seat window as the Range Rover roared south on Highway 12.

Becker did not notice. He walked up to Daisy, who was sobbing on the sidewalk, and put his arm around her to comfort her.

CHAPTER SIXTEEN

A VIAL CRIME

Deputy Yost called and filled us in on the arrest of the doctor after he checked Moreland into a cell at the Huerfano County Jail.

"We got your doctor, Moreland. Two other deputies and I were headed to his place on ATVs through the forest to surprise him with the search warrant, but before we got there, he came running into our arms, so to speak," the deputy said.

"And what does the doctor have to say for himself?" I asked.

"He said someone was chasing him. He gave us a wild story, claiming that, when he ran into us, he was fleeing three armed Mexicans who showed up at his place and set it on fire. We took him into custody and then checked it out. The cabin was partially burned and the building out back, which had been converted into some sort of lab, was pretty much destroyed by fire and explosions.

"It looks like there were multiple propane tanks inside, and they were blown all over creation. We found two or three blown tanks in the cabin, which explains how it caught fire. There were also some blown canisters found way back in the forest. We're lucky they didn't start a fire there, too."

"You weren't kidding about him having a wild story," I said.

"Oh, I have more: We searched the doctor when we ran into him. He had a small vial of a clear liquid in his pocket. The label said it was fentanyl citrate. He said it was a painkiller used on his patients and claimed he must have put it in his pocket at the hospital and forgotten about it when he left."

"Now, that could prove to be extremely helpful."

"Yeah, well, he said he is licensed to have it as an anesthesiologist."

"I will check with the hospital on that," I told Deputy Yost. "I think hospital protocol requires that he sign for any drugs he takes out of the supply room, and if he didn't sign for that, we might be able to file charges."

"That would be great since right now, we haven't got much to keep him locked up—other than the body in the lab," Deputy Yost said.

"A body? You are just getting around to sharing that?"

"Yeah, sorry. I haven't slept in a week. My brain is numb. It looks like one of the Mexicans the doctor talked about. A big guy. There was an AK-47 lying next to him."

"Had he been shot?"

"Not from what I could see, but his body was burned to a crisp and I didn't want to move it."

"What does Moreland have to say about this?" I asked.

"Again, he had quite a tale prepared for us," Deputy Yost said. "He said that he had taken in one of his counseling clients from the recovery center, a young guy with a chemistry degree, and was letting him stay at his cabin in Cuchara. Moreland said he was trying to help this guy, Lester Sharp, get his life together. Said he was paying him as a caretaker and house sitter to protect his property, but he claims the guy secretly set up a drug lab in a metal building on his property."

"That is highly creative," I said.

"Oh, he seems to think he's the next Mickey Spillane," the deputy continued. "Moreland said he recently figured out that Sharp was cooking drugs there, so he drove from the Springs to shut it down. The doc said he had gone into his cabin to get his shotgun and was planning on confronting his caretaker in the lab out back when the three Mexican guys showed up, grabbed young Lester, and set the lab on fire, destroying it."

"And how did the doctor escape the wrath of these cutthroat banditos?" I asked.

"He says he ran into the woods and two of them were chasing him when we found him, but they must have given up, and gone back to his place."

"And how much of the doctor's story do you believe?" I asked.

"I'd say about ninety-nine point nine percent of it is bullshit, but we haven't had a chance to grill him because once he told us his fairy tale, he lawyered up. Do you know a lawyer from the Springs named Salvador Augustine?"

"Oh yeah, good old Sal is the legal pit bull favored by all of our favorite drug traffickers here," I said. "His billboards offering guaranteed freedom for felons are posted all over town, desecrating most of our major roadways."

"Well, like I said, Moreland isn't feeling chatty anymore. I haven't been able to ask him about the deaths of my son and father, but my guess is he will try to pin that on his trusty sidekick, too."

"Have you searched his property for evidence of any connection to them?" I asked.

"I was getting to that. There was a fenced-in area behind the lab building. We found a wheelbarrow there. The handles were scorched, but it was mostly intact. The tracking dog that had been provided with clothing from my father and my son was all over it."

"You think it was used to move their bodies into the forest?"

"Yes, that's what I'm thinking. It looks like the tires on it match the tracks we saw in the forest," the deputy said, his voice cracking. "We are sending it to the state crime lab to see what they can tell us about it."

"This is all interesting circumstantial evidence," I said.

"I hear you, Detective Kenda. As things stand, I am worried that we won't be able to hold Moreland in custody for long, even with the dead guy in his lab," the deputy said.

"That is a problem," I said.

"Unless you find out he stole that vial of fentanyl from the hospital, we have nothing to charge him with down here so far. We might be able to hold him on suspicion because of the burned body, but his lawyer will likely beat down that charge. The fire destroyed the lab and about half his cabin, which we are still searching. The wheelbarrow may give us something to connect it to the deaths of my father and son, but even then we would still have to tie Moreland to it. My guess is he will have an alibi ready for that, too. Are you any closer to linking him to the OD deaths up there?"

"Maybe, but not yet. We are still working on it. We're talking to the district attorney about our options and still investigating," I said. "Even if we connect him to the fentanyl in the heroin that killed our victims, it will be tough to make a homicide case. We would have to convince a judge or jury that he was guilty of murderous intent or, at least, murderous negligence."

"Damn," said Deputy Yost. "I guess we will keep digging for evidence here while you do the same up there. His lawyer is on his way down here tomorrow morning, and once he gets in front of a judge, I'm sure he will be able to spring Moreland."

"Well, keep us posted. I think the doctor is a flight risk. Maybe you can convince the judge to hold him an extra day or two."

TRYING TO MAKE A CASE

After talking with Deputy Yost, I filled in Wilson on the events in Cuchara, and we again walked through our investigation, trying to figure out some way to connect Dr. Moreland to our overdose victims so we could bring charges.

"Lula Lopez is the one person who could have helped us directly tie Moreland to the fentanyl she used to cut her heroin, but I just checked Springs General again, and she is still in a coma, and the doctor monitoring her said the chances of her coming out of it aren't good," Wilson said. "I just wish we could have talked to her before the goons got to her."

"Agreed. Moreland was smart enough to use her as the middleman, but my guess is that once her customers started dying, she would have flipped on him rather than take the fall herself,"

I said. "I wonder if she gave the doctor up to the guy who tortured her."

"Yeah, and we still don't know who took him out, or why they took him out, or if that shooter knew that the fentanyl was coming from Moreland . . ." Wilson said.

"And why did the guy who killed the torturer then take Lula Lopez to the hospital and drop her off?" I said. "I can't make sense of that unless it was someone who cared for Lopez, otherwise why not just finish her off?"

We were not making any progress, and it was frustrating as hell because Moreland's lawyer would surely bust him out of jail as soon as he got down to Huerfano County.

"I'll bet Moreland already has flights booked for some remote island that doesn't have an extradition treaty with the US," Wilson said. "Once he's out of jail, we'll never get our hands on him."

Wilson and I were still reading over all our reports and planning our next moves when one of our switchboard operators told me I'd missed a call from the local newshound Becker. I wasn't much inclined to call him back anytime soon until she added, "He said he was calling from the Wagon Wheel Grill in Cuchara, and you could reach him there."

"What the hell would Becker be doing down in Cuchara?" I asked Wilson.

"He must have tracked Moreland down there somehow," Wilson said. "Unlike us, he doesn't have to worry about staying in a designated jurisdiction. He follows his leads anywhere they take him."

I called the phone number he'd left with our operator.

"Wagon Wheel Grill, how can I help you?"

"Hello, I'm Detective Joe Kenda in Colorado Springs, is there a pain-in-the-ass reporter named Becker hanging out in your restaurant?"

"Yes, sir, he is bugging the hell out of us, but I don't think my husband has shot him—yet," said Christine Palmer. "I'll get him, hold on."

Becker came on the line.

"Detective Kenda, I've got a license tag number for you," he said.

"What? Hold on. I'm not your research assistant, fuck head. What are you talking about? And what are you doing down there?"

"I found out that Dr. Moreland has a place down here where he might be making fentanyl, so I came down to try and find it, but then all hell broke loose when I got here. Two of the Mexican mob's sicarios showed up and kidnapped some guy who'd been working for Moreland and living at his place."

"Why haven't I heard this from the sheriff down there?"

"Shit, Kenda, I don't know. I mean, it just happened. I'm not sure the sheriff's department even knows about it yet. They are probably out at Moreland's place, which the Mexicans apparently torched, according to the locals here."

"What license plate number do you have?"

"It's the plate on the Mexicans' Range Rover," Becker said. "I wrote it down as they were driving off with Moreland's guy. They had an AK-47 stuck in his ribs. I got here just in time to see all of this go down.

"Now, do you want the license number or not? I thought you'd wanna kiss me for giving it to you."

"I'll kiss you later—with the toe of my boot," I said. "Give me the damn plate."

"You sure are a hard guy to please," said Becker. "Okay, Colorado plate number, CSR A12."

"CSR A12, got it. Thanks, but you are still P. Rick to me."

"Fuck you, Kenda. You're welcome."

I was about to hang up when Becker said, "Hold on."

"What?"

"Looks like the sheriff's deputy just showed up. Should I give the plate number to him, too?"

"Yeah, go ahead. We're all hunting the same group of bad guys, it seems."

"Okay."

I checked with the Colorado State Department of Revenue records department and learned the license plate number was registered to Santos Trucking Company in Denver. I then looked at the state's business registration records and found the CEO of that company was Jorge Santos.

Wilson walked that name over to our friends in Metro Vice and Narcotics, where it rang bells and set off alarms.

"We have an ongoing investigation with the DEA into Santos and his activities in the Denver area," said Det. Herb Miller. "We think he is using his HVAC and trucking empire as a front to move heroin and launder money for the Hinojosa family."

"What's the status of your investigation?" Wilson asked.

"We are moving slowly and cautiously on this because the guy is politically connected. He's a big contributor to nearly every politician in Colorado, covering all his bases. Santos has his tentacles everywhere, and he is considered a hero for all his charitable work in the Hispanic community. Why are you interested in him?"

"A Range Rover registered to his company was involved in a suspected kidnapping down in Cuchara. Two Mexican guys with AK-47s grabbed the caretaker of a cabin owned by a doctor from the Springs. We suspect drugs are involved, and the doctor may be tied to our string of overdose deaths here," Wilson said.

"Man, that's a big web you're tangled up in," Detective Miller said.

"No shit," Wilson replied.

"You said it was a Range Rover?" Miller asked.

"Yeah, 1977, black."

"That sounds like the vehicle driven by Santos's nephew Lorenzo Martinez, who seems to be the top lieutenant in his drug-trafficking activities," Detective Miller said. "We've noticed that he hasn't been around Denver lately. Maybe Santos sent him down your way to figure out what was causing the OD deaths among the family's heroin customers. That sounds like the sort of job he'd trust Martinez with, but I'll bet he sent some muscle, too, because Martinez isn't known to be a real hard-ass. He considers himself a strategist and likes to keep his hands clean."

"The sheriff said witnesses reported one of the guys had an AK-47, so that sounds like the muscle," Wilson said.

"Did you put out a bulletin on the vehicle?"

"Yeah, but he had a good head start."

"If they kidnapped someone working for the doctor, they might be taking them to the Hinojosa family in Durango, rather than driving back to Denver," Miller said. "Martinez is ambitious. If this caretaker has value, then Martinez could be presenting him to the family to win favor with them, which wouldn't make his uncle in Denver very happy."

A TALISMAN

After securing the vial of fentanyl citrate in the evidence locker at the Huerfano County Sheriff's Office in Walsenburg, Deputy Yost drove back down to check on the search being conducted on Moreland's property.

He'd put Deputy Smythe in charge of the search along with three other deputies. "Smitty, what have you found? Any other bodies? Something we can use to keep the doctor locked up?"

"We found a bag of marijuana in the nightstand of a guest room where it looked like the caretaker was staying."

"Is it enough dope for a felony charge, do you think?"

"Checking on that too. It's a good amount of weed, so it could be close."

As they spoke, the deputies stood near the remains of the metal building that had housed the lab. A canine unit deputy, Greg Lunas, and his tracking dog walked up.

"I don't know if this is even worth mentioning, but Diego here just alerted on this. It was in the area surrounded by the fence behind the building. It's an arrowhead with the initials JY etched into it."

Deputy Lunas handed the thin stone, slightly bigger than a quarter, to Deputy Yost. He looked at it, turning the stone in his hand, and then doubled over as grief overcame him. His put his face in his hands, shaking and sobbing. The other deputies put their hands on his shoulders to comfort him. After a minute or two, Yost regained his composure and explained.

"This belonged to my son. I gave it to him, just as my father had given it to me," he said. "It was our good luck charm."

Deputy Yost explained that his father had found the arrowhead decades before when they were on a hiking trip.

"I was only ten at the time. We hiked up to the Indian Cave, north of Cuchara, over the ridge top and on the east side of the Dakota Wall, which my father called the Hogback. My father told me it was a shelter used by the Ute Indians on their summer hunts. Now when you go up there, people have defaced the cave with graffiti, but back then, it wasn't so bad. There were often anthropology students and researchers up there looking for artifacts. On this hike, just as we were leaving the cave, I slipped and fell on loose rock. My father reached down to help me up, and as I got to my feet, he saw this arrowhead right where I had fallen.

"'The Indians considered these symbols of good luck, a talisman, so you should keep this,' he told me. 'Whenever you feel scared or worried, hold it in your hand and it will give you strength. That is what the Indians believed. I believe it, too.'"

Deputy Yost held the arrowhead in his palm and rubbed it with his fingers.

"When I was a boy, I scratched my initials on this, as you can see. I carried it every day, and when I passed it on to Buddy, he did the same. He never went anywhere without it. Sometimes, I'd check on him when he was sleeping, and he would be holding it in his hand."

As he told the story, all the deputies were fighting tears. They had to turn away from each other and wipe their faces on their sleeves.

Deputy Yost studied the arrowhead, holding it up, and said

to the other deputies, "And now, this rock has given a clue that could help us tie the deaths of my father and son to Moreland and his caretaker. The fact that it was found here, on Moreland's property, means that my son and father may have died here. Then, someone—probably the doctor or his caretaker—took their bodies up into the forest and buried them, only to have some other animals dig them up and drag them off."

CHAPTER SEVENTEEN

THE DOCTOR IS IN

Kathy reported for work at Springs General the next morning, and they asked her to help in the trauma unit where Lula Lopez was still in a coma. When she arrived there, Nurse Claire Behr filled her in.

"Ms. Lopez has hung on longer than I expected, but I think the end is near, especially after we received her latest blood test results," Nurse Behr said.

"They did another blood test on her?"

"Yes, she was not responding to anything we gave her to try and bring her out of the coma, so the doctors wanted another test."

"And the most recent one had different results than the earlier one?" asked Kathy.

"Yes, and you might want to tell your husband about it."

"Why?"

"The initial tests showed that she had heroin in her system, and it is suspected someone had drugged her while torturing her for information, but the most recent tests show heroin *and* fentanyl in her blood."

"And there was no sign of fentanyl in the initial test?"

"None. And we have no record of anyone on staff prescribing it for her or administering it to her," Nurse Behr said.

"So do you have any explanation for how it showed up in her results?"

"I have my suspicions. A nurse saw Dr. Moreland come out of her trauma-care room. He was in there a brief time alone with her, left, and then came back for another short visit—again, alone with her. When he left the second time, he reassigned all his surgeries to another anesthesiologist and told his secretary he'd be out of town for a few days."

"That must have been right before a security guy was posted outside her room?"

"Yes."

"Do you think he might have given her a dose of fentanyl, hoping to kill her?"

"I hate to think that a man I nearly married could be that evil, but if he thinks this woman has information that could take him down . . . I would not be surprised," Nurse Behr said.

"I need to tell my husband about this," Kathy said.

"I hope you do," said Nurse Behr.

Kathy called and filled me in.

"There was nothing on her charts saying fentanyl had been prescribed and administered to Lopez?" I asked.

"Nothing."

"Who saw him come and go and then return to her room?"

"The trauma unit's charge nurse. Ashley Kyle. It was shortly after Lopez was transferred out of ER, and before the security guard posted up outside her room."

"This could be very good news for us, though not for

Moreland," I said. "When the deputies took him into custody down in Cuchara, they found a vial of fentanyl from the hospital on him, and it appeared that a small portion had been used."

"That is strange. Why would he be carrying the vial with him down there?"

"He claimed he'd put it in his pocket at the hospital and forgotten to put it back in storage."

"That sounds shady to me. Anesthesiologists do not carry vials of opiates around with them, especially outside the hospital—unless they are up to no good."

"Let's hope a judge agrees with you."

Wilson and I were preparing for a meeting with our district attorney to discuss this new information and other evidence we had—and didn't have—in the OD cases and from the investigation in Cuchara, when Deputy Yost called again.

"Did you meet with your DA yet?"

"No, we were just prepping for it. We have just learned a new bit of information about the hospitalized woman I told you about, Lula Lopez. We suspect she was using fentanyl from Dr. Moreland to cut the heroin that killed a couple of her customers.

"What is the new information?"

"They did a new blood test and found that she was administered fentanyl *after* she'd been admitted to the hospital, even though no one there prescribed it or administered it, according to the staff and their records."

"So who gave it to her?"

"The charge nurse saw Moreland come out of her room in the trauma unit shortly after she was moved out of the ER."

"Which might explain the missing amount of fentanyl from the vial we found on him?"

"Yes, that is what we are thinking," I said.

"I have another new bit of interesting evidence we found here, as well," Deputy Yost said. "Our tracking K-9 that alerted on the wheelbarrow also alerted on a small arrowhead found behind the lab in that fenced-off area. The arrowhead belonged to my son. I gave it to him, just as my father had given it to me when I was a boy."

"When was the last time you saw your son with that arrowhead in his possession?" I asked.

"He took it everywhere because he considered it a good luck charm."

"Ok, that's something, but a good defense lawyer could come up with all sorts of scenarios as to how it ended up in Moreland's yard unless we can prove your son had it on him the day he disappeared," I said.

"Got it," Deputy Yost said. "Damn, we need something to nail this down. Moreland's hot-shit lawyer is on his way down here to spring him at a hearing tomorrow morning."

"I agree, in your case and in ours. We'll keep working on it, and I'll let you know what the DA says."

CALLING OUT THE DOGS

Salvatore Augustine drove into Walsenburg from Colorado Springs feeling supremely confident that this would be a short and lucrative visit. His wealthy client, Dr. Blair Moreland, had already agreed to a $50,000 retainer, which was non-refundable.

"I will pay you that exorbitant amount because I want you to get me out of here as quickly as possible," Moreland had told the lawyer. "You need to understand something, and I'm telling you this as privileged information that cannot be shared with anyone."

"Understood," said Augustine.

"I have an addiction. It has gotten out of control recently. So I cannot remain incarcerated without going into withdrawal and possibly dying. Is that clear?"

"Yes, Doctor," Augustine said. "How long do you have before withdrawal sets in?"

"I'm not sure. My addiction is to a relatively new drug, a painkiller, and there is not a lot of information out there. I took a fix just before I drove down here, but I am already feeling cravings, body aches, and fever. I'm sitting here sweating like I just ran ten miles."

The criminal defense attorney considered his retainer to be just the first installment on a much larger remuneration, though the doctor had no inkling of that.

The Hinojosa family will pay me hundreds of thousands of dollars for keeping this el cabrón *out of prison and delivering him to Durango so they can torture him for his knowledge of this powerful new drug. Then they likely will kill him for the damage he has done to their heroin business, but that is not my concern.*

His first stop was the Huerfano County Sheriff's Department where he asked the deputy behind the front desk, Sgt. Ross Verlander, to please show him the public record arrest reports on his client Dr. Moreland. The reports, written by Deputy Yost, a detective, were brief and concise, but consisted mostly of conjecture, circumstantial evidence, and a lot of veiled innuendo.

More importantly, it appeared there were no substantial charges that would convince a judge to allow a successful professional and upstanding citizen like Dr. Moreland, who had no criminal record, to be held without bond.

"I see there are references here to an investigation of two suspected murders that may or may not have occurred on Dr. Moreland's property, is that correct?" the lawyer asked.

"If you have questions, you will have to speak to the district attorney handling this case," the desk sergeant said.

"Yes, but can you at least tell me the names of the murder victims? I don't see them here."

"Jack and Buddy Yost," said Sergeant Verlander, who immediately regretted answering that question.

"Yost? Are they related to the Deputy Yost who arrested my client and filed these reports?" asked Augustine.

"Again, you will have to direct your questions to the district attorney handling the case, sir," said Sergeant Verlander.

Augustine returned to his Jaguar sedan in the parking lot to ponder his next moves.

If these local yokels allowed this deputy to investigate the murders of his own relatives, then this case may be even easier than I anticipated, especially since he has nothing substantial on Dr. Moreland, and a lot of the circumstantial evidence could be blamed instead on his missing caretaker, who has a felony drug conviction already. Piece of cake! I will bust the doctor out of here at the hearing this afternoon and hand him on a platter to the Hinojosa family in Denver tomorrow.

The lawyer next drove to the ancient Huerfano County Courthouse and Jail. The jail section of the building was built of sandstone from a local quarry in 1896, the courthouse was added eight years later. The imposing architecture style is called "Romanesque," but it looks more like a medieval fortress, fully furnished with guillotines and torture racks in every room.

I'm sure the doctor will be eager to get out of this hellhole, Augustine thought as he entered the jail and signed in. They met in a tiny room with stone walls, their voices echoing loudly unless they spoke in whispers.

"Welcome to my dungeon, Mr. Augustine," said Moreland. "Would you believe this place was built *before* Alcatraz?"

They knew each other from the Rocky Mountain Recovery Center, where the lawyer served on the advisory board. This was the first time Dr. Moreland needed the services of the state's most renowned criminal defense lawyer.

"First off, how are you feeling?" Augustine asked. "Have your symptoms worsened?"

"I was starting to get sicker, but I put the word out among the other inmates and got some methadone from another addicted inmate, who has been paying off one of the kitchen staff to keep him supplied."

"You are resourceful," said Augustine. "I promise we will get you out of here soon, Dr. Moreland. They don't seem to have any solid evidence against you that I can tell," Augustine said.

"No, it appears the caretaker of my property here decided to start up his own drug lab, and although I'm impressed with his initiative, I am not willing to take the fall for his criminal enterprise," said Moreland.

"This is the fellow you told me about on the phone? He had been your counseling client at the recovery center, correct?" the lawyer asked.

"Yes, Lester Sharp."

"It seems that his illegal lab is not the only matter under

investigation here. The sheriff's office is claiming that the older gentleman and his grandson whose remains were found in the forest had been on your property at some point. Is that your understanding?"

"I don't know anything about that. If Lester knew anything about it, he didn't tell me."

"You know he was kidnapped at gunpoint by two Mexicans in downtown Cuchara, and no one knows his whereabouts, right?"

"I have heard jailhouse talk about that, but this is the first time I've heard it from someone who is not trying to be my cell buddy," the doctor said. "My guess is that Lester somehow ran afoul of a Mexican drug trafficker and is probably hanging from a bridge across the border."

"Yes, well, we will do our best to distance you from any of his illegal activities. You were simply trying to help a client by giving him a job and a place to live. We'll stick with that, okay?"

"I'm on board with that plan. After all, the truth is the best defense," Moreland said.

"Okay, Doctor, I will see you in the courtroom after lunch," said Augustine. "Do not share anything with your fellow inmates. Trust no one. They will try to use anything you say to buy their own freedom."

"I understand. See you at the hearing. And thank you for representing me."

"Well, you are paying me handsomely, and it was a lovely drive down here in my Jag."

Augustine walked around to the courthouse section of the building and asked a deputy circuit clerk if there was a visiting attorney's room where he could prep for the hearing. She directed him to a small room with a desk, chair, and telephone off the main courtroom.

The lawyer went inside with his briefcase, locked the door, took a seat, and removed his address book from his briefcase. He then dialed a Durango number for Roberto Juarez, the lawyer who served as his contact to the Hinojosa family.

Augustine had represented many of their associates over the years, from actual family members to high-ranking lieutenants to drug mules, drivers and street dealers. He had attended many of the family's parties in Mexico and the United States, including baptisms, birthdays, quinceañeras, weddings, and funerals.

"Roberto, this is Salvador. How are you, my friend?"

"I am well, thank you. I trust you are the same. What can I do for you today?"

"Roberto, as you may or may not know, I am representing the American doctor, Blair Moreland, whose property in Cuchara was visited by three men who I assume were *sicarios* working for the family. One of the *sicarios* was killed. Two others abducted a caretaker working for the doctor, a young American named Lester Sharp."

"I am not aware of any of these individuals or the incident you are referring to, but please, tell me why you have called me about this?" said Juarez, cautiously.

"Roberto, I believe this Dr. Moreland has information and knowledge that could be valuable to the family's business operations, so I was hoping to arrange a meeting with him and your representatives once I have finished up my legal work with him here in the Huerfano County circuit court, where there is a hearing in a half hour. I expect to have him out of jail by late afternoon."

"I understand. Since I am not familiar with the doctor or any value he might bring to the family's business, let me discuss this with my clients and get back to you shortly."

"Yes, Roberto. I will be returning to Denver later today, but for the next hour or so, I will be at this number," said Augustine, who provided the phone number for his temporary courthouse office and then said goodbye.

TWO TOO MANY AT THE PROSECUTION'S TABLE

The Denver lawyer spent the next half hour waiting for the call and reviewing his notes on Dr. Moreland's case and the police record. When the call from Durango did not come, Augustine assumed that he'd hear from the Hinojosa family's lawyer when he returned to Denver.

Then, as he was packing up his briefcase to go to the hearing, the telephone rang.

"Salvador Augustine here," he said.

"Mr. Augustine, this is Roberto Juarez in Durango. Sorry to keep you waiting."

"No problem, Roberto. What did the family say about my proposition?"

"They are not interested in the proposition or your client, I am afraid, but good luck with your hearing today. Goodbye."

What the hell? I thought they'd be all over this opportunity. What did I miss? I thought they'd want to question this guy and then hang him from a bridge.

Stunned, Augustine put the phone receiver on the cradle and walked out into the courtroom for the hearing just as the bailiff was asking everyone to please rise for the Honorable Judge Marcus Spenser.

The troubling phone call from Roberto Juarez had thrown him off. Augustine was not used to such a cold rejection from the Hinojosa family. They had a long-term professional and personal relationship.

The lawyer struggled to regain his composure as he took a seat at the defense counsel table, where Dr. Moreland, wearing his orange jail suit, was waiting for him. The lawyer glanced over at the table across the aisle where the county prosecutor was seated, along with Deputy Yost.

Then, he spotted Wilson and me sitting next to Deputy Yost and did a double take. I don't think it was my Sears sports coat and tie that got his attention.

Criminal trial lawyers do not like surprises when they appear in court. In fact, they pride themselves on never being surprised by anything because they prepare themselves so thoroughly; they know all there is to know about their clients and their cases and any evidence or witnesses involved.

But Wilson and I were full of surprises on this day in court.

"Your Honor, if it pleases the court, I would like to introduce into evidence an arrest warrant just presented to me by Colorado Springs Police Department Detectives Joe Kenda and Lee Wilson," said the Huerfano County prosecutor Shane Herron.

"What sort of warrant is this, if I may ask?" said Judge Spenser, who had noted the shocked expression on the face of the doctor's criminal defense attorney.

"Your Honor, it is an El Paso County arrest warrant charging Dr. Moreland with murder in the first degree in the death of Lula Lopez, who was declared dead at Springs General Hospital by El Paso County Medical Examiner Dr. Maggie Medina at 6:35 p.m. yesterday."

"Objection, Your Honor. Neither the defendant, Dr. Moreland, nor I had any knowledge of this El Paso County arrest warrant prior to this moment, so we had no time to prepare."

Judge Spenser and the prosecutor could barely conceal their amusement. The notoriously smug Mr. Augustine was flailing in the water, and he knew it.

"Mr. Augustine, I believe you understand neither Mr. Herron, the Huerfano County prosecutor, nor the Colorado Springs Police Department's homicide detectives are required to notify your client, or you, of the issuance of this arrest warrant until it is presented. And I believe they are presenting it now. Is that correct, Detectives?

"Yes, Your Honor, we most definitely are," I said.

"Well, in that case, I remand Dr. Moreland to the custody of these detectives for transportation to the El Paso County Jail in Colorado Springs, where I am sure they will be holding him without bond, given that the state does not offer it on such serious charges. Thank you, gentleman. This preliminary hearing is adjourned. Good luck to you all."

Dr. Moreland glared at his befuddled defense attorney as the bailiff switched out the Huerfano County sheriff's handcuffs for ours.

"I want my fifty grand back," snarled Moreland.

"As you know, Dr. Moreland, it was nonrefundable," replied Augustine, who packed up his briefcase and walked out with his former client raining curses upon him. Wilson and I escorted the doctor out to our car and headed north to the Springs where he would await trial for the murder of his former lover and dupe, the late Lula Lopez—and any of the OD cases we could pin on him.

"So where did you get the secret formula for making fentanyl in your home chemistry lab, Doc?" Wilson asked as we pulled out of town.

Silence from the back seat.

"You know, Detective Kenda and I have been wondering about something else. Aren't anesthesiologists trained to ease pain and suffering? When did you decide to use your training and a powerful pain medication to kill people?"

More silence.

CHAPTER EIGHTEEN

NOT A PAIN-FREE DEATH

We still had considerable work to do before we could file charges against Dr. Moreland for his suspected role in the overdose deaths of Buck Medina, Airman Alfonso Peres, Curtis Whitford, and the Rev. Albert Hoskins, but at least we had him locked up and no longer producing fentanyl for sale to unsuspecting drug users all over town.

It was not a coincidence that we hadn't had an overdose death ever since Lula was hospitalized.

While we pursued those investigations, we assumed Dr. Moreland was busy trying to hire a new defense attorney while fending off unwanted attention from his fellow inmates in the El Paso County Jail. He was unaware of two new prisoners who had arrived a few days after him.

One of them was Emilio Dorado, grieving brother of the late Dionisio. The other was Alfredo Archivaldo Salazar, who could be Emilio's lost twin, if he wasn't even larger and more cutthroat. They were checked in to our jail after an hour-long brawl in Bub & Bingo's Saloon on the Colorado Avenue strip downtown.

Emilio and Alfredo were harassing the regular clientele by pelting them with pool balls and beer bottles. You'd almost think they were *trying* to get arrested. They achieved that goal, but only after a rigorous entrance exam administered by our police department's designated jail admission registrars, Patrol Officers Finn O'Keane and Chauncey Malone.

They were beat cops who conducted bar checks for underage drinkers, drug dealing and partaking, and the usual menagerie of gropers, brawlers, and other miscreants. The owners of Bub & Bingo's, the Corrigan brothers, generally handled bar disruptions without assistance, but in this case, the two grizzly bear Mexicans seemed so determined to get themselves arrested that the Corrigans felt obliged to summon their favorite tag team from CSPD.

O'Keane and Malone arrived in their official paddy wagon. Weightlifters and boxers specializing in the street-fighting arts, they walked in, sized up Emilio and Alfredo, and smiled at them while brandishing old-school billy clubs weighted with lead cores.

"Are you eye-fuckin' me?" Malone asked Emilio, who'd been glaring at him while tossing a cue ball in the air.

Emilio responded by throwing out the first pool ball, which Chauncey knocked out of the park with his billy club—or at least through a window at the rear of the bar.

Alfredo hurled the eight ball. Finn caught it barehanded, on a dead run, and then used it to bash out most of Alfredo's teeth. Chauncey dropped Emilio with a billy club shot to the belly followed by a pair of brass knuckles to the bridge of the nose.

The street cops were out to an early lead, but the *sicarios* rallied. More pool cues were broken. Alfredo got a belt around Officer Malone's neck and was close to choking him out before one of the Corrigan brothers stepped up and broke a heavy glass pitcher over Alfredo's head for the assist.

Tables were upended. Chairs were thrown. Mirrors and beer signs were ripped off the walls and broken. It appeared that Emilio and Alfredo might have defeated the legendary patrolmen if it weren't for the hometown crowd eventually stepping in to help pin them down so they could be cuffed.

The Bub & Bingo's patrons offered a stirring round of applause as the patrol officers escorted Emilio and Alfredo out to the paddy wagon.

"When you come back at the end of your shift, the whiskey is on the house," said Terrance Corrigan, youngest of the ownership team.

A FINAL CHECKUP

Word had spread quickly among jail inmates that Blair Moreland was a doctor and an addict. This was welcome news. It didn't matter that he was an anesthesiologist, not a general practitioner. From day one, the sick, wounded, diseased, and delirious lined up for consultations and examinations at his table in the general population dayroom.

Two bodyguards he had hired made sure the process was orderly and no one shanked the physician during working hours. Medicare and Medicaid were not accepted, so most patients paid in goods from the jail commissary. Those who were hooked up with gangs had cocaine and heroin, which had helped ease Moreland's withdrawal symptoms.

He played jailhouse doctor for the drugs and to help pass the time. Moreland also figured that, as long as he was providing a service to his fellow jail mates, none of them would try to kill him.

He was wrong about that.

Emilio and Alfredo took their time settling into the jail routine, getting to know their fellow inmates and the guards, figuring out who else was on the Hinojosa family payroll, or aspiring to join it.

They made it a point to ignore their designated target, and Blair Moreland had not noticed their arrival.

Julio Torres, a Hinojosa family drug courier who was doing six months in jail for flashing a local stripper, even though that would seem to be an occupational hazard, had landed a job in the jail laundry room. He provided Emilio and Alfredo with a canvas laundry bag and all four steel wheels off a laundry cart.

The big boss, Marcos Hinojosa himself, had decided that shanking the doctor, hanging him in his cell, or strangling him wasn't a fitting punishment considering all the damage his fentanyl additive had done to the reputation of their Mexican brown.

"Tell the *sicarios* to inflict as much pain as possible over a long period. I want him to serve as an example to any others who might want to interfere with our businesses," he had instructed his new lieutenant Lorenzo Martinez, formerly from the Denver division.

"I want Dr. Moreland to experience a slow and excruciating death, so break as many bones as possible, crush vital organs, and do it quietly so that you have plenty of time to work him over."

"Yes, sir, I will relay those orders to Emilio and Alfredo," Martinez said. "I'm sure Emilio will want to avenge his brother's death by doing exactly as you ask. I do have one observation, however."

"What is it?" the drug lord asked.

"Maybe at the very end, as the doctor is near death, we should have Emilio shove an open vial of fentanyl up his ass as a parting gift. After all, Dr. Moreland is the man whose formula for making the drug will soon be adding millions and millions of dollars to the family's earnings."

"I understand what you are saying and appreciate the creativity, but no," the Hinojosa family patriarch said. "Fentanyl is a painkiller, after all. I want him to die experiencing as much pain as possible."

Blair Moreland was asleep in his cell when Emilio and Alfredo entered. The cell door had been unlocked by a guard on the Hinojosa family payroll.

"Hey, Doc, remember me? My brother burned to death in your lab, so while I'm here to deliver a message from the Hinojosa family, I want you to know this is personal for me, too," said Emilio as he towered over Moreland's bed.

"Wait, wait, wait!" Moreland said. "I can help the family make fentanyl in their own labs. They will make hundreds of times more money selling it than they'll ever make with heroin. Get me out of here and I'll help them do that!"

"Sorry, Doc. Nice try, but I think they have that covered," Emilio said, as Alfredo gagged Moreland and then handed his fellow *sicario* the canvas laundry bag containing the heavy steel wheels.

The sound of Moreland being beaten to death were muffled enough that no other inmates were disturbed and no guards were alerted. It would be noted that the anesthesiologist was not blessed with a pain-free death.

DURANGO, MEXICO, DECEMBER 24, NOCHE BUENA, 1978

After celebrating midnight Mass at the Cathedral of the Immaculate Conception in the historic center of Durango, opposite the Plaza de Armas, Marcos Hinojosa hosted a lavish party for his family members, extended family, top lieutenants, and the recently returned heroes Emilio Dorado and Alfredo Archivaldo Salazar.

Seated at the head table was Lorenzo Martinez, the newly named head of the family's already thriving fentanyl production division. Seated next to him was his proud uncle, Jorge Santos, who had been given responsibility for the logistics of transporting fentanyl shipments throughout the United States.

Also at the head table was a man with features unlike any of the other guests. Fang Chen was a new business partner of the Hinojosa family. His Chinese criminal enterprise provided precursor chemicals to produce fentanyl in Mexico. Chen had also recently offered to help the family launder their rapidly swelling coffers of drug money in Asia.

The finest tequila, mezcal, and other libations flowed in abundance as three mariachi bands played throughout the family compound for more than three hundred guests. The music carried a few miles to the north, to a newly constructed building housing the most sophisticated clandestine drug laboratory in the northern hemisphere.

Heavily armed guards manned six towers located around the lab building. Foot patrols with guard dogs walked the perimeter twenty-four hours a day. Inside the building, more armed guards stood watch as Lester Sharp conducted training classes in fentanyl manufacturing for a dozen recent graduates with advanced degrees in chemistry. They'd been recruited from Mexico's finest universities. Like Lester Sharp, all of them were there involuntarily, under threat of death to them and their families.

That training session ended around 6:00 a.m., just as the

party at the Hinojosa compound was winding down and the participants returned home for their own, more sedate, Christmas Day gatherings.

Lester Sharp left the lab building in handcuffs and under armed guard as the sun rose over the mountains. He was pale and thin, though his captors were careful to feed him well enough and to monitor his health. Lester had ample opportunities to take his own life with the fentanyl powder he helped produce, but he held out hope that one day he would escape and return to Daisy's arms.

EPILOGUE

FROM THE EDITORS OF THE *ROCKY MOUNTAIN HIGH TIMES*
OCTOBER 10, 1979

We are pleased to announce the opening of a new bureau of the *High Times* in Cuchara, Colorado. This bureau, which will extend our coverage to southeastern and southwestern Colorado, will be staffed by our award-winning investigative reporter and columnist Rick Becker and his wife, Daisy, a Cuchara native, geologist, and restaurateur who will report on environmental and cultural matters.

As you know, Rick won the 1978 Pulitzer Prize for investigative reporting in his ten-part series on a drug-addicted Colorado Springs anesthesiologist who began manufacturing fentanyl, a powerful and addictive painkiller, in his own illegal drug lab in Cuchara.

Becker will continue to roam the state reporting and writing his popular columns on wide-ranging topics including the expanding activities of Mexican drug traffickers in

Colorado, which was also a big part of his Pulitzer Prize–winning series.

We hope you will join us also in congratulating Rick and Daisy on the recent births of their fraternal twins, Lillie Mae and Buck.

POSTSCRIPT

FROM AUTHOR JOE KENDA

As I noted in the opening pages, this book is a work of fiction and the story of the malevolent Dr. Blair Moreland is entirely fabricated, but it is also quite plausible because it is based on the true story of the continuing fentanyl plague in the United States.

You might say that our fictional anesthesiologist Dr. Blair Moreland is the human incarnation of fentanyl, a drug with the power to ease pain and suffering, but one that also continues to cause enormous amounts of both due to the illegal abuse of it.

Our story is set in 1978, just a few years after this synthetic opiate was first made widely available to hospitals and physicians. Reports of fentanyl addictions and deaths began shortly thereafter and have escalated ever since. Anne Milgram, administrator of the US Drug Enforcement Agency said in 2023 that "Fentanyl is the single deadliest drug threat our nation has ever encountered. Fentanyl is everywhere. From large metropolitan areas to rural America, no community is safe from this poison."

Fentanyl was used to cut heroin at first, and now it is often sold online disguised as prescription pills like OxyContin, Percocet, and Xanax. People who think they are buying their prescription drugs on the cheap are dying from taking those fake pills. Just a few milligrams of fentanyl can kill a person within minutes.

Equally disturbing are recent reports that patrons leaving bars and clubs in Manhattan have been assaulted by robbers who either put fentanyl in their drinks or attack them and rub fentanyl on their faces to disable them. Some of the robbery victims have died.

No wonder the Commonwealth of Virginia has labeled fentanyl, "a weapon of terrorism."

As our fictional tale notes, back in 1978, it was difficult to make a murder charge stick if a dealer sold drugs cut with fentanyl to someone who died of an overdose. That is rapidly changing today as states across the country enact laws that permit homicide charges to be brought against anyone who gives a lethal dose of fentanyl to someone.

Most of the illegal fentanyl brought into the United States is produced by Mexican drug cartels in heavily guarded laboratories. As in our story, once the cartels figured out how powerful and addictive fentanyl was, they learned how to make it. The cartels have switched from growing fields of poppies for heroin production to cooking up fentanyl in labs. Their profits have grown exponentially.

Near the end of our story, we note the presence of a criminal from China at the party hosted by the Mexican drug lord. This fictional character is also based on fact as Chinese criminal networks are believed to be supplying most of the ingredients for fentanyl manufacturing to Mexican cartels. The same criminal networks in China are reportedly also helping Mexican drug lords launder their rivers of cash from illicit fentanyl sales.

Hundreds of thousands have died from fentanyl abuse, but when there are such profits to be made, criminals care nothing of the human suffering they create. As you may have heard me say before, when it comes to man's inhumanity to man, truth is always stranger—and more disturbing—than fiction.

ACKNOWLEDGMENTS

I tapped into the knowledge and guidance of family and friends in the medical profession for this book, especially my wife, Kathy, and friend Maureen Birckhead, both veteran registered nurses, and also Caitlin Brey, a skilled nurse-anesthetist. And, once again, I thank my partner in crime writing, Wes Smith.